FLOPPER

Titles By Colleen Charles

Minnesota Caribou:

Benched
Played
Checked
Gamed
Saved
Hooked
Iced

Rochester Riot:

The Slot
The Crease
The Point
The Zone
The Line
The Net

Reel Love:

Bait
Hook
Line
Sinker

Vegas Venom:

Flopper
Wheeler
Grinder
Bender
Dangler
Sniper
Brawler
Duster
Ringer
Plumber

The Caldwell Brothers:

Hard Gamble
Hard Line
Hard Up
Hard Luck
Hard Hit
Hard Bargain
Hard Sell

Pagan Passion:

Solstice Song

Naughty Little Books:

Chopped
Roped
Educated
Bought

Urban Dictionary Dudes:

Mansplainer
Nicebomber

Romance Singles:

Hot Cakes

Hot Water

Hot Pursuit

Chaos & Class

Crabbypants

Gunslinger

FLOPPER

Vegas Venom: Book One

Colleen Charles

Flopper Copyright © 2022
by Colleen Charles

Printed in the United States of America
First Printing, 2021

Second Printing 2023

ISBN: 9798841246442

Second Wind Publishing

www.ColleenCharles.com

FOREWORD

Subscribe to my Newsletter online and receive email notices about new book releases, sales, and special promotions.

New subscribers receive an EXCLUSIVE FREE NOVEL as a special gift.

www.colleencharles.com/free

AUTHOR'S NOTE

Before you dive into this love story on ice I wanted to take a brief moment to let you know that this start to the Vegas Venom series, *Flopper*, touches on themes of grief and loss. While it's wrapped in the heat and humor you've come to expect from my books, it also delves into the emotional complexities that come with losing loved ones.

If these themes could be triggering for you, please proceed with care. Your emotional well-being is important to me, as is delivering a story that speaks to the highs and lows we all experience in life and love.

Skate safely through these pages and enjoy the read,

Colleen Charles
USA Today Bestselling Author

PROLOGUE

Noah

Three years earlier...

My hands slide along the weathered paper as my eyes struggle to focus on the words. I probably should be in bed already, but this always seems to happen when I get my hands on one of the signed first edition copies of a book I want to read. This one I've read countless times already. With a sigh, I decide I'll read just one more chapter.

Even though I know how *A Brief History of Time* ends, it always blows my mind that a guy who couldn't navigate the world without the help of technological assistance could somehow sit in a wheelchair, imagine complex theories about space, time, and matter, and then prove himself to be *right*. Plenty of the guys on my team, the Vegas Venom, rely on their muscles and their dicks as their primary means of marking their places in the world—*I fuck, therefore I am*—while guys like Stephen Hawking can commune with the universe on this whole other level.

Mind-blowing.

Just as I get to my favorite passage, the bit about the theoretical anatomy of a two-dimensional dog, my phone blows up. I don't recognize the number, so I press ignore and go back to reading. A few seconds later, my phone buzzes again—the same unlisted number with a local Vegas area code. I groan with annoyance, set my book aside, and answer the call.

"If you're calling about my fucking warranty or some other scam, you can lose this number—" I begin, wondering how in the hell anyone could have access to my unlisted number. As one of the top goalies in the NHL, I take my privacy and my safety more seriously than most. Anyone who's anyone is already listed in my contacts.

"Is this Noah Abbott?" a man's voice asks.

I roll my eyes and fumble on the side table for a holographic bookmark I got the last time I checked out the Freemont Street experience. "Speaking."

A pause. Just long enough to cause my heart to skip a beat. "Are you Natalie Campbell's brother?"

"Um... yes. Why are you calling?"

"Our records have you listed as her emergency contact."

The book slips out of my hand, landing on the floor so that the pages bend inward on themselves. Under most circumstances, I would care—would think that mistreating a book like that is a prosecutable crime.

But some guy is calling me out of the blue, using the words 'Natalie' and 'emergency' in the same sentence.

And the tone of his voice? I don't fucking like it.

"Is she okay?"

The man doesn't answer. Instead, he says, "How quickly can you get to Desert Springs Hospital?"

I don't answer him, because I'm already shoving my phone in my pocket, grabbing my key fob and running toward my garage.

I don't remember how I get to the sterile-looking building, only that traffic seems to crawl the entire way. I want to push every single person aside and lean on the gas, but for the people of Las Vegas, it's just an ordinary day. They have jobs and appointments and grocery lists to worry about.

And with our parents both long gone, all I have is Nat.

* * *

Nobody can prepare you for the moment that you learn someone you love is gone. Poof. In the blink of an eye, the air shifts and the structure of your cells change. You are no longer the person you were just one heartbeat prior. I might have known when I arrived at the hospital and it reeked of pain, suffering... and death. I might have known when a nurse ushered me to one of those small private rooms where they break the news to those numb with terror soon to become the bereaved. I might have already known when I chose to not even disconnect the call I got earlier.

But the thing is... I didn't want to even think the thought, so I shoved that *knowing* aside.

As I sit in front of the doctor with my hands folded neatly in front of me, I don't receive his words. I don't process them either. *Car crash. Freeway. We did everything we could.* I stare at him, open-mouthed, not quite believing any of it.

Natalie—my only sister, my only close relative—who isn't even thirty years old, has left this world? It's not possible. She just became a wife. Then she became a mother. She had her whole life ahead of her.

She's a happy, healthy, positive person who's going places. She's my sunshine and unicorns. She's my soft place to fall. She's my flesh and blood. She's the only one who truly gets me.

She's gone, Noah.

"... the other driver lost control, crossed the center line and was also killed. Since your sister was behind the wheel, and your brother-in-law was in the front seat, at the speeds they were traveling, there was nothing anyone could have done. I'm terribly sorry for your loss, Mr. Abbott."

Nothing anyone could have done? Lost control of the car? Who the fuck does that? Some damn teenager, that's who. I can see his cocky ass in my mind's eye texting and drinking and vaping and every other thing hoodlums are doing these days while they're not paying attention to the road. Allowing myself to slide into a pit of rage for a split second, I suppress a shiver. But blaming some nameless, faceless villain isn't going to bring Nat and Steve back.

"When do I get to see her?" I ask.

The man's mouth opens, but for the first time since my arrival, *he's* the one grasping for words. "I... don't believe that's wise. Her body sustained major trauma, so we don't need you to identify it."

Body. Like my sister is... was fucking leftovers. Like she's disposable packaging that doesn't matter anymore now that she's...

Now that she's...

Not only can I not say the word, I can't even think it.

"Christ." I press my hand over my eyes, glad that I have it in me to cry, because what I really want to do is pick this doctor up along with his fake empathy and his perfectly embroidered white coat and rattle his teeth until he takes back the horrible things he said and return my *sister* to me and not just her motherfucking body.

On the other side of the too-thin wall, a woman begins to sob. I stare at the perfectly neutral wallpaper as if my laser gaze can bore right through it. They're on the other side. The other family.

And even though I know they lost someone too, I can't even muster up a sliver of empathy for *their* loss.

Because mine is bigger. Mine is *everything*. Then again, maybe not everything. My mind clears and focuses enough to ask, "What about Vivian? Was she in the car? Did she die too?"

"She was in the back strapped into her car seat."

"Jesus Christ..." I can't take this and my knees start to shake. If I wasn't sitting down, I'd fall down. All three of them, gone, just like that. I'm alone. Couldn't the 'other driver' have picked a more private place to lose control?

The doctor searches my face. "She experienced some bruising from the belt of the car seat, but she seems alright otherwise."

I look up sharply. "Viv's alive?"

"It's the closest thing I've ever seen to a miracle," the doctor says, nodding. "We're going to keep her for overnight observation, but she should be able to go home with you tomorrow. I thought you might want to spend the night here... with her."

My stomach lurches, and I drop my forehead into my sweaty palms. "Viv's alive," I repeat the words like a mantra. Right before my niece was born, Natalie and Steve drew up wills, just in case. And none of us even had a passing thought that just in case would ever come.

As Viv's godfather, my sister asked if I could be named as a legal guardian if something happened to them. At the time, I thought it was pretty morbid to contemplate. They were young. Healthy. Happy.

And now she's *the body*.

With tear-filled eyes, I make arrangements to be with Viv. Once the doctor and I leave the room, my eyes scan the small waiting area. A cluster of people gather around a coffee pot. A whole family of people, at least three generations, clinging to each other and wailing out their grief. They have their own support system just by nature of DNA.

I only have myself.

"Is that the family? *The other driver's* family?"

The doctor shifts from foot to foot. "Ah. I'm not at liberty to—"

"Forget it." Truth be told, I don't give a damn about them. As far as I'm concerned, every last one of them along with the distracted perpetrator can go to hell.

I take one final glance over at the weeping people on the far side of the waiting room. Do they know how much they've taken from me? From the baby who just celebrated her first birthday with balloons and a unicorn cake that she didn't eat but used instead to paint her face in rainbow colors? That baby who now waits in her hospital bed, probably crying for Mama and Dada?

My throat tightens into a knot I can't even think of swallowing past. "Can I see her now? Can I see Viv?"

The doctor nods. "I'll take you back there."

I follow him on shaking legs back to the sterile room where Vivian lies sleeping like a tiny angel. Her eyes squeeze shut and her perfect little mouth opens and closes as she dreams even through the beeping of the machines checking her vitals.

I resolve, then and there, to be everything she ever needs. Natalie and Steve were robbed of the chance to watch their little girl grow up.

But I'll do my damndest to make sure she never wants for anything—most of all love. I'll love her enough for all three of us.

Because this is Vegas—and fate just dealt me a crappy hand.

CHAPTER ONE

Noah

Three Years Later...

I walk in the door of the house and drop my gym bag onto the sofa. Our road trip went well—better than expected. One of the Riot players, Ealon Jones, scored a greasy goal on me in the first and Cole Fiorino popped it in my five-hole on a sweet powerplay breakaway during our only loss, but other than that, I kept the puck out of the Venom net. Of course, my buddies, Anders Beck and Latham Newberry, let me have it over Jones's goal, laughing and saying I had my head up my ass and a blind man could have made that save, which only stung because it was partly true. With those two and their smart mouths, I just use rolling my eyes and shrugging as self-preservation. Then I shake it off in the shower and forget about it before the next game. The most successful netminders in the NHL have their minds right.

I scan the living room and then the kitchen. "I'm home! Where are my girls?"

Silence greets me, which always sends a little shiver down my spine. My worst fear is finding out that something's happened to Viv when I'm not here to protect her. Ever since the accident, I get triggered a bit more easily than before.

Before I can get myself all worked up, however, I spot movement through the glass door at the back. All three of the girls in question are out back, playing around by the pool.

The moment I step outside, Biscuit trots over, wagging her tail and issuing her standard greeting—one sloppy kiss. Ever since I rescued her from a local outfit who rehabs guard dogs surrendered by owners who couldn't handle them, she lets me know how happy she is to be here in this house. For some crazy reason, Biscuit's obsessed with knees and elbows, and one good slurp can leave me dripping.

I eye my dog suspiciously as she stands there—all twenty-six ferocious-looking inches of Cane Corso—entirely too pleased with herself. Even though her fangs scream danger, her eyes give her away. But that doesn't matter. I wanted a loyal, badass dog who would protect my niece in my absence just as fiercely as I would. Biscuit's barrel-chested, brindled, and has jaws that I'm pretty sure could take a man's leg off in one go if she really put her mind to it.

And if someone made even a whisper of a move to hurt Viv, it would be chompity-chomp-chomp.

With an internal chuckle, I shake my head. At the moment, she's also wearing a sparkly pink tutu and a rhinestone tiara.

"Alright, who turned the dog into a Disney princess?" I demand.

Viv looks up from whatever she's playing with in the garden. When she sees me, her face lights up. "Unkie Noah!" she calls, waving me over. "Come help with the gnomes!"

I look down at Princess Biscuit of Noahland, who wags her tail once. There's no denying it: When the queen calls, as her loyal subjects, we must obey.

If I were in charge of the house, everything would be minimalist and tidy. I'd fill the house with IKEA furniture, paint the walls white, maybe put up a few tasteful houseplants, and call it a day.

These days, however, I am but a lowly peasant who obeys the

will of her royal highness, Vivian. Instead of a tidy lawn, the backyard has been transformed into a gnome playground. Gnomes of every shape and size, from small plastic lawn ornaments to solar-powered light up monstrosities occupy every available surface—my last count was fifty-six of the creepy little critters. Judging by my niece's current posture, more of them have joined the family in my absence.

Francine, the full-time nanny I've hired to keep an eye on Viv while I'm on the road, looks up from the garden. I can't tell if she's weeding or working on planting more gnomes or what, but she's definitely the reason this whole thing started. I'm pretty sure that the gnomes were her idea, and she's been enabling Viv's addiction ever since.

"Oh, hello, Noah," she calls. "I didn't hear you come in. How was your road trip?"

"And the guard dog didn't alert you." I shake my head at Biscuit, whose only response is another tail-wag. "Road trip was good. We won two out of three, and I helped out my save percentage." I crouch down beside Viv and inspect her handiwork. Sure enough, there's a new gnome, which has been graced with a dandelion crown.

"What do you think, Unkie?" Viv asks.

"I think he's nice and creepy, sweetie," I say, suppressing a shiver.

Viv stands up and plants her little fists on her hips. "Not creepy! He's *cute*. Now say you're sorry."

"I'm sorry I insulted your gnome. His crown looks lovely. Did you make that yourself?"

Viv's face pinches in annoyance. "Say sorry to the *gnome*, Unkie. That's Samuel. And you hurted his feelings."

I stifle a laugh and make a show of bowing to the little man. At least this isn't one of the truly ugly ones. His hat is a cheerful yellow, and chubby apple cheeks are painted bright pink... as are the other cheeks peeking over the hem of his trousers. Why people like garden gnomes is a mystery to me, but their further obsession with gnome butt cracks and cheeks takes my confusion to a whole new level. Still, if an army of smiling secondhand exhibitionists is what it takes to make Viv happy, it's a price I'll gladly pay.

"I'm very sorry, Samuel," I say with as much solemnity as I can manage. "I admire your self-expression and your dedication to defying gender norms."

The gnome smiles back at me.

"I'm pretty sure he can see into my soul," I whisper to Viv out of the side of my mouth.

Viv nods. "That's because he's a Gnome in the Gloam."

I stare at her for a moment, then turn to Francine, who's come over to watch this exchange. "Gnome in the Gloam."

"Like Elf on the Shelf, but they stay outside," Fran explains.

"And watch us from the garden?" I lift my eyebrows at her. "So now they're voyeurs, too?"

"What's a voo-yers?" Viv asks.

"Someone who watches you for their own perverse pleasure," I explain, pointing to the gnome in question. "Like this guy."

"Elves live in the house," Fran says. "Gnomes live in the garden. Or would you rather they follow you inside?"

All three of them stare at me, waiting for my response. Either Fran has spent too much time with my four-year-old, or vice versa, because both of them seem to find this logic perfectly reasonable.

Sensing that I'm outnumbered by both bodies and estrogen, I get to my feet. "Sure. How silly of me. When I was growing up, we didn't have these, so it's all new to me."

"What *did* you have?" Viv asks.

After a moment's consideration, I tell her, "Hobbits in the closets."

Viv's eyes widen, and she turns to Fran. "Do *we* have those?"

Fran purses her lips and turns toward the house. "I'm not sure. We'd better check."

"Biscuit and me'll check my room!" Viv runs toward the back door and tugs it open. Biscuit follows on her heels, tutu bouncing and tail wagging. In her excitement, the tiara has fallen to one side, giving her a rakish look.

"I assume I'm on dinner duty tonight," Fran says. "Seeing as it's Tuesday."

"If it's not too much trouble..."

My Tuesday nights are dedicated to a local bereavement group. I've been going ever since the accident—at least, since I was able to convince myself that it was okay to leave Vivian for a few hours at a time. Even after I hired Francine and brought Biscuit home, I turned into a mess every time I didn't have Viv right in front of me. Now I recognize that any work I do on myself is going to benefit her, too. That makes it easier to force myself out the door. Stepping outside my comfort zone is good for me—at least that's what the other people in my grief group tell me.

Francine used to walk on eggshells around me, but lately she's been more to the point. "What step are you on? You've been doing this for years." She places her hands on her hips and winks at me. "Haven't you made it through all twelve yet? Leave it to you to flunk out of AA, Noah."

"It's not AA, you know that. And they say that going through the *five* stages of grief is a lifelong process." Even though Francine's dancing eyes give away her teasing, truth be told, I've managed to make it pretty solidly to stage four. Most days,

I manage not to be angry anymore. It doesn't change things. Natalie's gone. Steve's gone. Viv's parentless, and there's no way to fix that. But I'm not ready for acceptance.

At least not yet.

Then there's the shame. Because my life changed drastically when they died and I took custody of Viv and as a man in his late twenties, it's hard not to be angry by that even when I have no damn right to be. I'm still alive. I'm still here living my dream while two amazing people don't have that chance. So what kind of a selfish jerk does that make me? I still haven't unwound that part in all these years of half-assedly discussing my feelings.

Honestly, I hate the word acceptance. Would accepting Natalie and Steve's deaths mean that I'm okay with them being cruelly snatched from life?

How am I ever supposed to be *okay* with the fact that they died?

Fran must see that I'm not in the mood for her teasing today, and she relents. "Noah, darling, you pay me too much and I've got nothing better to do." Fran pats my shoulder. "And Vivian is a treat. Stay out as late as you want. I know how much the ladies love you. It wouldn't hurt you to get yourself out there again. You should find a nice single mom. One who loves books as much as you do."

That brings a small smile to my face. "I'm not there for the ladies. You know that." Although I can't deny that I look forward to their adoring gazes, their soothing voices, and most of all the homemade snacks they bring every week.

Francine's smile widens from sympathetic to wicked. "Oh, I'm well aware. But seeing as it's the only place you're likely to meet someone..."

"I'm not looking to bring yet another woman into my life," I remind her. "I'm already outnumbered three to one. Plus however many of these creepy gnome things identify as female."

Francine clucks her tongue. "I see your mouth moving, dear, but only nonsense is coming out. One of these days, we're going to find you someone lovely who you won't be able to resist. Who will complete you. I'd bet my last dollar on it."

"I've already got you hovering over me. How would I even find the time for someone else? What other woman could even measure up?"

She swats at my shoulder. "You big flirt. How about instead of pretending to be interested in me, you turn on that charm for the ladies tonight and see if you meet anyone interesting?"

While I'm longing for a night of uninterrupted time in my library that's not coming anytime soon, Viv's second-floor window opens, and her little face appears at the screen. "Unkie Noah, what's a Hobbit? How do I know if I've got one?"

"Give me a second and I'll help you look." I leave Francine standing there in the garden with her devious plans to set me up with some random bookish woman and realizing I better shut her down before she really gets rolling down a road leading nowhere. I used to be like most of the guys on the team, sleeping with any hot woman who showed interest. Viv doesn't need that kind of influence, though. When I'm on the road for work, it's one thing to indulge in a rare hook up, but all my free time should be spent here, with her. And since Nat died, I haven't had much desire to sleep around. Women tend to want things. They tend to *ask* things. I'm adulting now. Viv's needs come before mine.

Fran does a great job with her. She's practically become Viv's surrogate grandmother.

As for me, I'm the only real family she has left. Women will have to wait a few years until Viv's at least in first grade. For now, my quasi little family has to stick together.

* * *

I help myself to a gooey brownie, a raspberry meringue kiss, and a five-berry-and-oatmeal cookie before sitting down on one of the metal folding chairs that might collapse underneath my weight. No matter how much I shift and flex, it never quite feels comfortable. A local Mexican restaurant, *Mi Corazón es Tuyo, Pollo,* hosts our weekly meeting. The owners of what we affectionately call *Tuyo, Pollo* lost their daughter to cancer a few years ago, and even though they've reached that mythical fifth stage of grief themselves, they still agreed to make the space available for us in perpetuity.

As I nibble my meringue kiss, I'm already fantasizing about ordering some *chili rellenos* to go, popping the tab on one of the craft beers in my library minifridge—where they're safely out of Viv's curious reach—and opening my new first edition signed copy of *A Killer By Design*. I heard Anne Burgess talking about her work on a podcast a few months ago, and the woman seems like a badass. Other than Viv and hockey, filling my library with all the books I love fills my heart with what can almost be considered joy.

When I remember to feel it.

"Do you like my kisses?" The woman sitting next to me bats her eyelashes at me.

Doreen lost her father a few years ago after being his primary care provider for almost half a decade. She might not have a book out about her work, but she and most of the other women who come every week as they share in their grief with others who've experienced the same thing are badasses in their own right. Women have this innate ability to work through uncomfortable emotions and come out on the other side even stronger than when they went in and that's a trait I admire.

"They're delicious," I assure her.

She bites her lip and blushes. "You can have more. Have as many as you like."

"They're extra-sweet today," I tell her. "There's something special in there, right?"

"Lime oil." Doreen fans herself. "I thought it was time to try something new."

I'm well aware that most of the women who come to this event are single. Plenty of them are single moms just like Francine wants me to date, many of whom are grieving for their husbands. Some were lost to horrible diseases like cancer or ALS. But most of them were lost in tragic accidents like Nat and Steve. So in our grief, we also have commonality. And that sense of community makes my load to bear just a little bit lighter. Most people don't come as regularly as I do, or for anywhere near as long.

Maybe they have a stronger support system, or they're just better at getting over things than I am.

"Did you like my brownies, Noah?" Another member, Susan, leans across the circle. "I added extra chocolate chunks this time."

"And caramel chips." I nod, licking my lips. "If there are some left over at the end of the night, would you mind if I took one home for my niece? She'd love these."

There's a collective swoon among the ladies present. Every single one of them loves the idea of a man who talks about his feelings and is open about his trauma, but more than anything, they love knowing that there are guys out there who adore their kids—even the ones who become entwined in their hearts in unconventional ways.

I get it. Every time I hear one of them gush over their son's performance on the school basketball team, or their daughter getting her learner's permit, or any of the other milestones that litter the day-to-day lives of their kids, my heart aches. They're getting to experience all of the things Natalie and Steve will be missing in Viv's life.

The reminder of what we've lost hurts, but it's good to know that there are people who appreciate what they have.

"Of course you can," Susan tells me. "Take the whole pan."

I feel a bit of a blush landing on my cheeks. "You spoil me, Susan."

Her eyes light up. It couldn't be more obvious that I have a fan club in group therapy, and I don't have anything against a little harmless flirting, but it's never going to go beyond that. It's not that I have anything against these women. On the contrary, I think Viv would benefit from having any one of them in her life, but I'm still struggling with summoning any romantic feelings toward anyone.

They're not the problem. I am. When tragedy struck, something snapped inside of me. It's still broken, and I have no idea when or if it will stitch itself back together again.

I'm better off alone and completely focused on Viv.

At least for now.

There are still a few minutes before the meeting starts when Jana rushes inside, fanning herself with a book. She scoots right by the snack table and comes up to me.

"Noah," she pants, "you've *got* to read this." She thrusts a paperback under my nose. "It's going to change your life."

I squint down at the cover. "What is it?"

"*The Quest of the Silver Fleece*. It's amazing... it feels so contemporary, but it's almost a hundred years old. I'm going to talk my book club into reading it next."

I whip out my phone to look it up online, but my first search only turns up some mass-produced paperbacks. I hate buying that crap—I'd much rather get a first edition signed copy in good condition, if possible, and a new hardback if I can't.

"If it's that good, I'd like to look for a good print version…" I mumble.

"You could try checking at a local bookstore," Jana suggests. "There's this great place nearby called The Last Chapter. It's got all kinds of unusual things. Plus, the owner can track anything down. She's amazeballs. It's like she's the guru of literature or something. She actually found me a first edition copy of *A Light in the Attic* for my daughter's birthday. Can you imagine? My kids love the Saturday story hour there."

The name rings a bell, although I've never been inside. "I think my niece goes there for that. I'll check it out. In the meantime, let me make a note of the title."

Jana grins. "Or we could just follow each other on Goodreads."

I nod. "Yeah, good idea. I can always use a recommendation."

Immediately, every other woman in the room whips out their phones. By the time the meeting starts, I've got fifteen new friends on the app.

Dating might be off the table, but I'm never going to turn down a recommendation for a good book.

CHAPTER TWO

Molly

My eyes roll over the business calendar for The Last Chapter this month, when my laptop pings with a new email. One glance tells me everything I need to know: one, that it's from my agent, and two, that I really, really don't want to deal with it.

Not now, and maybe not ever.

Unfortunately, running away is a strategy that can only work so long before I find myself in deep trouble with a woman who's put up with my writer's block for almost a full year. My last book, *Where Did You Go?*, sold almost five million copies. Writers like Dan Brown would scoff at that number, of course... but in the niche world of picture books, it basically thrust me into rockstar status.

Not that I ever wanted to be in rockstar territory. I like to remain unseen. To stay small and inconsequential outside the confines of my store. Most of all, I just wanted to help kids deal with their grief and make something good out of a horrible tragedy.

There's only one problem with my current level of success. My publisher wants a *second* book, and I'm starting to wonder if I have another one left in me, because the first one was a total fluke.

The good news is that running away can still work for a little while. I go back to clicking around in the bookshop calendar. Our new event series, which we're calling "Blind Date with a

Book," launches this week. Once a month, we'll be holding a get-together with wine and snacks, and each meeting will focus on a different popular book from one of twelve genres. We'll select the first book from a random drawing and get together the next month to discuss it and select the next title, and so on. Our signups for the first month filled within only five days of the page going live, which feels like a good omen. Business is surprisingly good, but most of our big sales come from the unique events the store features rather than random people wandering through the door.

Readers seem to love browsing my quirky bookstore and chatting me up, more than actually purchasing books. I keep hearing that my customers' visits are more like an experience than a shopping trip. Most of my business is done with online orders asking me to find rare books—my superpower—and The Last Chapter's event nights.

I'm about to place my preorder for cheese platters and veggie trays when Mona's head pops through the door.

"Greetings, Fearless Leader," she intones, "you have a call on line one."

There *is* only one line on the work phones, but rather than pointing this out, I simply smile. "Great. Thanks. I'll take it right now." My assistant, Mona, has been going through a goth phase for the last... oh, roughly two years or so. Actually, I think it may have started earlier, but I don't remember her being quite this bleak until I took over the bookstore full-time and worked with her every day. Maybe it has something to do with the fact that she's gotten all these new piercings.

Drenched in black and ennui, Mona disappears, the door clicking behind her as I reach for the receiver. "Hello, you've reached The Last Chapter. Molly speaking, how can I help you?" I didn't always pitch my voice quite so high, but since they've already had to deal with however Mona's answering the phone these days, I figure that it doesn't hurt to be extra cheerful.

"Hello, Molly. Long time no talk."

I wince at the tone of my agent's voice. "Hello! Angela! What a lovely surprise to hear from you."

"If you were reading my emails, it wouldn't be a surprise," she retorts.

"Ah." I glance toward the monitor and her unopened message. "Right. I've just been so busy..."

"Which is why I thought it would be better if we could talk voice to voice. Presumably the writer's block won't impact our ability to converse on the phone." Her tone is light and teasing, but wicked steel hovers right beneath it. I suppose I deserve this, given that I've kept her waiting all these months. She's been incredibly patient with me, and I'm sure the fact that I've ghosted her isn't helping.

"Sorry, Angela, I just—" I pinch the bridge of my nose and press the receiver to my ear. "I'm trying, okay? The shop is taking up most of my attention now. I haven't had the time to work on anything."

"Be honest with me. Time isn't the issue, is it? A picture book isn't *that* many words. I'll take anything, Molly. A first draft. An *outline*. Just give me something to work with."

Words aren't the problem. Once a week, I sit down and draft a newsletter much longer than a picture book manuscript. If spilling out a wordcount was the issue, I'd be fine.

A book is more than words, though. A good one requires an idea, and ever since Uncle Arthur died and seemingly took all inspiration with him, I'm fresh out.

Is it wrong to wish something stimulating would happen to me just so I could get Angela off my back? But alas, I am frumpy and boring and the last person the Universe would think of to mess with.

I'm just so.... basic.

"I'm sorry," I mumble.

Angela relents. "Honey, you wrote one of the most highly acclaimed children's books of the decade. You've helped thousands of kids deal with loss and process grief in a healthy way. I know you have the talent. All it takes is an itty-bitty spark."

"I wrote *Where'd You Go?* because I lost someone dear to me," I explain. "If that's what it takes to ignite creativity, maybe I don't *want* to write another book. How am I supposed to follow that up?"

"You're getting in your head. Putting too much pressure on yourself." Angela's tone teeters halfway between sympathetic and exasperated. "If I'm going to keep representing you, I'm going to need something soon. You can't be a one-hit wonder. I won't allow it."

"Define soon," I squeak. I don't want to lose Angela—she's amazing, and I know that my quiet little book would never have been anywhere near as successful as it is without her help.

"I shouldn't have to," Angela retorts. "Just get me something, okay, Molly?"

"Okay."

"Promise me."

"Yes, yes, I promise. I'll send an outline as soon as I have one."

Angela grumbles at the skepticism in my voice, but she must accept that I'm doing my best, because she says, "I look forward to seeing it," and then the line clicks as she disconnects.

"I really am trying," I mumble into the dead air. "It's not like I'm deliberately trying to be obtuse."

"She knows you're trying," says a familiar monotone voice. "That's why she didn't fire you as her client. She could have, you know. I'm sure your publisher is breathing down her neck with threats and warnings."

"Mona?" I leap to my feet, dropping the receiver into the cradle and storm out to the front desk where she leans against the counter and smirks.

"Come on," she says, "you have to know that she let you off easy."

"What makes you think that you can listen in on my private phone calls?" I demand.

Mona shrugs and goes back to flipping through the open comic book on the desk in front of her. "You've been uptight lately. I thought I could help."

"By spying?"

Her fingers flutter to a stop mid-swipe, her black fingernail polish glowing underneath the overhead lighting. "By psychoanalyzing you. Have you considered that your writer's block could be related to your complete lack of a healthy sex life? Creativity flows from the root chakra—in our case, the pussy."

I bury my face in my hands and take several deep breaths to stop myself from throttling my assistant. "I'm pretty sure that isn't the problem."

"Maybe not," Mona retorts, "but celibacy is rarely the solution, either."

"Why are we even talking about this?" I ask.

"Uh, because I'm trying to help you salvage your dream career and find, like, your Zen center or whatever." Mona licks her thumb and flips another page.

"Is that what you learned in psychology class? Do your parents know they're paying $17k a year for your therapy?"

Mona cracks a tight smile—sans teeth. "At least I'm using my education. You got a degree in English, a Masters in Creative Writing, and now you spend your Saturdays dressed like a princess reading books to toddlers."

"Plenty of respectable people have made a living out of encouraging children's love of reading."

"Yeah?" Mona stares at me and flips again. Flip. Flip. Flip. She's not even looking at the pages, and for sure isn't even trying to hide the fact that she's only listening with half an ear. "Name one."

"Levar Burton," I say at once.

"Yeah? That guy from *Big Bang Theory*?"

I shudder at her ignorance. "Maybe if more people had read to you as a child, you'd understand."

"People did," Mona says, finally glancing up. "My mom took me to an Anarchist's Storybook Hour all the time when I was, like, two."

If I didn't know Mona's family, I'd assume that she was yanking my chain—but I do, and she's not.

"Regardless, my sex life is *fine*," I lie. Reading smutty mafia romance while playing with my bullet-vibrator counts as a sex life, right? "So save your psychoanalysis for when you become a therapist."

Mona pretends to gag. "No way. Not gonna happen."

"Isn't that the whole point of your degree?" I ask, stepping past her to rearrange the display shelf.

"You think I want to get certified to listen to people talk about their stupid problems all day?" Mona rolls her eyes and snaps her comic book shut. "*My husband is ignoring me. My mom traumatized me. My children don't like me. Boo hoo, my self-esteem is entirely dependent on how many likes I get across social media platforms, and I have no personality beyond my ability to make parodies of other people's ideas.* Booooring. I'd rather just take Zoloft as a preemptive measure. Thanks, but no thanks."

I shake my head at her cynicism. "If you hate people so much, then why work here?"

"Uh, hello." Mona waves her arms to encompass the store. "Ninety percent of the time, there are no people here."

She's got a point. "Shots fired. So why don't you work on booking better workshops so we can get more paying customers? Maybe if I didn't have to spend all my time on the internet using my magic talents to find the rare books no one else seems to be able to come up with in order to make my business the best it can be, I'd be able to work on *my* next book."

"I'm already on it." Mona drops her comic book into her bag and removes another one. "I've sent out emails to a bunch of my classmates and posted ads on campus. There are plenty of people willing to hold workshops for free, just to get their name out there. I'm meeting up with a chick tomorrow who does, like, tarot and moon-cycle shit and stuff. She seems cool but I wanna make sure that she's not gonna flake at the last minute before I put her in the calendar officially."

This is why I keep Mona around. She might use more eyeliner in a day than I do in a year, and she's nosy as all get-out, but she really does care about the bookstore. Her blasé attitude is just a cover—although some days I wish that I could get her to drop the front entirely and just be her kind, professional self *all* the time.

"Thanks, Mona. You're a lifesaver." I stop by the front desk to make prolonged eye contact, affecting my scariest I-might-seem-like-a-bookworm-but-I-carry-pepper-spray smile. "But stay out of my personal business."

"If you're blaming the bookstore for sabotaging your writing career, doesn't that make it *business* business?" Mona arches a pierced eyebrow. "As your assistant, I'm pretty sure it's my job to, like, *assist.* Maybe you should learn to delegate better. I've been organizing the workshops, taking inventory, *and* coordinating socials. Seems like that should free up a little time, doncha think?"

With friends like these, who needs enemies? Mona's right, though, at least about the fact that if I really *wanted* to have time for my writing, I could *make* time.

As far as her advice on using sex to unwind? I respectfully agree to disagree. Sex is overrated. In my experience—which is, admittedly, limited—it's not worth all the fuss people make over it.

More trouble than it's worth.

I head back to my office to finish placing my order. Maybe on my lunch break I can start brainstorming ideas about what to write next, but I'm not holding my breath.

CHAPTER THREE

Noah

"You look like hell," Anders says, his face popping into view above the bar I'm benching. "Anything I should know?"

Latham wanders into my peripheral vision and spots me as I continue my reps without me even having to ask. If he starts talking about local podcaster, Scarlett Stone, again and how much she hates him, I'm going to drop a weight on his toes. He needs to stop Googling himself, bragging about how many mentions he gets even when they're negative, and focus on his game.

I don't answer until I'm done, sitting up and mopping my face with a nearby towel. "Gee, thanks for the vote of confidence. What would you two do if I started telling you how shitty you look all the time?"

Latham flexes. "Um... I never look like shit. Even after I eat In-N-Out. Even after a tequila bender. Even after I spend all night handcuffed to the bedpost with a few hot chicks riding my dick and then licking each other so I don't have to."

Anders rolls his eyes so hard they almost disappear into his brain. "Shut. Up. I do not want to hear about your sexcapades, dude. Have you ever heard it's better to be a giver than a taker? Jesus. I feel sorry for any woman that winds up twisted in your web."

"Our season's about to get real, and I for one, am ready," I lie, not wanting to give away how low-key depressed I am. Despite everything I do to sweep away my grief and step up to be the best possible parent I can to Viv, it never seems to be enough.

Thank God for hockey.

Even for Anders and Latham, as annoying as they both can be.

They're damn good friends.

The ice, the locker room, the weight room—they're my places. I associate them with everything that feels good and right.

On the ice, doing what I love, I feel normal. Like I never got the call that changed my life in a heartbeat and I'm wrapped up in the innocence of *not* knowing what it feels like to ache from my soul.

Gripping the hem of my t-shirt, I yank it up and rub my forehead. Latham hip-checks me as we walk toward the showers. "Quit showing off your abs, Noah. Goalies shouldn't have abs like that. You're going to make us forwards look bad."

I glance up at him and his dancing eyes. The guy is in a constant state of positivity that I'm not sure I understand or ever could, because I'm the only one dealing with challenges that my teammates have never even come close to experiencing. Emotions come in waves, and lately, I've been cresting.

But I know if I hold on long enough, the surge will ebb, and I'll be able to catch my breath and be the best surrogate dad possible, rising from the ashes of tragedy to overcome all adversity.

And there's nothing more important than that. Even hockey.

If I had to give up everything for my little princess, I would.

"I think Scarlett Stone makes you look bad enough without bringing my abs into it," I tease.

He pouts a bit, and I think the only time I ever see his face fall for real is when she calls him out for some minor mistake he makes on the ice. The woman has a hard-on for Latham but not for anyone else. It kind of defies logic.

Clayton "Cash Money" Hale, one of our veteran wingers who only speaks in three-word sentences, grunts out, "You doing group?"

I nod. "Yup. I know I should probably stop, but it's the only thing that helps sometimes."

Anders looks me up and down. "Because it's just you and a room full of chicks. What's not to love about that? The healing you're getting is of the sexual nature."

I force a chuckle. When I think of all the ladies at group therapy, I think of them like sisters. Like family. Even though they're women—some of them attractive and close to my age—the thought of hitting on any of them has never once crossed my mind.

I look at Anders. "No can do, my friend. Those relationships are purely platonic."

Anders stares at me for a beat as if he's sizing me up, but ultimately, he knows me better than anyone else on the team. As locals, we go way back. We're both lucky to be able to play for the Venom, and we damn well know it. We even live in the same gated community, so if I need him or vice versa, we're within a couple of blocks of each other.

Finally, he breaks out in a smile and claps me on the shoulder. "I know. I was just razzing you."

I snap him with my sweaty towel and hightail it into the showers before he can retaliate. "Thanks for looking out for me."

* * *

Friday night, Francine meets me at the front door, already

helping Viv into her shoes.

"I ruined the casserole," she says. "Surprise, we're going out for dinner. Your treat."

I sniff the air, preparing to be met with the odor of smoke and a traumatized dog. Every time the smoke alarm goes off, Biscuit acts like it's a personal attack on her very existence. To my surprise, however, there's no lingering aroma of burned cheese, and Biscuit's napping on the couch looking perfectly content.

"Are you sure about that?" I ask. "Nothing *smells* burned..."

Francine plants her hands on her hips. "Listen, young man, if you really want me to go to the trouble of cooking a whole meal only to burn it, I'll do it, or you could just accept that it *would* have burned and save me the trouble."

Vivian giggles behind her hands. I'm not sure if this is part of a conspiracy or if she's just amused to see me being scolded like a little kid.

"What do you think, Vivian?" I ask.

Viv opens her eyes wide and rubs her tummy. "I'm *hungry*, Unkie!"

"Whatever makes my girls happy." I drop my gym bag on the couch beside my snoozing dog, who opens one eye to give me a baleful look. "I can see I'm outnumbered."

I don't mind taking them to dinner. Francine does more than her fair share when it comes to taking care of my little family, and if she wanted to be treated to steak dinners every night, she'd be well within her rights.

Francine eyes me over, stopping to take stock more than once. "Don't you think you'd better change?"

"I showered after practice!" I protest, gesturing to my still wet hair, my gray sweatpants, and my tight t-shirt.

"Hmm." Francine shoos me away. "But we're going out for a

nice meal. Why don't you go put on something appropriate?" She shoos me toward the stairs. "Hurry up, we're waiting!"

I'm not sure what nefarious plot Francine has in mind, but I do as she suggests. To my surprise, she's been in my room; a pair of dark jeans and a gray sweater of mine are lying out on the bed. I change into the pants but reach into the closet for a button-down instead. When I return, Francine frowns at my adjustment to her suggestion.

"It's too warm for a sweater!" I protest. "This is Vegas for Chri... I mean Pete's sake!"

Francine sniffs before reaching for Viv's hand. "That will do. Set the house alarm, Vivian, darling."

Viv's face lights up. "Beep beep!" she exclaims in a high-pitched voice. Biscuit immediately sits up to look over the back of the couch.

"Good girl." Francine herds us both to the door. "Come along, loves."

We head off, with Francine leading the way. Fran's a little odd sometimes, but in the same way that Amelia Bedelia or Mary Poppins is odd. She and Viv get along like a house on fire, and while I know that Viv's going to have a lot of questions about her parents someday, I'm also confident that she's never going to want for love while Francine's around. I adore my niece, but I often feel out of my depth with her, and sometimes she reminds me so much of my sister that it breaks my heart. I'm lucky to have someone around like Fran to step in when it all gets to be too much.

"What did you do today?" I ask Viv as I drive.

She puckers her little face up in a thoughtful frown. "Umm... we fed the gnomes, and then we looked for Celine..."

I have no idea what goes into 'feeding the gnomes,' and I'm frankly afraid to ask. At least I know what she means when she says that they looked for Celine—Fran is convinced that Celine Dion lives in our gated community as rumored by the neighbors and late-night helicopters flying overhead, but so far she has yet to find proof. As if Celine Dion, global superstar, would just walk outside for a little neighborly chat.

"Any luck?" I ask.

Viv shakes her head. "No, but we found a turtle!"

"Technically, dear, it's a tortoise," Francine interjects. "A desert tortoise. The state reptile of Nevada."

Viv nibbles her lip and tries again. "*Tor-tis...*"

"Why don't you tell Noah what we named her?"

"Esio Trot!" Viv exclaims. "Like the book Fran reads me. 'Cuz that's turtle spelled backwards!"

I grin at her enthusiasm. "Of course."

Once I valet the car, we pass a handful of shops as we talk until Viv grabs my hand and tugs it twice. "Daddy, can we stop at the bookstore?" This immediately gets my antennae up. Viv only calls me *daddy* when she wants something really badly. She knows that it makes me melt, even if she doesn't understand that it's from guilt as much as affection.

"I thought you were starving?" I tease, holding out despite her pleas.

Viv opens her mouth, closes it again, and then looks up at Francine.

"Are you really going to tell her that she can't read?" Fran asks. "Literacy should be encouraged! And so should her Unkie's love of books." She bats her lashes at me, the picture of innocence, which only reinforces my suspicion that this is part of some plan she and Viv have cooked up although I'm having a hard time figuring out why going to a small, local bookstore would require a nice outfit.

"Of course." I step back and usher them toward the door.

"Far be it from me to stand between you and your books, girls."

Viv grins and rushes toward the door. As Francine and I trail after her, I nudge my housekeeper-slash-nanny-slash-shepherd gently with my elbow. "What's going on today?"

"Nothing's going on, Noah," she assures me. "The girl just loves her books. Just like her Unkie. She comes by it naturally."

As we pass under the sign, I happen to glance up at the name of the store: The Last Chapter. It's the one Jana mentioned at the meeting on Tuesday. Maybe while we're here, I can see about ordering a copy of that book she recommended.

The place is fairly large, but even so, it's packed to the gills with an assortment of books and people. Bookshelves of all sizes are scattered throughout the store, and on two walls they reach all the way to the ceiling. Even I couldn't reach the top shelf without the aid of one of those little rolling library ladders which, on second glance, they have. It's eclectic and charming and every single thing I love about indie bookstores. The books vary greatly in size, color, and topic. On the other hand, I'm sensing a definite theme when it comes to the patrons. Women, ranging from their thirties to their fifties, make up the vast majority of the crowd.

A bit of discomfort flows over me as I realize I'm the token penis. Francine, that devil, deliberately polished me up to a shine to deposit me in the middle of a female-rich environment where she knew I would share at least one common interest with the horde.

Feeling like I'm on display, I try to fade into the background, but for a man of my size, it's next to impossible.

Francine hustles us to the desk across from the door, where a bored-looking young woman with dyed-black hair and an astonishing amount of eye shadow leans against the counter. Her shirt says, *Read My Lips*, and an arrow points up from her chest toward her face. Underneath is the image of an open book.

"What's all this, Mona, dear?" Francine gestures around the store. Of *course* she knows the name of the woman behind the counter. Why would I expect any less? She's the sort of person who makes friends wherever she goes. She probably knows the woman's life story, what she ate for breakfast, lunch, and dinner along with her favorite holiday already too.

Evidently, even this blank-faced young woman likes her, because she rolls her eyes extravagantly and waves to encompass the group. "It's the Blind Date with a Book event. Molly's gonna be drawing the title any minute now."

"Ooh!" Francine claps her hands. "Can I join? I didn't realize you were doing a mystery read... although I'm glad to hear that Molly will be around..." She glances over her shoulder at me as if I have a target in the middle of my chest ripe for Cupid's arrow. I have no idea who Molly is, but something tells me that she's the primary reason we're here.

"Sure, why not?" The young woman shrugs and points toward the back room. "It's adults-only in there right now, but if you're not drinking, you can just hang wherever."

Francine turns to my niece. "Vivian, my sweet, will you please go find something to read while Unkie and I join the book group?" She points to an assortment of beanbags in the children's area. A couple of other kids are hanging out in there, but it's easy to see over the child-sized bookshelves, so I only get a little nervous when Viv trots off to select a princess book and drops into a seat, her eyes sparkling with curiosity and happiness. I hate taking my eyes off of her in public, because I'm always worried that something's going to happen.

"Your name is Unkie?" Mona whispers under her breath. "What a waste."

"I don't remember saying that I wanted to join," I protest, still watching Vivian get cozy in the reading nook.

"Of course, you do, darling, you *love* books. And having a blind date with one? What fun!" Francine loops her arm through mine and hustles me off out of the way. "Let's just see what they're reading. Come on—live a little. It will be an adventure, and you don't have enough of that in your life."

Another few minutes pass, and a petite woman so tiny she looks like she could shop in the girl's section of a department store pushes through the crowd, a fishbowl clutched tight in her arms. She has long blond hair piled on top of her head, coke-bottle glasses, and a dress that looks like a cross between a burlap sack and a Mumu. Despite her non-descript outfit and barely there hair and makeup, something about her tugs at me.

It's because she's so different than every puck bunny you're always dealing with. Like the polar opposite.

That has to be it, because this particular woman looks literally nothing like my usual type.

"Hello, everyone!" the woman practically yells out over the chatter. "Thank you all for joining us this evening! It's time to announce our first Blind Date title. And it's going to be... Drumroll, please..." She dips one hand into the fishbowl and produces a slip of paper while Mona unenthusiastically taps a pen on the counter. "Oh, my—*The Claiming of Sleeping Beauty,* by Anne Rice!"

This selection is met by a murmur of approval from the collective group.

The woman points toward Mona. "If you'd like to pick up a copy tonight, we should have enough paperbacks at the desk for each one of you. Mona will help you with that and any other purchases you wish to make. We'll be back here on the first Friday of November to discuss the book and find out what's in store for next month's blind date!"

While most of the other customers form a queue, Fran pushes me toward the tiny woman. "Molly! Do you have a moment?"

The woman looks around for the source of the voice, then lights up when she sees Francine. "Oh, hello! I didn't see you on the list, Fran." The glasses that overtake her heart-shaped face slide down her nose, and she quickly pushes them back up as her full lips pucker.

"I'd like you to meet someone. This is Noah. He's Vivian's uncle." Francine pulls me forward like I'm a shy schoolboy, which is a bit of a joke since I have a good eight inches and sixty pounds on her. "Noah, say hello to Molly. She loves books just as much as you do, so I'm sure you have a ton to talk about. I'm going to collect Vivian and get in line for our books." She disappears into the crowd, leaving me with a woman I don't know and nothing whatsoever to say.

Molly smiles up at me. She doesn't even come up to my shoulders, but while she's short enough to be mistaken for a kid, nobody would look at her and assume she's anything but a woman. Despite her tragic fashion choices, I can still see full breasts pressing against the fabric and a round behind along with large, curious eyes in the most mesmerizing shade of green.

"What can I do for you, Noah?" she asks.

"I, uh." No words tumble forward, until I remember Jana's suggestion from the other day. "I'm looking for a book. *Quest for the Silver Fleece,* I think?"

"Oh, Du Bois!" Molly's face lights up. "Yeah, I should have a copy over here." She immediately sets out for one of the tallest shelves, and I have to hurry to keep up with her.

She sets her fishbowl of titles in the corner before pulling a ladder into position and scurrying up to the top. After a few moments of searching, she says, "Ah *ha!* I knew it." She pulls the book out of its spot in triumph, brandishing it above her head. In the process, she manages to overbalance.

I quickly step forward, opening my arms just in time to catch her before she hits the floor. Next to the weights I bench-press daily, she hardly weighs a thing.

"Are you okay?" I ask.

Molly blinks up at me, a warm and comforting weight in my arms. "Yes," she says breathlessly. "Oh, my."

Oh my is right.

We stare at each other for a long moment during which my dick actually comes back to life much like Rip Van Winkle after a long sleep, before common sense prevails and I set her back on the floor.

This woman is serious. A business owner. A lover of books and dates with them.

Which means she's not for the likes of an unlikely single dad like me—the man with the old-fashioned values and perpetually broken heart that would never allow me to break hers.

"Thanks." Molly straightens her skirt. "You're awfully strong." Her eyes linger on my arms. "Do you work out a lot?"

"I have to, for the NHL."

Molly blinks a couple of times and adjusts her glasses again. "NHL?"

"The National Hockey League," I explain as I wonder if this woman's been living under a rock instead of in Las Vegas. We won the cup a few years back, so we're local celebrities even in a town with a ton of them. "I play for the Vegas Venom."

"Oh, sorry." She shrugs. "I don't know much about sports. Um, anyway, here's your book." She holds up a Dover Thrift

Edition of the work I'm looking for.

"Actually, I was hoping you might have a hardback copy. I collect first editions, although I'd settle for any nice printing."

Molly's smile expands. "Tell you what... if you join the book club, I'll do my best to track down something that will suit you. It's kind of like my superpower."

I hold my hand out. "Deal. I enjoyed the *Vampire Chronicles*, so you're not exactly going to have to twist my arm."

She shakes it, and once again, I'm painfully aware of her touch. "Let me see what I can do. I'll let Francine know when it comes in."

I'm tempted to give her my number. There's something about the easy way she speaks to me, even the way she brushed off my status as an NHL player as if it were nothing, that makes me want to talk to her more. The interaction we're having is just Noah and Molly. She's seeing me for me, just an average guy with an above average love of books, and I can't even remember the last time I had that. I've had women quite literally throw their panties at me when they find out who I am, but Molly's... different.

"Works for me," I say instead. "I'll see you around, I guess?"

"It was nice meeting you, Noah." Molly sails off into the crowd as if I'm just one of the usual customers, leaving me off-kilter and bemused. "Thanks for keeping me from going splat."

I make my way back to the line, where Francine and Vivian are waiting to buy two copies of *Sleeping Beauty* and a picture book about a talking pig.

"Did you plan this, by any chance?" I ask.

"Plan what?" Francine smiles at me with an almost convincing expression of pure innocence. "It's not like I *intended* to introduce you to a smart, attractive woman who likes books as much as you do. After all, you haven't dated anyone since..." She glances meaningfully down at Vivian, who's too engrossed in her book to pay us any attention. "And yes, *some* might think that meeting a nice woman and getting back out there would be good for you but suggesting anything along those lines isn't my place."

As always, it seems, I'm outnumbered by people who want the best for me, regardless of my own intentions.

And if I'm being honest with myself, this was the most interesting and stimulating interlude I've had with a woman in years.

* * *

That night, after Vivian drifts off to sleep and Francine heads out to the guest house out back, I head to my library with my new trade paperback copy of *The Claiming of Sleeping Beauty*. *Interview with a Vampire* didn't prepare me for this book. Rice wastes no time before launching into a description of the main character losing her virginity. The writing is curt and minimalist, and I'm not a huge fan of the inherent violence of Rice's descriptions.

"What have I gotten myself into?" I murmur, flipping forward a few pages only to land on a description of Beauty—which is apparently the main character's only name—being paddled in a public tavern. "Is the whole book gonna be like this?" I skim another couple of pages and land on a scene with Beauty washing the Prince's *bulging and painfully twisted sex.*

"Wow." I skim another line. "That's not exactly..."

I trail off, thinking of that sweet-faced, tiny woman in the bookstore. She was so excited to share this book with people. Is she into this stuff? Spanking and public sex? God, it's always the quiet ones.

And suddenly, I find myself a hell of a lot more interested. My groin tightens again as I imagine ripping that three-sizes-too-big dress off of her, bending her over my leather couch and swatting her round rump until she squeals.

Would she like it?

Would it make her wet?

God, I'm a degenerate. I shake my head but the images keep flashing hard and fast. And all these naughty little mini fantasies that are coming feature Molly *coming.*

Her heart-shaped face flushed with desire.

Her sea-green eyes open wide as they lock with mine.

Her shapely thighs falling open.

"Might as well give it a chance," I say aloud, like I'm trying to justify to the book why I'm going to keep reading it even with every page mocking me for that decision. After all, if I'm going to go back and discuss this in a book group, I might as well read the whole thing, right?

And if I happen to be imagining Molly on her knees, washing someone's raging hard on with her delicate fingers, those full lips pursed into the perfect pout, that's only because she's the person who insisted I read the book.

Right?

Someone's hard on. Definitely not mine.

Although, come to think of it, why not? I mean, it's not like I'm imagining her in a situation she'd object to. She likes the book. She's attractive. This is all purely theoretical anyway.

I read the next few lines and groan aloud when I realize where this is headed. Now that the Prince is washed up, he wants her to suck him off. Of course. Beauty, who doesn't seem to have stopped crying since page one, agrees.

Fine, I won't imagine Molly. That's weird, given that Beauty is basically being forced onto her knees. It's manipulative. I'm not that kind of guy. Oral sex? Good. Sexual enslavement? Bad. There's not much room for ambiguity there.

Except I keep reading, and sonofabitch, Beauty *likes* it.

"This is so wrong," I mutter, letting my hand slide between my legs. I'm not jerking off, I'm just adjusting myself. It's been way too long since I was involved with anyone that it's only natural to be a little turned on by reading an old-school *Fifty Shades of Grey*-esque bodice-ripper. Or bodice-cutter, since the Prince literally sliced Beauty's clothes off at the beginning of all this.

No, as I read the scene where Beauty describes taking the Prince in her mouth so deeply that his cock nudges the back of her throat, I'm not imagining Molly between my legs in front of the armchair. I'm *not* imagining her naked, huge eyes glittering behind her gigantic glasses as she gags on someone's hypothetical dick. I'm not imagining how her mouth would feel.

Warm.

Wet.

But I sure am adjusting myself a lot.

The scene moves onto another spanking fantasy, and I'm *not* imagining Molly in my bed, with her ass in the air and her hands behind her neck, moaning as I slap her plump ass.

When the chapter ends without anyone else getting off, I'm on the verge of losing my mind. What a *tease*.

Although to be fair, it's probably for the best. If I let myself keep reading and imagining the bookstore owner crying out with pleasure as her release...

"Shit." I close the book and force myself to place my hands on the armrests. I take a few breaths to clear my head.

When that doesn't work, I get up and practically sprint to my room. I need a cold shower. *Now*.

If I'm going to see Molly again, I don't need the guilt of

jerking off to some fantasy of her following me around. It's not like it would lead anywhere. I don't date. A hook up here or there with a woman who knows the score? That's all I have the bandwidth for right now.

And still, for some reason, even after my cold shower takes effect and I'm getting ready for bed, I can't stop thinking about Molly.

CHAPTER FOUR

Molly

The next time Noah Abbott comes calling, I'm already up to my eyeballs in problems. It's a shame, because otherwise those eyeballs would be happy to ogle him up and down all day if they got the chance. Noah is *fine*.

After he caught me right before I almost took a swan dive onto my own hardwood floors, I *might* have looked up the NHL on the internet. Then I might have looked him up. Apparently, he's a huge deal. He's a goalie—the guy who tries to keep the puck out of his team's net and avoid the enemy scoring a goal. I'm not sure what that means. They also call him Flopper a lot. I'm *really* not sure what that means. Picturing him flopping on the ice like a sea lion at Sea World causes the corners of my mouth to tug upward.

And before I could find out the truth, Mona interrupted me and I slapped the top of my laptop down before she could see me stalking a man I just met. If she outed me, I'd never live that one down.

I spot him the second that he enters the bookstore. His hair is spiked up and freshly washed, and he's wearing a Venom shirt in neon green with a snake logo. That's right, he's a hockey player... he must have just come from practice. It boggles the mind to imagine the kind of body he must be hiding beneath that loose t-shirt. I've never seen a body like that in the wild.

But I might want to.

I might.

Whoa, Molly, pump the brakes. I was up late reading Anne Rice, so my brain is all out of whack. On one hand, my sexual history has a little bit too much in common with Beauty's... for me, arousal and shame seem to go hand-in-hand. On the other, there's something about Noah that leaves me twitterpated. Aflutter. Fine, *horny.* When he caught me in his arms on Friday night, I wasn't just grateful. I would have been more than happy to thank him with a kiss. Not that kissing is exactly my forte...

And a man like him? One with a reputation? Gah, I can't even.

But that doesn't stop me from imagining what it would be like to experience a man his size as the big spoon.

Noah's arrival is enough to knock my other concerns clear out of my brain. I barely have the wherewithal to close my mouth and act like a normal human being as he approaches the counter.

"Hey," I say, greeting him with the same cheerful enthusiasm I'd greet anyone else. No special treatment from *me,* no way. Only when he meets my eyes do I realize why he's probably here. "Sorry, I've been swamped... I haven't had a chance to track down your order yet."

"Order?" He cocks his head, frowning at me slightly.

"The DuBois book? The one you asked me to find?" If he's not here for that, then why did he come? To see *me?*

The thought makes me entirely too happy. In fact, my body starts to buzz, and I have to suppress a shiver.

He flicks his wrist. "That's fine. No rush. Listen, I just wanted to tell you that I won't be coming on the next date."

"Date?" It's my turn to frown, until his meaning occurs to me. "You mean the Blind Date with a Book?"

"Exactly. I like the concept, but the book..." Unless I'm very much mistaken, he seems suddenly uncomfortable. "It's, uh. It's not for me. Maybe if I drop out, it will open up a slot for someone else. It seems like a really popular concept."

"Not a big fan of erotic romance, huh?" Remembering my current predicament, I glance toward the meeting room, where Mona's little experiment is currently taking place. "Seems like you're in the minority."

Noah laughs and drums his fingers on the counter. "Yeah, probably. It's just not my cup of tea. Not to sound like an arrogant douche, but I was a philosophy major in college. That's more my jam."

"Not a big fan of spanking in literature?" I ask, so distracted by the gathering workshop that I don't realize what I'm saying until the words are already out of my mouth. When Noah splutters in alarm, I turn back to him. "Sorry, not my business! I'm all over the place today. There's, uh..." My cheeks redden until I'm forced to place the backs of my hands against them. If my face gets any hotter, my head might burst into flame, and I'm not sure that the insurance covers spontaneous human combustion.

Of all the times that Mona could unleash her inner freak, it had to be right now when I'm standing here in front of *this* particular man. The only man in my orbit who makes my lady bits roar to life just by being close to him.

No, no. Just by *looking* at him.

Noah stares at me, waiting for an explanation for my *faux pas*.

"There's a tantric love workshop taking place in my meeting room, and I didn't realize it was happening until people started showing up to pick up their preorders of the *Art of Conscious Loving,* and now I'm not sure what's going on." I'm not sure how Mona slipped that one by me, but apparently people are into it, because the room is packed. "I... um... didn't approve this."

Noah's head turns, as if in slow-motion, in the direction that I'm pointing. All he says, after a moment's consideration, is, "Huh."

"Little ones come here all the time for our extended children's book section," I groan, hiding my face. "I thought it would be fine for the wine event, but this is getting out of hand."

"How come every time I come to your store, people are reading books about sex?" he asks. "Are you some kind of undercover seductress?"

A giggle bubbles up at that thought. I couldn't seduce my way out of a paper bag. "Reading books is one thing, but this is apparently a hands-on activity. If I'd known this was happening in advance, I would have put paper over the windows or something."

"How hands-on are we talking?" Noah seems more skeptical than intrigued, which is mostly a relief.

I can feel my breath coming out in little pants. "Your guess is as good as mine."

Noah laughs—a deep rumble coming from his sculpted chest that sets my panties ablaze. "Relax," he assures me, "no one is going to have sex in the store."

I blink. "You'd think that, but how can you be sure?"

Through the windows, we watch the two people leading the workshop as they contort themselves into pretzels. It's all the more impressive given that one of them is a woman in her mid-sixties. Her partner, at a guess, is less than half her age. Both are barefoot and wearing skin-tight clothes that leave very little to the imagination.

"I guess I'm not positive," Noah admits.

As we watch, the woman stands up from her yoga mat and walks over to the door. She pokes her head through, winking at us as she pulls her mass of wavy gray hair back into a ponytail. "I saw you watching. Come on in."

"Oh, no thank you," I say, at the same time that Noah says, "I was just leaving."

"Nonsense." The woman beckons to us. "You're Molly, aren't you? The owner? I saved you a seat."

"Sorry." I shake my head, recoiling even as she approaches. "I'm working the desk. Can't *possibly* participate."

"Sure she can." I jump when Mona appears from nowhere and waves me toward the meeting room. "I just finished my break, so I've got the counter covered."

"Don't do this to me," I plead under my breath. "I'm not above firing you. Or hating you."

"She's been really excited ever since she found out you were hosting this event," Mona says loudly, ignoring my desperation.

Spicy novels are one thing, but I don't want to sit in a room full of strangers as we discuss the details of our private lives and talk about how to make sex last six hours. I will literally die of embarrassment—I'm not a prude, per se, but I'm practically a virgin, and I would rather throw myself in front of a bus than admit that to the people who frequent my store. God, it might end up like some tantric version of 'Never Have I Ever' where I'm the butt of every joke.

Because I've never done anything of consequence.

I've only orgasmed underneath the weight of my own hand.

"Wonderful. Come along, Molly." The woman places her fingertips on my back and steers me toward the door.

I turn to Noah as I'm marched away into captivity. "*Don't leave me,*" I mouth.

He doesn't get the chance to respond, because the workshop leader grabs him by the arm and drags him after us.

"And you won't be leaving either, young man. This is a couple's event."

"We're not—!" I squeak, but the door closes behind us.

I glance back out the window to find Mona grinning and waggling her fingers at me. She mouths the words, 'creativity' and gestures to her crotch. *Rude. Possibly fired. For certain hated in this moment.* The workshop leader releases us and goes to the middle of a circle of chairs.

"You don't have to stay here," I whisper to Noah.

To my surprise, he drops his palm on the small of my back. "I'm not going to abandon you in your hour of need... besides, I've already told you I'm gonna bow out of the book club. I don't want you to think I'm a *total* flake. Let's grab a seat."

He points to the chairs, and only then do I realize that there are far more people in this room than seats. Maybe I should offer to go grab more?

The workshop leader, however, seems unconcerned. "Alright, everyone, we're going to start off with an introductory exercise. I want one of you to take a seat. I believe that we have a celebrity in the house. What an amazing treat for us all. Mr. Abbott, would you like to demonstrate for us?"

Noah looks around. A few people grin when they recognize him, but fortunately nobody snaps pictures. I can't imagine he'd want pictures of this moment circulating on socials.

"You just want me to sit in a chair, right?" He lowers himself into a folding chair that suddenly seems far too small for his hulking body, looking around at the other people in the room as he does so. "Easy."

"That's right. Gentlemen, I recommend that you sit first. This is going to be a mirroring breathing exercise. Once you're comfortable, your partner is going to sit on your lap."

Oh, no. No way am I doing this. Because if I sit in that man's lap, he's going to *know*.

Just kill me now.

The woman waves me forward, and Noah's wide eyes meet mine, like he's a deer caught in the headlights, but he doesn't bolt. I hate to admit that I'm even the least bit into this, but if he isn't going to back out, I'm certainly not. My heart races in my chest as I approach and turn my back to him, getting ready to lower myself onto his lap.

"No, Molly my dear." The workshop leader chuckles, bangles jangling. "Eye contact is a key part of this experience."

My breath stalls in my lungs. "Uh. What?"

"Eye contact." She turns me to face Noah. "You'll be facing this way. Don't worry, I'm sure Mr. Abbott won't let you fall."

I gulp and take a shuffling step forward. I'm not really sure how to do this. Do I walk bowlegged around his huge thighs? Or perch on one knee and then throw my leg over him like I'm mounting a horse? I stop a few inches away and stare at him, nibbling my lower lip.

"Sorry," I mumble. "I'm not sure how to do this."

Noah's jaw tenses, and he licks his lips. There's something in his eyes that almost seems like anticipation... but that's impossible, right? There's no way he's looking forward to some mousy, strange chick straddling him, not if he can't handle reading a little smut. Not if he's turned off by spanking as a turn on.

"You sure you want to do this?" he asks.

I lift my chin defiantly. I'm certainly not going to be the one to chicken out. "I'm game if you are."

Noah leans forward, puts his hands on either side of my waist, and lifts me into his lap as if I weigh no more than a book on the shelf behind us. I bite back a squeal as I settle against him, bracing my hands against his shoulders. With my heart galloping off from inside my chest, I lean back from him as far as I can, but that just means that more of my bits are pressing against *his* bits with an alarmingly small amount of fabric between us.

"Is this okay?" he asks.

Okay isn't the word I'd go for. *Terrifying. Extremely intimate. The sexiest thing that's ever happened to me, and that includes my one time of 'zero foreplay followed by less than one minute of painful and erratic thrusting' cherry-popping sexual experience.* "Yeah." I shift my weight slightly and shiver. "This is fine." Fortunately, my bra hides the fact that my nipples have tightened, and there's no way for him to know about the ache low in my belly. No way for him to know how hard my ovaries are squeezing. How hard the *creativity* is starting to flow. How hard my clit throbs. Is there? No, he can't know. My brain realizes that this won't lead anywhere. I barely know Noah. He seems like a good guy and lord knows I adore Vivian and Francine but looks can be deceiving.

Professional athletes all have reputations, right?

Too bad my body ignores logic just as thoroughly as I ignore my agent's emails.

"Once you're settling in, you're going to look into your partner's eyes." The workshop leader chuckles. "And before anyone asks, yes, blinking is allowed. This isn't a staring contest. Now although sexual feelings may come up—and don't repress them or make them bad—stay present. I want you to relax, be in tune with your body, and feel a *soul* connection."

Being present in my body is easy enough. I'm exquisitely aware of every nerve ending, every point of contact, of the heat from Noah's imposing frame. Meeting his eyes, however, is harder than I thought it would be. It's easier to look at the floor, at his hands, at his muscular arms...

This man's blue eyes are hypnotic. Even more than that, they're *haunted*.

I'm not sure why. But God help me, I want to know.

I want to crawl inside him until he gives up every single secret to me.

Come on, Molly. You're being absurd. This whole situation is ridiculous. It's a game. He's a player. Just keep up the act.

I force myself to look up into Noah's face, across the stubble on his cheeks to his slightly parted lips and into his eyes again. I catch my breath at the intensity in his stare. He's not leering at me—his pupils have expanded, but I don't think it's a mark of arousal. He looks almost frightened. Come to think of it, he looks how I feel.

I thought his eyes were blue, but now that I'm closer, I can see flecks of green in them, making them almost turquoise.

I wonder what he sees when he looks at me.

"We're going to start with deep, slow breaths. Three seconds in, three seconds out. Steady. Deep." The woman who dragged us inside demonstrates. I assume that she's sitting on that young guy's lap now, but I don't turn to see. Now that I'm looking at Noah, I can't tear my gaze away.

We do as she suggested, taking long, slow breaths. For the first few exhales, we're out of sync, but gradually we fall into a rhythm. Other couples around the room do the same, but I'm only vaguely aware of them on the outermost edges of my peripherals. Noah's eyes dart back and forth, never breaking contact with me, although the connection seems fragile. I'm tempted to laugh just to diffuse the tension. Noah doesn't, however. Desperation lingers in the depths of his gaze. Something almost helpless.

It's like I can see inside him to the ticking gears below the surface, but I don't know him well enough to understand how he's wired. What is he thinking? I'd give anything to know.

"Perfect," our guide says. "Now, drop to two seconds per breath. In, and out. Breathe through the mouth. If you're ready, lean in closer. Don't break that connection. You're not going to kiss your partner. As I said before, this isn't a *sexual* exercise. This is all about that connection. Not taking anything, not giving anything. Just feeling that energetic connection between two human beings."

I do as she asks, fully aware that my breasts heave beneath my blouse. That my nipples have formed into ice picks. That my panties have flooded with moisture. How the hell is this not sexual? Noah's grip on my waist tightens ever so slightly, and I lean toward him as if pulled by a magnet. Now, instead of bracing myself against his shoulders while he leans back in his seat, we're sitting almost upright.

"Perfect. Nice, smooth breaths. Now, we're going to go down to short, sharp breaths. I still want you to breathe deeply, from your diaphragm. If you're familiar with yogic practice, this is going to be similar to *ujjayi* breath, but you're welcome to keep your mouth open if you're more comfortable. You should feel a rising heat in your chest. Shoulders back, spine straight... I want you to be just as aware of yourself as you are of your partner. Everything else should fade away."

Her voice seems to come from a great distance. Soon, all I can hear is the whoosh of my breath. Noah's mouth drops open a fraction wider. One hand drops to my thigh, while the other rises to the small of my back, pulling me closer. His eyes never leave my face. I want to roll my hips against him, I want to crush my mouth against his, I want to climb him like a tree and—

51

—and—

—I want more of this intense connection.

"Excellent!" The workshop leader claps, snapping all of us out of it, as if she's hypnotized us and is only now releasing us from her spell. "Relax, get up, and release some of that energy."

His gaze slams back into mine. I practically rocket out of the chair away from Noah. My face burns, and I need a minute to return to myself. I can't believe how powerful that was. I'm practically untried. To call the only sexual encounter of my life *mediocre* would be an overstatement.

Suddenly, I'm wondering if I've been missing out. Maybe there's a grain of truth to Mona's constant teasing.

I sneak a glance toward Noah, who's still sitting in the chair. He stares down at his trembling hands with an expression of complete bewilderment.

The guy's huge. I'm that awkward size where I'm usually short enough to shop in the children's section, but too curvy to fit into most of the pants. In the right heels, I can break five four; Noah's easily pushing six-three or four.

He's so big, I wonder if...

I bite the inside of my cheek and whip away again. What is *wrong* with me? I blame Mona. I blame hormones. Hell, I blame Anne Rice.

Although, holy shit, how hot would it be to have Noah Abbott under me, naked and sweaty, sighing, *You have conquered me as surely as I have conquered you...*

Through the window into the main part of the shop, Mona catches my eye. She waggles her eyebrows at me and blows me a kiss.

Later, when there are no witnesses, I'm going to kill her.

CHAPTER FIVE

Noah

When the class ends, I check my phone to make sure that I haven't missed anything. Vivian and Francine are at the movies. We're supposed to meet up afterward, but according to Francine that will be around seven, and it's still only five o'clock.

"Thank you for coming, and make sure to shop local!" The workshop leader and her silent assistant bow. Looking at them is a bit like gazing into an alternate reality where Francine's cougar act that she teases me with constantly *isn't* just for show. But this age gap couple does have chemistry, so who am I to judge?

I'm far more concerned about the impact this event will have on my budding friendship with Molly. I was so quick to assure her that nobody would be getting down and dirty in the back room, but now if she grabbed me by the figurative lapels and dragged me into a maintenance closet, I'm not sure I could say no. Whatever happened between us during that breathing exercise turned me on far more than the book she sold me.

Before Nat and Steve died, I was a little bit of a fuckboy. I wasn't a total horndog like some of my teammates, mainly Latham Newberry, but I didn't take any of my hookups seriously. I didn't *date*. After Viv came to live with me, I cut that crap out. A little fun between consenting adults is one thing, but I prioritized my time. I didn't want to *fuck* anymore.

Turns out, sex in and of itself isn't broadly appealing to me these days. But the connection I felt with Molly just now? A woman who couldn't care less about what I do for a living?

I want more. One hit, and I'm already addicted.

I didn't just want to slide my dick inside her, I wanted to slide my soul inside hers and merge them together. Something broken within me recognized something broken within her— that little hint of loss that only a fellow sufferer can understand.

She helps the workshop leaders put away the chairs and tidy up the room, and I stick around to help. I need to talk to her. I'm not sure if I'm going to apologize or what, but I need to know that she's okay. I need to make sure that I didn't make a mistake just now. I'm also tempted to ask her if she feels the same way, but what will that achieve?

God, what the hell is wrong with me?

It's like some beast has awakened, charged forth from my blackened depths and that sucker has an eternal supply of lives.

When the last of the chairs are stacked on the storage rack, and everything's rolled back into the closet, Molly finally turns to me.

"Can we talk?" she blurts. "Possibly at a bar? With alcohol?"

"Sure." I chuckle as I shove a hand in my pocket. "I've got an hour or so." After that intense experience, I can definitely use a drink. My nerves are fried and raw to the point of painful.

"Great." Molly ushers me out into the main room and stomps over to the front desk.

"Did you kids have fun at the workshop?" her assistant teases.

Molly snatches up her purse and spins toward her coworker. The other woman has a good six inches on her, and some people might find the hair dye, the piercings, and her smirk intimidating, but Molly clearly doesn't. She waggles her finger in the young woman's face.

"I'm going to deal with you later, Mona. This is a family establishment!"

"I thought you wanted us to be progressive and positive." Mona leans against the counter, totally unfazed. "Aren't we, like, a bastion of free thought here?"

I don't want to take sides against Molly, but her obvious annoyance is pretty adorable. She's all upturned nose, blushing cheeked, five-foot nothing of blustering indignation. Sensing that she has won the upper hand for the moment, Mona shrugs.

"Hey, if you want to censor the flow of information, I can print out a copy of the banned books list and start pulling things off the shelves for the book burning. We can get all *Fahrenheit 451* up in here *really* quick."

"Impossible," Molly mutters. "No respect." She slings her purse over her shoulder and stomps off toward the door.

"Hey, where are you going?" Mona calls.

"Work meeting," Molly calls over her shoulder. "You're in charge. Consider it phase one of your punishment."

Mona crosses her arms. "Rude." She rolls her eyes as far back as they'll go, then turns to me. "Enjoy your date or whatever."

I breathe in a gulp and hold it in my lungs before I say, "It's not... we're not... thanks?"

"Oh, and by the way." Mona leans closer to me and narrows her eyes to slits. "If you hurt her, I *will* utilize all the powers of darkness to make you pay. That includes voodoo, seances, and hex bags. Just imagine your dick. Slowly turning into a raisin."

"Aww." I grin at her. "You care about Molly."

"I'm serious. I keep a shoebox full of animal bones and human teeth under my bed for exactly this purpose." Mona points toward the door. "Now hurry up and don't keep her waiting."

I'm not entirely sure what I've stumbled into, but this has got to be the liveliest interaction I've had in years. My relationships on the ice are male dominated, but I seem to surround myself with women in my personal life.

Natalie would love this. It's a sobering thought that brings me crashing back down to Earth as I follow Molly out into the street.

* * *

Usually, any thought about my sister keeps me low for a day or two, but by the time our drinks arrive, I'm back to feeling pretty even keeled. For one thing, Molly cracks me up in the best way. She seems shell-shocked by our tantric experience, and when our drinks come, she tosses back a shot glass full of peanut butter whiskey and orders another.

"Was it that bad for you?" I tease. "Sorry to be such a disappointment in the impromptu tantric soul connection department."

Molly stares at me. "Bad? You thought that was *bad?*"

"No," I admit, staring down into my regular-flavored top-shelf bourbon. I don't need my booze to taste like a candy bar, thanks but no thanks. "That's most of the reason I wanted to talk, actually. Should I have put my foot down?"

Molly snorts and taps her empty shot glass against the polished wood of the bar. "So you regret it."

I open my mouth to reply, but nothing comes out but a sigh. This feels like a trap.

"It's okay, you don't have to be polite." Molly flaps her hands in a helpless gesture of distress. "You're some kind of NHL god who lays women like bricks. Women who are the anthesis of me. You've only come into the store twice, and first I forced you to read a book that made you uncomfortable, and then I

practically dry-humped you in a group orgy. I swear, this isn't...
me. I mean it was *me,* but not the real me."

I try and fail to bite back a burst of laughter. "Molly, it's *fine.*
You didn't do anything that made me uncomfortable. It's just...
I don't know you that well, and I don't...."

Molly stares at me intently, waiting for the end to that
sentence.

"I haven't had sex in more than a year," I blurt. *Why the hell
did you just admit that to a perfect stranger?* "So I no longer
'lay women like bricks' as you so eloquently articulated just
now." Then I lower my voice to a whisper. "And don't tell
Anders or Latham, whatever you do."

She blinks a few times. "Oh. Okay. Are you ace? Because if
you'd told me that before, I would have spared you the
trauma."

"I'm not asexual," I explain. "Just celibate by choice recently.
I'm in a weird headspace of late."

Molly's second drink arrives. She nods to the bartender but
doesn't throw it back this time. Instead, she fidgets with it. It's
obvious that she's not used to sitting still. "Can I ask more
about that?"

"I lost someone a few years ago," I explain. "Someone
important to me. My world came crashing down around me."

Her face puckers with sympathy. "Ah. Vivian's mom. Were
you married, or—?"

I've lifted my glass to my lips, and fortunately I manage to
stop myself just shy of snorting bourbon out my nose. Even so,
the liquor burns. "God, no," I cough, thumping my chest with a
fist. "My sister."

"Vivian's your *niece,*" Molly says. I can see the wheels
turning as she takes this in. "Right, okay. She called you 'daddy'
the other night, so I just assumed..."

"She was just a baby," I explain. "She knows I'm her uncle. She flip-flops between calling me uncle—well, *Unkie*—and Daddy. I don't know how much she remembers her parents—or if she even remembers them at all."

"She lost her father, too?" Molly sighs. "That's rough. I can't imagine processing grief at such a young age."

Whenever the magnitude of my loss comes up in conversation, most people say, *I'm sorry* and move on. I think the intent is to give me space and respect my feelings, but mostly it just feels like they're tossing the ball back into my court. My grief, my problem. One and done.

Molly leaves the door open, but she doesn't ask probing questions. Her eyes have unfocused slightly as she stares down at her drink. It's almost as if she understands what I'm going through on a deep level.

"You've lost someone, too," I guess.

Molly shivers and snaps out of it. "Yeah, but not like that. My uncle and I were close, though. He was my godfather. He was also the one who opened the bookstore. I was just thinking about our relationship... we really understood each other, so I can sort of understand how Vivian must feel about you."

"He died too?"

"Yeah. Natural causes." Molly lets out a breath and takes a drink. I know that look; I've seen it in the faces of so many people at grief counseling. She's ready to change the topic. Sure enough, her next words are, "So, you're celibate. I take it you didn't read the book. If you want to return it, I can give you a refund."

"Um." I clear my throat and take another sip. "Not a chance. That would be a dick move. I can appreciate good literature in all its forms. Whether or not I want to read it myself, I can still use it for my personal library."

Molly's eyes light up with interest. "You *did* read it? But you hated it."

"I'm not in love with the idea of talking about it in a book group of strangers, I guess," I clarify.

"Too kinky?" she asks, not bothering to hide her glee at the direction this conversation has taken.

"Too... emotionless?" I shrug. "Everyone's walking around with a raging boner, or getting fingered by their mother-in-law, and...?" I lift my hands up. "Not my thing?"

Molly cackles and throws her head back. "Oh my God, you really *did* read it."

"Look, if public spanking is your thing, I'm not going to yuck your yum. I'm just not going to participate. Because my yum is... different."

But I might make an exception for you, Molly. Because when your ass was pressed down on my dick earlier, my mind flooded with all the things I could do to it and spanking it was probably the least filthy option.

"Yeah, not so much." She leans back in her bar chair and examines me. "You know, you could come to the book group and just *say* that."

"And ruin my aura of mystery?" I fake-gasp.

"I'm just saying, there's a conversation to be had about consent. Maybe that's something we could discuss." Molly stops herself. "I meant in the book group, not right here and now. But you already said that you weren't interested, so forget it. If you want, I can tell you what the next book in the series will be. The second genre is going to be historical nonfiction, so you probably won't have to suffer through descriptions of people gagging for the D."

Her tone is self-effacing, but the mental image conjured by her words is a little too vivid for comfort. My fantasy from the other night flashes across my eyes egged on mainly by that perfect cupid's bow on top of her full upper lip.

As if she just now realizes her own filthy words, her eyes meet mine and hold. That pink tongue darts out to moisten her lower lip and dammit all to hell, I can't look away.

"That was supposed to be a joke," Molly says, face palming herself. "Aaaand I made you uncomfortable again."

I may be uncomfortable, but it's more about the rod I'm about to sport rather than the subject matter. I skipped lunch, and the bourbon must be getting to me, because I find myself throwing caution to the winds. "See, this is the problem," I tell her. "After that workshop, anything you say about—uh, about *intimate activities* is going to land differently. We're friends. I shouldn't be thinking about that stuff when we're together."

"About what, exactly?" she asks. Coming from someone else, those words might be construed as a suggestion, but she seems genuinely confused.

My gaze sweeps her tiny body. "About anyone gagging for it. I don't want to be that guy."

Her head tilts to the side. "Which guy is that?"

My loafer grips the bar stool until my foot goes numb. "The one who fantasizes about his female friends, when he really should know better."

Understanding passes through her expression. Then Molly's cheeks turn pink, and she adjusts her glasses. "If you want to fantasize about me, I don't object. It'll make me feel better about earlier."

I nod and clear my throat. "When you were, as you put it, *dry humping me?*"

Molly bites her lip and looks away. "No. Uh, when I was imagining what it would be like to repeat the exercise in private."

"Are you like... hitting on me?" I ask, breath coming in little pants.

I'm not sure how to feel about this. I don't date, but... well, I feel comfortable around Molly. Like I don't have to worry about how I act or what I say. I don't have to walk on eggshells. She makes me feel safe.

It's been a long fucking time since I felt that way around another person outside of my treasured inner circle. God, it feels so damn good to let go for a hot second and let the weight of my new life just fall away.

For just this once—in this woman's presence—I want to just be Noah.

"I don't know." She pouts and leans forward on the bar, resting her chin in her hand and frowning. "If I am, I'm probably messing it up."

"You're an enigma," I tell her, chuckling again. "If you were going to flirt with someone, I would expect you to be the first one to know."

Molly doesn't turn her head, but her eyes slide toward mine. "Look, we've already done the soul connection thing. Do you mind if I'm brutally honest?"

I slug the last of my drink and set the glass aside. "Hit me with your best shot."

She chuckles. "Is that goalie humor? Anyway, I have no idea what I'm doing. When we were..." She waves her hands between us. "Doing whatever you want to call that in the workshop, it felt good. It made me want to branch out. Try new things. With you, specifically, even though you're not interested."

"Pretend I am interested," I suggest, fascinated. "Hypothetically, what kind of things?"

"I don't *know!*" Molly slumps forward, cradling her head in both hands. "This is what I'm talking about."

Now would be a great time to get up and walk away. If I had more self-control, I would. But it feels like there's an electrically charged cord between the two of us, and I can't break it. It just snap, crackle, pops and pulls me toward her with a powerful intensity. Instead of shying away, I shift closer. "Let's start with what you do know. What do you like?"

"Hypothetically?" Molly asks.

"Yup." I nod. "In the abstract."

I stare, mesmerized as she removes her hair clip and her silky mane of blond hair waterfalls over her shoulders. "I have literally no idea."

My body hums with an awareness, so I shift in my seat. "Sounds like your previous lovers have been lackluster."

"Yeah, no kidding." She sighs heavily. "If you must know, I'm basically a virgin."

"*Basically*?" I repeat. "Please explain."

"I have had sex with exactly one person, one time." She meets my eyes but then quickly glances away, pretending to be interested in the whiskey bottles behind the bartender. "It was bad. It lasted less than a minute. And there was nothing leading up to it. It felt... um..."

Immediately, my hackles go up. "Bad, as in he hurt you?" If someone did anything to this woman to put that vulnerable darkness in the depths of her eyes, I don't care who he is. I'll hunt him down and make him pay.

"Nah, nothing like that." Molly shakes her head. "Just... I don't know. See, I can't even explain what I *don't* like. It was so forgettable, I just assumed that sex was overhyped. I basically felt like a human masturbation sleeve. But after today, I'm not so sure." Her eyes rove toward me again. "Mona keeps telling me that lack of sex is my problem. Like getting slipped the D is medicine or something."

"It isn't?" I let a little chuckle bust loose. "Damn, and I always thought the term *sexual healing* was literal."

"I love that crazy kid, but she's too up in my business." Molly picks up her glass and finishes her second drink. When the bartender walks by and points inquisitively to it, she shakes her head.

"She cares about you a lot," I say, remembering the threat Mona made as we left.

"Yeah, but she's also the reason we're hosting sex classes in my uncle's bookstore." Molly rolls her eyes. "She's lucky I like her so much."

I swipe my fingers across my forehead. "Seems like she's maybe more than a coworker?"

"She's practically family."

"It's a bit like that with me and Francine," I admit. "She's the nanny, but she's more like a surrogate mom."

"To Viv?"

"To me."

Molly laughs. "I can see that."

"She's up in my business, too. Thinks I need to get out there and start living again."

"Maybe she's right," Molly says. "Maybe they're *both* right."

We fall silent for a long moment. We've both been dancing around the subject, and the push and pull of my desire tugs at me like an ocean current. If it was just about getting my rocks off, that would be one thing, but the connection I felt with her today in that workshop...

It's enough to raise more questions than answers.

"What are you suggesting?" I ask at last with my heart stuck in my throat.

She peeks at me from underneath impossibly long eyelashes.

"If I'm going to dip my toe in the waters, I'd like to do it with someone I can trust."

Shit. Why did she have to put it that way? Can I live up to that? Do I want to?

"It doesn't have to be you," she says in a smaller voice. "I was just thinking out loud."

Somehow, that makes me all the more drawn to her. She's so unsure of herself, but it makes me think that she wants more than just a good time. She wants that connection as badly as I do.

"I'm not interested in a relationship," I say. "I don't want to make things confusing for Viv by adding another person to the mix. She's lost too much already, so I have no intention of doing anything to jeopardize the stability we've established at home. I'm still not in a headspace where I could be a good boyfriend. If you're okay with a situationship, though, I could be convinced."

"I've got my hands full with work anyway," Molly assures me. "I think what I really need is a personal workshop. A test drive. Actually, a situationship would be perfect. If it turns out that sex isn't my thing, we won't even have to break up. But this is good. It'll get Mona off my back. And I won't have to be so worried that I'm bad at it."

"Bad at it?"

"At sex. That my bad sexual experience was all my fault."

"That can't be possible." I tap my finger against my temple. "And if we do this, Francine will stop pestering me about getting out more."

Molly rubs her hands together, eyes gleaming with a wicked light. "So, hang on... are you telling me that you'd be willing to be my fake boyfriend and real lover?"

"Are you asking me to make this fake official?"

64

"Yes." Molly nods. "Yes, I'm *definitely* hitting on you this time."

"In that case, I graciously accept."

My phone chimes. It's Francine, telling me that the movie has let out. I pull out my wallet and drop a hundred on the bar.

"I can pay for mine," Molly insists, reaching for her purse.

Despite what we just agreed to, the thought of me not taking care of her twists my stomach. "Let me get it. It's all part of being the best fake boyfriend I can be."

The stubborn set of her jaw tells me that this is going to be an uphill battle. "We're not a couple."

"No, we're friends. You can chip in next time." I get up from my seat. "So how does this work?"

Molly considers this. "We exchange numbers, and then we set up a date? Or, no, a *booty call.*" She seems entirely too pleased with this phrasing.

I type my number into her phone. "There you go."

Molly checks the screen and snorts. "You put yourself in here as the *eggplant emoji?*"

"I know my place," I tease.

She tugs my phone out of my hand and types her number into the contacts. "Fine. Point taken."

I snort when I see that she's entered her name as a peach, and her last name as an open book. "Is the book in case I confuse you with some *other* peach emoji?"

"None of my business." Molly tosses her hair. "It's not my job to keep track of all your fake girlfriends. Gotta go, break's over." She hops off her stool and saunters toward the door. God, her heart-shaped ass matches her heart-shaped face. She's making me want things. She's making me *feel* things. I already wonder if I'm in too deep. "Text me with your schedule. I'm looking forward to our next workshop."

So much for drawing a clear line in the sand to put some limits on my libido. I'm now certain I just got myself in over my head.

But I won't catch real feelings for Molly. I can't.

I won't.

You will.

CHAPTER SIX

Molly

"Where were you?" Mona demands as I walk in the door to the shop. "Some lady wanted help preordering like fifty new releases for her book club, and I thought it was going to kill me."

"You're the one who wanted me to date," I point out, dropping my purse behind the desk. There are still a few people browsing the store, so I keep my voice down for their benefit.

Mona's head whips toward me, and her heavily lined eyes bulge. "Wait. You're dating? That big hockey dude? That was fast."

"I just went out for a drink with a man I find attractive. One whom I attended a tantric love session with. Don't you think that counts as a date?" I cross my arms and eye her up and down. "Speaking of which, I'm going to need to approve all workshops in the future."

"You told me to get customers, and people came." Mona pauses and frowns at the ceiling. "Hopefully not literally. But sex sells, am I right?"

I wag my finger at her. "You, young lady, are walking a *very* fine line. Some of our biggest events are story hours. This is a family venue, and I don't want us to get a reputation. Once you get known as *that* bookstore, there's no coming back from it."

"I think there's plenty of those on Tropicana." Mona rolls her eyes. "I'll cancel next month's Kama Sutra session."

I squint at her. "You didn't." My tone is confident, but I wouldn't be willing to bet money on it.

She shrugs and flips her hair, turning back to the textbook laying open behind the register. "I guess we'll never know."

My phone buzzes, and even though I've scolded Mona for using her phone behind the register, I check it immediately. It's from Noah, aka *eggplant emoji.*

🍆 *: I'll be on the road this weekend. Are you free next Thursday night?*

My heart drops. That's more than a week away, which gives Noah plenty of time to change his mind and pull the plug. And me plenty of time to get up in my head and ruin it all.

As I reply in the affirmative, I say aloud, "Hey, Mona, I need you to cover next Thursday evening. Are you okay closing up?"

"What? But I have *finals...*" Mona's voice trails off in a whine.

I shake my head at her tone. "So I'll give you Wednesday off."

She slinks closer, peering over the top of my phone. I quickly turn my back on her, but she's just enough taller than I am that she can easily peer over my head.

"Hold on. Who's the eggplant? *Are you hooking up with Noah Abbott already?* Girl, mad props."

"A, keep your voice down, and B, none of your beeswax." I hunch my shoulders protectively around my phone. "You're too nosy. Go away."

"You *are.*" Mona cackles. "Operation Tantric Loving is a success! He wandered in at the perfect time. I couldn't have planned it better if I'd actually planned it."

"I said keep your voice down." I peer around, wondering if anyone has overheard. I'm sure that Noah wouldn't love his business being broadcast at top volume on Mona FM.

"I'm happy for you, you wanton little harlot," Mona cackles.

"Finally taking my advice? Maybe that'll get your creative juices flowing." She wiggles her eyebrows at me. "Or some of your juices, anyway."

"You're the literal worst," I gripe. Despite my protests, I can't seem to stop smiling. I have no idea what's going to happen with this whole situationship, but I know for a fact that I'm looking forward to finding out.

* * *

Saturday mornings are my favorite part of my job. I get to dress up like a princess, put my hair up in a braided crown, cover myself in glitter, and read stories that matter to me to kids while their minds are still open and malleable enough to care.

"Have you ever thought about scheduling a drag queen story time?" Mona asks as I sweep past the desk. "We could call the Entertainment Director over at the Legends show and see if they can send someone over. Maybe even Ms. Las Vegas him... er... herself."

"And let Frank Marino rule over my kingdom for a day?" I sweep my arms out to encompass the store. "Verily, peasant, why wouldst I relinquish my power harnessing young minds for good over evil?"

"Oh, good Lord." Mona pinches the bridge of her nose. I have no doubt that if she was ever in charge of story time, she'd show up dressed as Edgar Allan Poe and read emo poetry to the toddlers.

"Why dost thou sigh? Wait, I hath an idea." I bat my lashes at her and wave my magic wand. "*Reverso attitudium!* There, art thou feeling any more upbeat?"

"If you're going to commit to the bit, lose the glasses." Mona swipes at my wand, but I dodge out of her reach. "Fine, let's say Sir Eggplant wants to go on a Saturday morning date. Wouldst thou consider a replacement for that occasion or whatever? Or wouldst thine kingdom take precedence?"

I hold my wand close to my chest and turn up my nose at her. "Verily, I wouldst postpone, for the sake of my adoring subjects."

She gives me an unladylike snort. "Oh my *God,* stop saying 'verily.'"

"Verily, *nope.*" I stick my tongue out at her and turn to flounce toward the meeting room, only to narrowly avoid collision with a little girl. "I've been waiting years to use that word in context."

"Hi, Molly!" Vivian waves up at me, clutching a pink star-tipped wand of her own. "Look what Fran got me! It's a wand, just like yours. Now we can grant wishes together!"

"Oh my goodness." I drop to one knee and compare our wands. "Truly, we must be equals! Over what lands do you rule, my liege?"

Vivian frowns for a split second before her face lights up. "The Gnome Gloam!"

"Well, Princess Vivian of the Gnome Gloam, will you be joining me for story hour ten minutes hence?"

"Yeah!"

"Why don't you go in, and we'll catch up?" Francine suggests.

The little girl nods before trotting off to the meeting room. Francine doesn't make a move to follow her. Instead, she looks me over and nods approvingly.

"You know, I've been trying to get Noah out of the house for *ages.* I'm glad he's finally listening to me."

"Er." I clutch my wand tightly. "He told you?" I can't imagine how he explained that, given his insistence that this wasn't going to be a romantic relationship, but it makes sense. That's the point of our fake dating, after all.

"He mentioned that he spoke to you this week, and about ten seconds later, he told me that he had plans for Thursday night. I'm not an idiot." Francine winks. Apparently I'm not the only one with nosy well-wishers getting all up in my business. "I'm glad it's you, Molly. I was hopeful—he's an attractive man, but usually women stop short of literally throwing themselves at him."

My hands flutter up to the throat that now feels as tight as a bow string. "I didn't *throw* myself! I fell!"

"Whatever it takes, my dear." Francine follows Vivian into the meeting room. I can't tell if I'm offended that she thinks I'm that desperate or amused that she thinks she's got us all figured out. I settle on *amused,* because her intentions seem purely good. She cares about Vivian. She cares about Noah.

I watch through the window for a moment as Francine and Vivian settle down on a giant beanbag. Noah mentioned wanting to protect Vivian from any complications involved in his love life, and I totally understand that.

Whatever happens, I don't want this sweet little girl, who lost her parents at such a young age, to get caught in the crossfire of a situationship. I'm going to compartmentalize and keep any additional feelings in check no matter how adorable she is. No matter how much I might yearn to connect with her as intensely as I want to with her uncle. As I walk toward the door, I make a silent promise to myself that I'm not going to get in too deep.

I can't.

I won't.

You will.

CHAPTER SEVEN

Noah

After practice the next day, my buddy, Anders, and I strike up a conversation in the locker room.

"Did you see the chick following Latham around after the last game?" Anders snickers. "Apparently, she talked her way into his hotel room. Long story short, he missed his show time the next morning, and Coach had to track him down. Turns out, she'd tied him to the bed during the course of their *escapades* and then just left afterward. Coach had the hotel manager use the master key and they both found him like that. Naked as the damn day he was born."

"Almost makes you feel bad for the guy," I observe. "Not."

Anders snorts. "I guess she wrote her number on his abs in Sharpie, and now they're texting every chance they get. Just so you know in case Lath goes MIA again. He's the last dude we want to get benched because of his extracurriculars. I like being on the solid first line, and I don't want another center fucking up my flow."

"Well, there's no accounting for taste," I say, pulling my shirt on. My own abs tingle, but only because I'm picturing Molly writing filthy Anne Rice quotes on them with Sharpie since I already have her digits.

"Says the guy whose tastebuds have atrophied." Anders elbows me, but there's no heat in his taunt.

"Actually..." I look around, then lower my voice. "I'm going to start fake dating."

His face scrunches up. "What, like catfishing? I don't advise it, man. Those dating apps are whack. You can do better."

"Not catfishing." I shake my head at him. "Where do you come up with this stuff? No, I'm just going to pretend I'm dating a bookstore owner to get Francine off my back."

Anders slams the door of his locker. "Yeah, because *that's* normal. Does Francine know that she works for you, and not the other way around?"

I yank on the back of my neck, trying to ease the tension. "No, I think she believes I pay her to mother both me and Viv."

"How exactly does one 'fake date' anyway?" Anders puts exaggerated air quotes around this phrase. "Asking for a friend."

I close my eyes against the sudden barrage of filth that infiltrates my brain when I think about Molly and our situationship. "We're probably going to hang out. Go to dinner. And get this, she wants to sleep with me. Without any strings."

Anders rolls his eyes as he stuffs the last of his things in his gym bag. "Not news. You could bag a different woman every night, if you wanted. Without *strings*."

Blowing out a sigh, I glance over at him. "Yeah, but I haven't for a long time. I'm out of practice. I like the fact that she doesn't seem to care who I am or what I do. The night we met, she didn't even know what NHL stood for."

Anders pretends to yawn. "So what differentiates fake dating from real dating? Because they sound suspiciously similar."

I glance at the screen of my phone as if this conversation might have conjured up a text from my peach emoji. No notifications. "I told her, no strings attached."

Anders lets out a guffaw of laughter. "Yeah, right! You always catch feelings."

God, why do I even care what Anders thinks of who I'm

fucking? Because he's my best friend. So I do. "What the hell does that mean?"

He slaps me on the back on the way to the locker room door. "Because it's too late for you. You're *already* attached. Because if you weren't, you would have just walked away. You like this girl. She intrigues you. And even though it's as rare as that first edition hardback of *Ulysses* I bought you for Christmas last year, when a woman intrigues Noah Abbott, he goes all in. And he's gonna catch feelings."

I lope after him, through the halls where our teammates are milling around and then out into the early afternoon sunlight on our way to the team parking garage. "You can't know that."

"Uh, excuse me, but yes, I can." Anders holds up one hand, ticking his reasons off on his fingers. "One, you haven't gotten laid in literal *months*, and now you're staging some elaborate fake-date scam? No way. It's real, you're gonna love her, end of story."

"I'm not—"

"*Two,* you said she's into books, and you've got a boner for anything old and stinky with yellow pages. And let me guess... Does she wear glasses? Long hair in a tight bun? White button down with only the top button undone? Pencil skirt? Black pumps? Huge boobs that she's always trying to hide?"

I swat at him. "Stop it. No, she's tiny with the most delectable heart-shaped ass that I can't wait to squeeze. She's like my little tater tot."

Anders stops dead. "Fucking *hell*, dude, you've already got a pet name for her? *Tater tot?* Does that sound like what a guy calls a girl he's hoping to casually lay? I think not."

Anders finally starts walking again and thankfully, falls silent. We're almost to the team parking garage, and I have a bad feeling that Anders might be right about this. Before I can muster a suitable retort, however, my phone buzzes and my heart right along with it. Playing it cool, I pull it out of my pocket to see that I have a text from Molly.

🐚📖: *Looking forward to seeing you tomorrow.*

I stare down at the screen, deliberating over what to say.

A few paces ahead of me, Anders pauses to look back and see what's holding me up. "She texted you, didn't she? You've got the dopiest damn look on your face right now."

"I'd rather be dopey than ugly," I tell him as I start to type, *Me, too, I've been missing you,* but delete it before I hit send. It sounds too corny. She's expecting me to be smooth, right? Unaffected? Dammit, I'm so out of practice with this stuff. I can't even send a simple text!

"And I'd rather be ugly than self-delusional." Anders swipes the phone out of my hands and takes off across the parking lot. Within moments, I'm hot on his heels.

"What are you doing?" I demand.

Anders dips behind a Honda Fit and stares at the screen before cackling. "Ooh, Noah's fake GF is already missing him! She probably already luuuuurves him!"

"Give that back." I lunge to one side of the car, but he darts to the other.

His sparkling gaze duels with mine, daring me to stand down. "Does she know that you call her *your little tater tot*? Maybe I should tell her for you."

When I zig, he zags. "Give me back my fucking phone, you dickhead!"

Anders grins at me and tosses the device back toward me. "Fine, but I rest my case. You care what she thinks about you. You already like her. But go ahead, have fun trying to keep yourself from catching feelings. Remember high school?

Remember college? You always say this shit, and then you always break your promise to yourself. Face it—you're a softie when it comes to chicks. You have an overweight guard dog and a herd of ceramic gnomes littering your yard."

I sigh and stare down at my screen. "I hear you, Anders, but I'm not ready to get involved in anything too serious. Even if it's more than a convenient arrangement..."

Anders is a good friend, and he's always been supportive, but I don't know how to tell him that I'm afraid of becoming too dependent on someone, only to lose them. I only have so much emotional bandwidth, and Vivian deserves everything I can spare. My niece is my priority, and since I'm the only person she has left, I have to take care of myself second. Nothing else tops that.

I can't force the words out, but Anders senses the change in my mood.

"Ignore me," he says. "I'm just giving you a hard time. If you're determined to fake-date the lady, I firmly believe in your ability to fake the hell out of it. Just don't get distracted and start letting a bunch of greasy goals blow past you or I'll lose my shit."

"Thanks for the pep talk." I roll my eyes at him and text Molly.

🍖 : *Are you ready for lesson one?*

Only a few seconds later, my phone buzzes again.

👌📖 : 😵

"Any big ideas for your first fake date?" Anders asks, waggling his black eyebrows. "You only get one chance to make a first impression."

I lift my eyes from the screen long enough to grin at him. "Yeah, I have something in mind."

CHAPTER EIGHT

Molly

On Thursday night, I examine myself in the mirror, wondering what I've missed. My hair is halfway down my back in lazy waves, actually *styled* for once. I was a little awkward with the curling iron, but I think I figured it out in the end. I've exchanged my glasses for contacts, and while I was rusty at putting them in, it doesn't feel as uncomfortable as I remembered. The woman staring back at me over my bathroom sink doesn't exactly look like a sex machine, but she doesn't look like a shy bookworm either. I even sprung for a new dress—one that actually accentuates my curves.

"*I'd* do me," I say, trying to strike a sexy pose.

My phone buzzes with an update from the eggplant emoji. Noah's apparently outside. I scoop up my purse, lock the townhouse door, and hustle off to meet him on the front stoop. I also try to ignore the tingles in my body when he puts his huge hand on the small of my back and leads me to his car where he opens the door for me like a gentleman.

Fake dating: so far—so good.

When I slide into the passenger seat, Noah glances over me appreciatively. "You look great, as always. I think I might be underdressed."

"I was hoping you'd be *more* underdressed." I wave to his business-casual outfit. "Don't you own any assless chaps?"

"Ah, you were banking on a Chippendale's look?" Noah chuckles as he pulls back out onto the main road. "Sorry to disappoint. I don't have anything like that in my closet."

"I guess I know what I'm getting you for Christmas, then. Where are we going?"

I stare at his fingers gripping the leather-wrapped steering wheel. "Have you ever been to the Armónico?"

I've *heard* of it, certainly... as far as resort casinos go, it's a fairly new building on the Strip, but it's hard to miss. "It's a little out of my price range."

"I happen to know the owner, Nixon Caldwell. He snagged us VIP seats for a show tonight."

I'm surprised that Noah wants to attend a show, given that he's supposed to be planning my sexual education, but I have no real objection to doing whatever he likes. If he'd shown up at the townhouse, whipped his goods out, and started putting the moves on me right away, I would have felt awkward and skeevy. Wining and dining is part of the usual course of events for a fake dating situationship, right? A classic. Even I know that.

We need to ease into the filthy parts.

When we arrive at the Armónico, however, I can see that this is going to be more than a stereotypical experience. The hotel is even more beautiful on the inside than the outside, filled with deeply saturated blues and a stunning peacock theme in the lobby. Noah steers me through to the restaurant and cocktail bar as I gape at the crystal chandeliers and scantily clad cocktail waitresses. One glance at the prices makes my eyes pop wide.

"Are we, uh, gonna go Dutch this time?" I ask, nibbling my thumbnail.

Noah lifts an eyebrow. "Over my dead body. I'm getting the surf-and-turf... pick whatever you like and let me treat you. I don't know what bookstore owners make, but I have enough money for both of us."

I decide on the crabcakes. Noah orders a hideously expensive bottle of wine, and we spend the next hour discussing our favorite books. I don't mention to Noah that I've published one of my own. If I did, he'd probably ask about it, and then I'd have to admit that I've been stringing my agent along forever because I'm most likely a one-hit wonder.

Because of our mutual love of literature, the thought of him not respecting me as an author really stings.

A few times, the conversation lulls, and Noah ends up fidgeting with his silverware.

"Sorry, I don't always know how to fill silence," he says after the waiter takes our dishes away. "Maybe I used to be charming. I'm sorry if I'm not doing this right. I haven't gotten out much since my family died."

"It's fine," I assure him. "Silence never hurt anyone. I'm new to the relationship thing anyway. I'm not always sure what's interesting about me."

Noah smiles, his easy demeanor returning. "So far, it's *all* been interesting." He finishes off his glass of wine. "If you'll excuse me, I'm going to use the restroom before we head through to the show."

While Noah's gone, I go into the women's room, and in the lounge portion, I rummage through my purse for a tin of Altoids I threw in there earlier. I don't know what Noah has in mind, but I don't want my breath to smell like crabcakes while we're doing it. After chomping a few of them down and throwing back a couple of Listerine Cool Mint strips for good measure, I check my teeth to make sure there's nothing stuck between them. I wasn't expecting to feel so nervous. What if I'm so bad at whatever Noah has planned that he excuses himself from our arrangement?

Even the thought of that squeezes my heart in a vice grip.

By the time I exit the bathroom, Noah's already waiting outside. He offers me his arm. "All set?"

I accept, shivering when our skin meets. He's so warm, and the idea of his hands all over me sends goosebumps along my arms.

The Armónico is truly huge, and as we make our way through the casino, following the overhead signs pointing toward the theater, Noah ushers me toward red velvet ropes. I squint at the poster outside the door.

"*Cirque Du Soleil?*" I ask.

"I thought it might set the tone." He grins down at me as we head inside, and when he shows the attendant our tickets, we're directed to a private booth at the back.

A very roomy, private booth. In fact, I can't see a single person from where we're located.

The room is relatively dark, and not long after we take our seats, spotlights come on and illuminate the stage. There's no reason for anyone to look back here and see what we're up to.

"Ready for lesson one?" Noah asks in a low voice.

I glance around, just to make sure that the rest of the audience is focused on the stage, where a troupe of gymnasts in tight outfits are now performing a slow, sensual routine. Talk about setting the mood—I never would have thought to take our lessons into the public eye, but there's no way I'm going to tell him to stop now. "Um... Okay."

Noah slides toward me in the booth, turning his upper body toward me as his thigh presses alongside mine. I mirror his movements. He places one hand on either side of my face, gently; it would be easy to pull away if I wanted to, which I don't.

"Lesson one starts here," he murmurs, over a bust of applause from the audience. A moment later, his lips meet mine.

The only other guy I ever kissed was big on tongue. I found it unpleasant, almost like he wanted to suffocate me, but I went along with it. I've *never* been kissed like this, as slow and sensual as the performers on stage. Noah's in no rush. His lips graze over mine, light as a feather, exploring. He smells divine, so I lean in. After I shift closer, eager for more, he stays steady. When I open my lips in anticipation, his teeth graze my bottom lip. I gasp, pulling closer to him, wrapping my arms around his neck.

He pulls away, chuckling, but doesn't try to extricate himself from my grip. Instead, his mouth travels to my ear, where he nibbles my earlobe and leaves a line of little kisses down to my collarbone.

Nobody's watching us. Their eyes are fixed on the stage where a trio of shirtless men in tights are spinning through the air on aerial hoops.

Noah nips my ear. "What do you think?" His hand creeps higher up my thigh until it touches the hem of my dress. He stops there, waiting for my answer.

I've never understood the fascination with groping in public. It always seemed tacky, something a high school student might do, or a creepy old man. In this darkened booth, with my pulse hammering in my ears and throbbing between my thighs, I'm starting to see the appeal.

"What did you have in mind?" I whisper.

He traces the outside of my ear with his nose and lets out a deep, shuddering sigh. "Just my hands."

As a response, that's both cryptic and thrilling. And this is supposed to be my sexual education, after all. It's only right that I should murmur, "*Please.*"

He adjusts his arm so that my head can settle on the outside of his shoulder. "Wrap your arms around mine," he instructs.

"Like you're using my shoulder as a pillow... yeah, like that." His hand creeps up between my legs, and he presses his palm against the crotch of my lacy panties. I moan and push against him. I'm vaguely aware that I must appear totally desperate, but that's only because I am. It's like this man has awakened my repressed sexuality and cracked it wide open. His middle finger strokes me through my underwear, teasing me with the promise of penetration as he rubs his palm against my clit. I turn my face into his shirt and gasp.

"Good?" he asks.

"Oh, yes."

He smiles down at me, his eyes sparkling. "You're already that turned on?"

I slide my hand onto his lap, hovering inches from the growing bulge in his dress slacks. Noah sucks in a breath and squeezes his eyes shut. "Can I touch it?"

"Not yet," he says. "Let me focus on you right now. There's only so much we can get away with in public." When he opens his eyes, there's a brilliant gleam in them. "People are going to notice if I start fucking you right here in the booth."

I shiver at his words.

"You like that?" he asks. "Are you into dirty talk?"

"I'm discovering that I am." I didn't know this about myself, but isn't that the point of all this? Who would have thought that filthy talk makes Mousy Molly wet and needy?

A low groan escapes his mouth. "Really? And you like the idea of me lifting you into my lap? Could you tell how difficult it was for me not to get hard with your sweet pussy only inches away from my cock?"

"Yes." I try to press myself against his hand, but he pulls away, keeping just enough distance between us to drive me out of my mind.

"You like the idea of me sliding into you? I bet you'd be so tight for me, Molly. I bet I'd have to take my time, squeeze into you inch by inch." As he says this, one finger slips beneath my panties. I cry out in shock as one finger slides into me, slowly but deeply, just as his words suggest. Even as the sounds escape my dry throat, the spotlights dance on the stage. The acrobats flip and soar through the air. The audience gushes and gasps.

And I become awash in a sea of sensation.

The first time I had sex, we rushed into things. Zero foreplay. I was dry and tight and completely confused. My college boyfriend slapped on a condom—one of those ribbed ones, supposedly for her pleasure. I wasn't ready for him, but by the time I fully decided that I wanted to stop, he was already apologizing for coming too fast.

Now, I feel empty but open at the same time. Noah has big hands, but one finger isn't enough.

"More," I plead, trying to keep my voice down. On stage, the aerial artists have been replaced by contortionists. The show is impressive, but I have to close my eyes and bite down on the inside of my cheeks to keep from screaming with a mixture of pleasure and anticipation.

Another finger joins the first. Noah manages to pretend that he's entirely focused on the show, even as his fingers explore me and his palm presses ever more firmly against me.

"Do you like this?" he whispers. "Do you like having me inside you?"

I grip the back of his shirt. My eyes are probably glazed over, but I don't care. It must be obvious to anyone who glances our way that I'm falling apart, but I don't care about that, either. It's not just the man's fingers inside me—my emotions run deeper than that.

"Yes," I gasp. "Yes, it's— ah—!"

"If we were alone," Noah whispers, "I'd lay you down on this table right now. I'd lick you until you came, and then..." His movements are becoming urgent and erratic as he thrusts and circles my swollen, throbbing clit at the same time. More wetness floods his fingers as I see stars. "And then I'd see just how much of me you were prepared to take."

He pushes his arm back slightly, and the change in angle is too much. I bite down on his shirt, writhing against his hand as a flood of warmth rushes out of me and I come harder than I have in my life. Harder than with any vibrator. With stars exploding before my eyes, I clamp down on Noah's fingers, trying to pull him deeper. I want more. I want the thick weight of his dick inside me. I want to make him feel as good as I do right now.

I want it all.

Noah looks down at me, the strangest expression on his barely illuminated face. He leaves his hands in place until I finally relax. A wicked smile steals his expression, and he slips his fingers out of me, lifts them to his lips, and licks them.

"Christ, Molly, you taste good. I can't wait for more lessons."

I collapse against him, pressing my knees together. It's a good thing I'm wearing a dark skirt, because I'm quite literally dripping wet. That's *never* happened to me before.

We slip out before the end of the show, even though I feel guilty... the tickets must have cost a fortune. On the other hand, I'm not sure what's going to happen next with Noah, but I'm dying to find out.

The whole drive back to my place, I keep glancing at him. He's so handsome, with those sharp cheekbones and sturdy jaw. But even more than that, he's sexy in a well-read, old soul sort of a way. He's like the perfect man for someone like me.

He's proven more than once that it would be easy for him to pick me up like it's nothing. With another guy, that might be alarming, but with him it feels exciting. I don't know what's more thrilling—the idea of him lifting me into his lap, or the idea of him on top of me as I receive the entire weight of him.

Maybe we can experiment after we get home. For the sake of science, of course.

"This is me," I say, pointing to the end unit townhome, as if he wasn't the one who picked me up only hours ago. "You can park on the street, if you want to come in..."

"Not tonight," he says.

"Oh." I tuck my hair behind my ear as my stomach swoops and dips. Did I do something wrong? He doesn't seem upset, though. Maybe this is part of his strategy. He's the sexpert, after all.

Before I get out of the car, he leans over to kiss me on the lips, soft and sweet. "I'll see you soon," he promises.

"Thank you for, uh." I press my knees together. "For dinner and... and everything."

Everything? Oh my God, Molly.

He gently places a lock of hair behind my ear. "Any time. I'll wait here until you get to the door."

It feels like he's trying to pull away, and I don't understand why that would be, but he waits patiently as I gather my things, scoot out of the car, and head up to unlock my front door. He doesn't pull away until I'm safely inside.

I'm not sure I understand what just happened, but Noah is clearly much more experienced than I am. I'm theoretically familiar with the concept of the cold shower, but after shimmying out of my skirt and my panties, I need one of my own for the very first time.

CHAPTER NINE

Noah

It's entirely possible that I'm losing my mind.

Ever since I dropped Molly off at her place, I've been kicking myself. She was having a great time. Hell, so was I.

She wanted more. I wanted more.

But things were getting too hot too fast. I didn't expect to like her so damn much. I *certainly* didn't expect to wake up the next morning wishing that she were lying beside me wearing one of my oversized jerseys with her silky hair all sexed up into bedhead, and that she and Viv and I could all have breakfast together like a family.

Good thing I pumped the brakes, because everyday fantasies like that could get me in trouble.

Francine stays smug all the way through Monday night. Vivian doesn't seem to notice that anything's different about me, but I suppose that she's used to me being moody and doesn't think much of it when I'm quiet at dinner. She's happy to fill the silence by telling me about their ongoing quest to find Celine, the imagined adventures of her friends in the Gnome Gloam, and a new game she and Biscuit invented, the rules of which are decidedly murky. On the ice, word has gotten out about 'my librarian,' as Anders calls her. And since they haven't had much to razz me about recently due to my normally humdrum existence, they grab onto Molly with both hands and refuse to let go. I fully expect Cash to speak an entire paragraph, but he doesn't. Even when I try not to think about her, nobody will let me forget.

On Tuesday night, even the ladies in group therapy can tell that something's up. I'm nibbling my way through the baked goods—including some particularly excellent homemade fudge—when it's my turn to talk.

"How have you been this week, Noah?" Dr. Ellis, our group leader, asks.

I swallow the fudge and shrug. "Fine. Good."

"Anything new? You seem different tonight." She smiles at me, and I'm aware of all the other single moms leaning toward me, looking even more expectant than usual.

I'm not going to lie, and Francine loves to insist that dating is part of the healing process, so I throw caution to the wind. "I might have decided to dip a toe in the dating pool," I admit. They don't have to know it's fake dating.

Doreen gasps audibly, and a flurry of covert glances flash around the room.

"Like, a pinkie toe," I add. "No big deal."

"What brought this change on?" Dr. Ellis asks.

"Well, I met someone..."

My next words are drowned out by a chorus of groans, and Susan lays one hand over her heart, looking utterly devastated. "You're already seeing her?"

I nod. "We met at her work, and I've gone there a couple of times since then. We went on one date last week." I crumple the edges of my paper plate, feeling strangely shy. These ladies know intimate details about some of the hardest times in my life, so I'm not sure why admitting this feels like the big deal I just lied about.

"That's great!" Jana exclaims. "Where does she work?"

"Yeah," Doreen chimes in, "is she a model? Or an actress?"

"A singer?" suggests a regular named Pam.

"A stripper," Susan hazards. "I bet she has a perfect body and works at The Library."

Blazing heat overtakes my face as I think about how close Susan is while still be being oh-so-far away.

"Nothing like that." I grin at the idea of Molly working at The Library. God, in my mind, she tugs off her glasses, strips off her oversized dress, and there's a thong covering her sneaky hot body. "She owns a bookstore. And before you ask, no, it's not a naughty bookstore... although she did sell me a copy of *The Claiming of Sleeping Beauty* the first time we met."

"She's just an everyday person?" Susan digs into her purse to produce a packet of tissues. "Like one of us?"

"We could have had a shot?" Doreen murmurs. She holds her hands out for the tissues, and both women dab at their cheeks.

Dr. Ellis clears her throat. "I think what we all *mean* to say is how proud we are of Noah for taking this first step. You've really been concerned about dating, haven't you?"

"I don't know if that's the right word. Between work and parenting and staying on top of my mental health, I'm just not sure how much I'll have left over for someone else... Viv has to come first."

Which is one of the reasons that I agreed to Molly's suggestion. When she said that if we parted ways, we wouldn't really be breaking up, that sounded appealing as hell. Now, not so much. I can't imagine breaking things off with her now, but on the other hand, I don't have to be afraid of losing someone again, since I know this thing is short term. It was supposed to be fun. It was supposed to feel safe.

Now, I'm starting to wonder if I'm playing with fire.

Dr. Ellis's voice pulls me back to the present. "Have you discussed any of these concerns with your new partner?"

"A little, yeah." I run one hand through my hair. "She's had a loss of her own, too. We're both in uncharted territory."

"Oh my god, he *communicates*." Doreen sniffles again.

Susan scoffs. "Of course, he does. What do you think he's been doing with us all these years?"

"Well, this all sounds like progress, Noah." Dr. Ellis smiles around the circle at us. "That's what's really important here, being open about our feelings, rather than trying to bottle them up or shove them down. Once you've lost someone dear to you, it can feel like the whole world has imploded. Forming strong connections, whether romantic or platonic, is both a sign of and a step toward healing."

A few people talk after me, but at the end of the night while I'm waiting for my empanada order to come out, I watch a cluster of women gather around Jana, furiously typing into their phones.

"...you think it was that place you told him about a couple of weeks ago, right?" someone asks.

Jana nods. "The Last Chapter. I'll text you all the address."

"This, I gotta see for myself," Doreen says with a shake of her head.

"You snooze, you lose," Susan adds, slipping her phone back into her pocket. "We all knew it was a long shot. I can't believe some random woman got there first. I guess this is lesson learned about being brave enough to shoot your shot, ladies."

I turn my face away so that they can't see my smile. I've never tried to lead anyone in the group on, but I'll be the first to admit that I don't mind the attention. If only they knew the terms of engagement, I wonder what they'd think of what Molly and I have going?

CHAPTER TEN

Molly

"Date number two, eh?" Mona grins at me as I emerge from the back office. "Sounds like round one went well."

"Yup. You're sure you're okay closing up for tonight?" I've got no banter left in me. Today felt like it was about a hundred years long.

"It seems like it's calmed down now." Mona shoos me to the door. "If it gets out of hand, I'll just lock up early and drop the metal gates."

Usually, I'd take her to task for her attitude, but after the day we had, I'm lucky she didn't quit. I grab my purse, fly out the door, and book it to the Bellagio just in time for my cocktail date with Noah.

"Hey," he says as I dart toward the table he's staked out overlooking the fountains. "How was your day?"

"Endless." I drop into the chair beside him. "It was weird, too… it felt like there was a whole army of women in there with their kids today. They kept asking me all these personal questions… like some kind of conspiracy."

Noah chokes on his drink.

"Don't worry, I didn't say anything about you," I assure him, waving away that concern before he has a chance to introduce it. "And they all bought something, so it worked out in the end." Our server approaches and I order a Manhattan before turning my attention back to him. "So, what's the plan for today?"

Noah gestures out to the fountains. "First, we have a drink or two. Then, I'm taking you shopping."

"Shopping?" I frown out at the water. "Listen, I appreciate you paying for dinner the other night, but I'm not sure how I feel about you spending a bunch of money on me. I'm not trying to take advantage of you."

"You only want my virtue, not my wallet?" Noah waggles his eyebrows at me. "Don't worry, this is part of your education—but I think you're going to need a drink or two first."

* * *

I stand before the door of Noah's chosen shopping venue, staring up at the sign which announces the name of the store: *Le Gasp*. The display windows are full of lingerie, dildos, and handcuffs.

"Where have you brought me?" I wheeze.

"Shopping," Noah says, jutting his chest out. "Whatever you pick, I'll buy, but we're using it next time. That's the deal. Choose wisely."

I step into the shop. Never have I felt so totally out of my depth. Vibrators of every imaginable shape and size, ball gags, anal beads, paddles, crops, panties, garters, and what Mona would no doubt call 'banana hammocks' cover the walls.

"Have you never been in a place like this?" Noah asks.

I shake my head. "I had a bullet vibrator that I ordered online, but it stopped working and I never bothered buying another."

A middle-aged woman looks up from the desk. "Do you folks need any help?"

"Just looking," I squeak.

"Well, let me know if you have any questions." She goes back to reading a battered paperback copy of the *Story of O*, as if this is all totally normal—as if my heart isn't whomping against my ribs—but I suppose it's normal for her.

Now that I've gotten over the shock of the place, my mind races as it appreciates the possibilities. I make a beeline for an enormous strap-on and hold it up gleefully beneath Noah's nose.

"Not a chance," he says. "You put that back."

I pout and wrap my arms around it. "You said I could pick anything I wanted."

Noah shakes his head. "Nope. No way. Anything you want *within reason.*"

"Fine." My answering eyeroll would make Mona proud. "If you're not secure enough in your masculinity to take a—" I squint at the label, "—'*Donkey-Dong Love Aid*' yet, we'll have to start smaller." I set it back on the shelf and blow it a kiss.

Some of the items are utterly puzzling. I hold up a glow-in-the-dark anal plug. "Why would anyone need it to glow?"

Noah shrugs, but the woman at the register looks up. "Easier to find when the lights are off, honey."

"Ooh, right." I put it back, clasp my hands behind me, and march through the store. "What about this sixteen-inch tongue? Where exactly is this supposed to go?"

She doesn't even glance up this time. "Anywhere you can fit it, love."

I stop to examine an enormous, floppy object, each end of which is shaped like a life-sized human fist. "Is this designed as a couple's toy, or is it meant for one truly enthusiastic user?"

"That one's also off the list," Noah says.

I shake my head at him. "Where's your sense of adventure?"

"I've created a monster, haven't I? Maybe we could look for something a little less specialized to start with." He points toward a wall of vibrators in a wide array of shapes and colors. I trot over obligingly to examine them. Some are pretty standard, while others are shaped like cute animals, monster appendages—*Cryptid Cocks* seems to be a brand heavily favored by the local clientele—and even, inexplicably, corn on the cob.

While I browse, Noah slips off through the aisles in search of something. He returns with a parcel, which he holds up for my inspection.

"This could be fun, if you're comfortable with it," he says.

I hold up my find. "Works for me. Is this one alright, as long as I don't try to use it on you?"

Noah nods. We take our purchases up to the register, where the employee rings us up without batting an eyelash. It's exhilarating to engage with something that's usually taboo in a way that's so casual. There are plenty of things in here that I'm not interested in but knowing that there's so much out there to explore is exciting.

On our way out the door, we pass a sign that says, *Come Again*. Noah points it out to me, and the two of us titter.

"Is it okay if I leave these with you?" Noah asks. "I don't want Vivian stumbling across them and asking questions I'm not prepared to answer." He pauses for a split-second. "Or Francine, for that matter."

"I take it you'll want to use these at my place?" I ask, accepting the bag from him.

"Is that okay? I could rent a hotel room if you're more comfortable with that..."

I give my head a quick shake. "No, a booty-call is fine by me. When are you free again?"

"We have a short road trip this week, but I get home Thursday. How's Friday night?" he asks. "Vivian goes to bed by eight, and I'm sure that Francine will stay late if I ask nicely."

"The store closes at five on Fridays, so that's perfect. Eight-thirty?" I whip out my phone and start typing.

"What are you doing?" Noah leans over and tries to peek at my screen.

I lift it up to show him that I've put him into my calendar on Friday as:

8:30 'Booty Call' with 🍆

"You're too much." He chuckles and turns to walk me back to the car. "Are you going to set a reminder?"

"Good idea. Otherwise, it might slip my mind." I do it, too, just to yank his chain. "By the way, am I ever going to get to see the... you know?"

In the growing dusk, I could swear he blushes before saying, "Yeah, but we have to take baby steps, right?"

What's he worried about? The man is known for the size of his... hands. The truth is, I think we both know that this is going to be all I can think about between now and the weekend.

CHAPTER ELEVEN

Noah

I'm not sure what to expect when I show up at Molly's townhouse for her self-titled booty call. I try not to have any expectations about what she'll want, or how I'll respond. Maybe we'll take things slow. I wouldn't mind talking to her more—she always makes it so easy. And when the only adult conversation you get is with Francine, Anders, and Latham, that leaves something to be desired.

Her townhouse door is unlocked, and she's not in the sitting room when I step in.

Oh, little Tater Tot, come to Daddy. I'm here to devour you.

"Hello?" I call, peering around. She has a little art up on the walls, mostly featuring muted landscapes, and a couple of house plants, but for the most part, Molly's home is packed with books. It's a decor style I can appreciate. The only reason mine are contained better is because I have a huge house with a dedicated library.

"Noah?" she calls from down the hall. "Back here."

I open the door at the far end to find a cozy bedroom filled with still more bookshelves, the largest spider plant I've ever seen, and a plush bed with soft pink rose-patterned sheets.

And Molly—a very *naked* Molly, grinning at me from where she's lying against the pillows among a pile of blankets.

"Already undressed?" I pout as my dick twitches in protest too. "You're taking all the fun out of this."

Molly spreads her legs slightly and grins. "Is that so?"

My heart rate accelerates as I step closer. "Unwrapping the present is half the fun. Take that under advisement for next time."

"Maybe I was impatient for lesson number two." She salutes me. "Yes, sir. You're the sexpert here."

For all my teasing, it's the first time I've seen her naked, and I can't seem to look away. Her figure is delightfully voluptuous. Huge tits and ass with a tiny waist I could span with my hands. Jesus, how did I get so lucky that this woman just literally fell into my arms and then into my lap? I can't deny that I'm an ass guy, generally speaking, and Molly's got one that won't quit. The fact that those silken tresses are pulled up in a bun and she's still wearing those cat-eye glasses slays me. My fingers itch to set her hair free. Maybe Anders was on to something when he accused me of having a librarian fetish. All she needs to complete that look are black pumps and a book in one hand. Maybe a string of pearls around her neck.

Our selections are laid out on the side of the bed. A rabbit vibrator—Molly's choice—is lying next to the beginner's bondage kit I picked out. There's also a sizable bottle of lube.

"I don't recall buying that," I say, pointing to the bottle.

"You didn't. I was Googling, and it sounded like a good choice." Molly drops her seductive posturing and sits up in the bed, folding her legs crisscross-applesauce. Her expression turns serious. "Women don't stay wet indefinitely, you know."

"Of course." I consider putting on a striptease, but if she wants to get right down to business, that's her prerogative. I shuck off my clothes—all but my underwear, not for modesty so much as an attempt at self-restraint.

"Wow." Molly adjusts her glasses as she admires my physique. "You work out a *lot*. Your abs are like lickable and stuff. Come here for closer inspection."

I approach the side of the bed, and Molly runs her palms over my six-pack.

"Damn," she mutters, "you could grate cheese on these things. I've never seen this in real life. I was starting to doubt its existence outside of TikTok."

I grin down at her. "I appreciate the compliment, but I'm getting some mixed messages here."

"Right." Molly waves her hand at the toys. "Sorry, I'm a little out of my depth."

"What are you hoping for?" I ask. "These lessons are all about you. I want to make sure you get your eggplant's worth."

"The only time another human being has gotten me off, he was fingering me at the theater," Molly deadpans, adopting a posh British accent for the final word. "Before that, my prior experience was some spasmodic thrusting that ended in about thirty seconds. My dry vagina did not recommend it. Zero stars."

"But you read," I remind her. "And I know for a fact that you've read some pretty vivid material."

"Maybe we can just start and see how it goes?" she suggests. "I don't have any ideas right off the top of my head."

A jolt of nerves zaps me, and I wonder why. "If that's what you want."

It takes both of us not only to open the bondage kit packaging, but to untangle the various straps and restraints. Molly keeps giggling nervously, but she's game to start attaching the Velcro wrist cuffs.

There's something strangely comfortable about the feeling of being there with her, with one of us completely naked and the other not far behind. She doesn't seem shy, exactly. If I even suspected that she was having second thoughts, I'd put the kibosh on this so fast her head would spin. Instead, the moment is somehow funny. Affectionate. When she gets frustrated with the straps, she throws her hands in the air.

"I have no idea what I'm doing," she grouses. "Help a girl out, Noah."

It takes us a while to get her in position, and as we do, I keep finding little excuses to touch her, to caress my knuckles along her curves or stroke my palm along her spine.

"You have great tits and an even better ass," I grit out. "Has anyone ever told you that?"

For a second, she blushes and pulls her lower lip between her teeth. Fuck me. "They're both too big. I try to hide them. I've never been one for attracting attention."

I place a reverent kiss on the side of her boob and then one to her hip. "No way. Don't ever let me hear you say that again. I have huge goalie hands and you're perfect."

When I'm done, her arms are tied behind her, with her thighs spread and her ankles held toward her ass while she lies on her belly. Only then do I toss my boxers aside, which takes a huge yank because I'm hard as fuck. I can't remember ever being this hard before.

Molly glances over her shoulder. "Holy shit, Noah. You're huge all over. How am I supposed to take all *that*?"

I smack my lips. "Oh, don't worry, baby girl. It will fit."

After spreading the cheeks of her perfect ass, I rub my dick along the tender flesh between them. Damn, she feels amazing. "Is this good? Are you comfortable with being restrained? Um... maybe we should have a safe word or something."

Molly turns her head to the side and lets her cheek rest on the sheet. "I trust you, but just in case, how about peaches and cream?"

I can't believe how good this feels to be playful with her. How right. "Good. I'm not going to betray that trust, either." I caress the small of her back, dragging my length back and forth between her cheeks. This is totally self-serving, but she feels so good, I let myself indulge in another few seconds.

When I finally move, I settle behind her, slide my biceps under her thighs, and pull her toward me. Molly squeals as I drag my tongue across her clit, then lick her entrance, teasing the tip just inside her. This angle makes it a little harder to reach, but on the bright side, I get an eyeful of that peach-like ass. Still supporting her thighs on my arms, I reach up to squeeze her cheeks.

After a few seconds of this, I pull back. "Is this comfortable?" I ask. "I don't want to overextend your back."

Molly groans in frustration. "Stop talking," she demands. "Go back to... whatever you're doing back there, oh my *God*."

That's more like it. I push my tongue into her again, then bring one of my arms back around so that I can slide two fingers into her. They go in easily, and Molly whimpers. I can tell that she's holding back.

"How good is your insulation?" I ask.

"What?" Molly's voice is hoarse.

"I want to make you scream," I explain. "Are the neighbors going to complain?"

"N—no. I don't think so. I never hear them."

"Good. So stop holding out on me." I thrust my fingers deeper, spreading them to open her. "Let me hear you."

A strangled moan tears its way out of her throat.

"Good, baby, good. That's it." It's tempting to ask if we can save her toy for later... I have two condoms in my jacket pocket, just in case. The whole point of this is a no-strings situationship, and if Molly's comfortable with it, why not?

But I don't ask if it's okay if I slip inside her as much as my dick begs me to. That feels like crossing a line, not for her, but for myself. I'm not ready to be that intimate—even with her. So I have to settle for impaling her with something else.

Anders is right. That bastard knows me far too well. I'm in danger of catching feelings, so while I'm focused on her pleasure, I'm also thinking about how best to erect a wall.

Molly is still panting and squirming. When she twists her head around to look back at me, her cheeks are flushed, and the little noise emerging from the back of her throat is fucking delicious. I reach for the toy.

"You washed this, right?" I ask, because she might not know.

"Yeah," she gasps. "In scalding hot water, just like the directions directed."

I should have known. "Are you ready?"

She yanks against her restraints. "*Yes*. Stop *asking*. Just lube it up already."

I go still for a minute. "I want to make sure you're comfortable. That I'm not doing anything to hurt you."

Her breathing slows back toward normal, and the expression on her profile softens. "I know," she says, sounding much more like the Molly I know. "And I appreciate that. But, Noah... I want..." Her muscles slacken against the force. "I was the one who suggested this. It would be nice if you could enjoy it, too. Right now, it feels like you're taking care of me, and I want..." Again, words fail her. "I just want you, okay? To be my full partner in every way that matters."

I can tell that she's coming out of the moment, which wasn't my intention. I kiss the inside of her thigh, and she shivers.

"How about this?" I suggest. "As long as I'm using the toys we bought together, or doing something we've already done, I won't keep asking. But if I'm going to suggest anything else, I'll ask. If you don't want me to do something, say it and I'll stop. And later, I want you to tell me what you did and didn't like.

Seem fair?"

"Yes," Molly says, which makes it all simpler. It gives me a boundary, a border, something I know not to cross.

I tease her entrance with my tongue again, and she gasps. I squeeze her thigh with one hand and reach for the Rabbit with the other. It's bright pink, and whoever designed it didn't go out of their way to make it look particularly realistic, but as the tip of the dildo portion slides into her, it's all too easy to imagine myself in its place, entering her inch by inch.

Molly cries out.

"Too big?" I ask.

I watch as the muscles of her thighs contract as the toy slides deeper, and her asscheeks quiver. "No."

I'm trying to keep myself in check, but from where I'm lying, the view is too good. Once the toy's in place, sunk as deep as it will go, I take a moment to adjust myself. God, I'm envious of that stupid toy as it glides right through her wetness.

On the other hand, if I was going to end up balls deep inside Molly, this isn't what I'd want our first time to be like. I wouldn't want her at my mercy like this. I'd want to be able to look into her eyes, to feel that connection I felt in the tantric workshop the other day. Even though my dick protests, this works.

I allow myself a few seconds to imagine what it would be like, to pull her into my lap like that and watch her expression as she slides onto my cock. I know what her O-face looks like, but to see her come apart like that while I was inside her?

That mental image is going in the spank bank, for sure.

"Noah?" she asks. "Are you okay?"

"Just taking a moment." My voice comes out as a growl. I already know that she likes a bit of dirty talk. "I was picturing what it would be like to take you from this angle. To slide inside your sweet pussy inch by delicious inch."

Molly shivers. "You could."

I wasn't asking for permission, but the fact that she's given it... damn, how am I supposed to avoid temptation like that?

"Not yet. I have other plans for tonight." As I say this, I reach forward and turn the rabbit on.

Molly's response is instantaneous and explosive. Her spine stiffens, and the restraints creak as the 'ears' caress her clit and the vibrator shudders inside of her.

"You like that, don't you, dirty girl?" I ask. The restraints position her legs so that it would be entirely too easy to prop her hips up on a pillow and sink inside her wet heat in one wicked thrust. As she twitches and moans, there's no way on Earth I'm going to be able to just watch. Instead, I sit up on my knees and pull her back toward me, rubbing my erection between the luscious globes of her ass. My sensitive skin against hers feels good, but not *so* good that I forget myself.

"Yes," she pants.

I reach between us and switch off the toy.

"*Noah!*" she screeches. "What are you—who said you could stop?"

I laugh at her indignance. "Too easy, baby."

Molly mutters something unintelligible, but I go back to what I was doing. Now, each time I rub against her, I hold the toy in place so that it thrusts into her with the same rhythm as my hips.

"Do you know how good you look right now?" I ask. "Do you know how hard it makes me, to watch how well you take this toy? To see it slip into you?"

"Noah," she pants.

I lean closer to her ear, taking care not to put pressure on the restraints or her limbs. I don't want to hurt her, not even a little... Who knows what she's into, given how much she seems to have liked that Anne Rice book, but I hate the idea of causing anyone pain just for the hell of it. Pleasure, though? Absolutely. I want to make Molly feel so good that she forgets that this arrangement is only temporary.

"It would be so easy to lose myself in you," I groan. "I want to fuck you so bad."

I only realize what's about to happen a split-second before it does, when Molly's breathing hitches and she bucks back against me. She comes, tightening around the vibrator, reigniting my jealousy. It helps a little that she's moaning my name as her orgasm rolls through her.

Just as her pleasure peaks, I switch the toy back on, and her low groans crescendo into a cry of ecstasy. I have to lift my hips off of her, because otherwise I'm going to come all over her back, and I'm just... I can't. I tell myself that again and again as she keeps shuddering, clenching down on the vibrator with everything she has.

"That's right, baby," I tell her, forcing myself to take deep, slow breaths. "Let me hear you."

When Molly finally goes limp, I turn the vibrator off and slowly wiggle it free. I can feel how wet she is—so much for needing that vat of lubricant. "Good girl," I soothe, massaging her lower back.

"Noah?" she mumbles against the sheet.

"Yeah?"

"Can you help me get out of these restraints?"

"Okay, one second." I set her toy aside and begin to undo the Velcro around her wrists and ankles.

When she's free, Molly sighs with relief and rubs her wrists, then stretches her legs before flopping back on the bed, eyes closed.

"I've never come that hard before," she sighs.

"I bet I could get you off again," I tell her.

Molly scoffs and opens one eye. "Impossible."

"Never speak in absolutes. Didn't you know that women can come multiple times in one session? You're miracles in that way. Mind if I try?"

She clicks her tongue and closes her eye again, letting her limbs drape lazily. "Suit yourself, but I'm telling you, I'm wrung out."

With a grin, I reach for the lube, pour a little onto my fingers, and then rub it in to warm it up. Then I swing on top of her, with my knees on either side of her legs and one hand braced against the bed. I lick one perfect nipple as I work my fingers into her.

Molly gasps and writhes beneath me, which makes me smile—I *knew* it—but I don't call her out. Instead, I keep fingering her until she arches her back. When I drag my teeth lightly across her nipple, she cries out.

I reach for the toy again. This time, rather than teasing her, I waste no time in sliding it between her thighs and into her, turning it on the moment it's seated against her g-spot. As I circle her nipple with the tip of my tongue, she lifts one hand to my shoulders, digging her short nails into my skin as I fuck her with the toy.

"Noah," she whines.

I'm so hard I'm aching. As she writhes and bucks beneath me, it's tempting to lower myself to her, to press myself against her thigh in the hopes of some relief.

"*Noah!*" she wails, as she shudders with a second release. Goddamn it, I want to feel her tighten around me, want to feel the slick heat of her. I want that connection. I want *her*.

I want Molly.

"That's right, baby. Tell me how good it feels," I breathe as she clings to me, shaking with the force of her orgasm.

Gradually, her grip slackens, and she lets out a deep sigh as she settles back on the bed.

"Guess I win that bet," I growl, sliding up to kiss her neck and then her cheek.

"Mmmhmm," she murmurs. Her eyes are closed, and she looks content and exhausted. She hisses softly when I slide the Rabbit out of her.

I need a minute to pull myself together, so I head for the bathroom to wash up, taking the Rabbit with me. I wash it in the sink, then take a few deep, slow breaths. After such a long time of self-imposed celibacy, I can't seem to get out of my own head. If I'd done what Molly had suggested earlier and reached for a condom, I would have lost it. This whole interlude wouldn't have been casual for me, and I don't have space in my life for a real relationship right now. Until I can figure out how to keep my walls up, staying out of her body means that she stays out of my heart.

When I head back into the bedroom, Molly's curled up like a kitten, breathing heavily. I place everything on her nightstand—there's no point in keeping it at my place, since I won't be bringing her there for any of our lessons—before tugging the blanket over her and tucking her in.

My lips linger too long on her forehead, but in the end, I pull away.

It's easier this way. I don't have to feel strange about leaving her in bed alone as I get dressed, lock the door on the way out, and jog to my car.

CHAPTER TWELVE

Molly

The morning after our booty call—can I even call it that when Noah didn't come inside me, or even come at all?—I wake to find myself tucked into bed, entirely naked, completely satisfied and utterly alone. I suppose I shouldn't be surprised... I pretty much passed out before I could make sure that Noah got his.

God, I'm a selfish bitch. He must hate me. So far, I'm not sure what, if anything, our arrangement does for him.

Feeling bemused as much as anything, I reach for my glasses and then my phone. To my embarrassment, the Rabbit rests gently on my nightstand with the bondage kit neatly folded and sitting beside it. Not sure what else to do with them, I toss them into the top drawer of my nightstand—vibrator on top—and slam it closed. Then sit up against the pillows, turn on my phone, and start Googling for all I'm worth.

I don't know much about sex other than what I've read, seen, and assumed. My previous experience was lackluster enough to make me think I disliked it entirely, which is *clearly* not the case. On the other hand, when Noah asks what I like or what I want, I have no idea how to answer him. Last night, when he kept checking in with me, I got flustered and frustrated. How come Noah seems to know my own body better than I do?

I want to know his body just as well.

In school, when I didn't know what to do, I turned to the internet. Braced for all the graphic details the web has to offer,

I buckle in and begin my research, my mouth continuing to form into a larger and larger oval the deeper I dive into everything X-rated.

* * *

"Oh my god, you two are so gross together," Mona observes as she wheels a cart of books past the desk. She's working on a new display which, to my relief, is focused on Halloween rather than the weird things she's been putting out lately. I'm happy to have her peddling *Rebecca, The Complete Works of Edgar Allan Poe,* and even *Will My Cat Eat My Eyeballs?* if it keeps her out of trouble.

"You're the one who wanted me to see someone," I remind her, pressing my lips to hide my smile as I merrily text away in the affirmative that I'll gladly accept his abnormally late phone call later from the road. Apparently, he needs to get away from Anders Beck, his best friend and teammate.

"Did you do the nasty yet?"

I make a strange noise, and Mona's head whips toward me so fast it's a wonder she doesn't hurt herself.

"Is that a *yes?*" Her eyes light up with glee.

"No," I tell her. We've done plenty, but she doesn't need to know that. "No, we haven't slept together."

"Dammit, Molly!" Mona lifts her hands in the air all while doing a little crotch thrust. I can tell that she's about to go on a tangent, but then the bell in the front jingles, the door opens, and a mother and child walk through. Mona sighs, but all she says is, "That book isn't going to write itself, you know."

Right. The book. Angela isn't going to wait forever, but for some reason I've been distracted lately...

As my day drags on with the usual stuff, Noah and I don't text much. I'm busy, and he's got hockey stuff and a game to play in, but my anticipation builds as evening approaches. I'm looking forward to any contact with him. It almost feels like a date.

I mean, it's *not* a date. We're not *dating.* But FaceTime doesn't fit into the category of *booty call*, so I'm not sure what else to call it. But something deep inside me lights up and stays brightly illuminated at the prospect of talking to him. Our arrangement doesn't allow for personal phone calls, but I'm happy he's thinking of me enough to want to.

Maybe he thinks of me as a friend now. I sure hope so.

I push through the rest of my day, before going home, ordering Chinese and settling in to mindlessly watch Netflix. At almost eleven, my phone finally rings. I'm lying in bed with my laptop in hand, staring at a blank document to pass the time. Theoretically, I should be writing, but so much for that.

As I answer, I giggle at the eggplant emoji that Noah set as his contact info, and I'm still laughing when his face pops up on the screen. His bemused smile does funny things to my heart and body. I recognize the pinch in my belly from all the way back in middle school... dammit, I have a crush on this guy. Although, do you still call it a crush after the third mind-blowing orgasm?

"What did I miss?" he asks.

"Nothing much, I'm just punchy from the long day. The bookstore was hopping."

"That's good, though, right?"

"Of course, but it means I got takeout for dinner and crashed the minute I walked through the door." I shove my laptop aside and settle back against the pillows. "How was the game?"

From the looks of things, Noah's in his hotel room, alone. His hair is still damp from the shower. "We won, obviously." He winks. "But Anders is driving me nuts. I finally sent him out to get us drinks from the café so I could talk to you alone."

"Aah, of course, you won, because according to Google, you're a hockey god." I can't keep a straight face when I say this. "Did you keep all the biscuits out of the basket tonight?"

One corner of his mouth quirks up. "You've been researching again, haven't you? Be honest, how much do you know about the game without the internet?"

My frantic Googling over the last few days has included some digging into the rules of hockey, but Noah doesn't need to know that. Instead, I tell him as much as I knew *before* we landed in a situationship. "A bunch of burly men ice skate and do their best to knock each other's teeth out. Sometimes they score goals. Sometimes they just give up and get in fights instead."

Noah groans and presses his palm to his forehead. "*Nooo!* I can't believe you're really that clueless."

Because I enjoy tormenting him, I add, "What I can't remember is how it's scored. Is it like basketball, or golf?"

"Both," Noah teases. "You want your team's score to be high for knocking out the other guy's teeth, but you want to keep as many of your own as possible."

I don't suggest that I should go to a game, and Noah doesn't invite me. Why would he want me to get that involved in his life? I'm not someone he's going to show off to his friends. He can use me to get Francine off of his back, but it doesn't make sense to get more entangled in each other's lives than we already are.

And I'm fine with that.

I totally am.

"We'll have to work on that later," is all Noah says, before changing the subject. "That's not why I wanted to talk, though. I was hoping that we could debrief on the other night before we get together again. I get the impression that you're not comfortable talking about certain topics in the heat of the moment."

I let out a sigh before I can stop myself.

Noah cocks his head. "We don't have to, if you don't want to…"

My stomach ties itself into a knot I'm afraid I won't be able to unwind. "It's not that. I'm just not sure what to say."

"You could tell me what you liked, for starters. Or what you didn't like." Noah wraps his free arm behind his head. He looks cozy. This feels so coupley. I can easily imagine being with him—his girlfriend for real.

Stop it, Molly.

I wish I was there with him right now. Instead, I shove the emotions away and imagine his citrusy smell. His rock-hard body. His huge and talented hands against my skin.

"It was good." I glance toward the drawer where my contraband is hidden. "The bondage kit was fine, but I don't think I want to use it often. Everything else was amazing…"

His face scrunches up into an adorable little pout. "Was there something you wanted to do that you felt uncomfortable asking for?"

"Not at the time. But I've done some research since then."

Noah's eyebrows climb toward his hairline. "Research?"

"I watched porn," I say bluntly.

Noah snorts. "And did you learn anything from this *research?*"

I stare at his face as I admit, "That I want to touch you more."

Noah clears his throat.

"Now *you* look uncomfortable. Why? I thought pretty much every straight guy on Earth wanted to either get laid or have his dick sucked at the drop of a hat. And even though I've never done that, I want to. I want to learn, Noah. So far, I've only learned how to come hard. I don't want to be a selfish partner."

Noah doesn't say anything for a long moment. His eyes drift away from mine. He's still looking at me, but not meeting my gaze.

"Don't you like the idea of me sucking you off?" I ask, feeling slightly indignant. "I'm not experienced, but I bet I could figure out what you like. Besides, you're really good at communicating, and I'm really good at following orders."

"Christ, Molly." Noah looks away toward the wall of his hotel room. At first, I think he's uncomfortable, but then I notice the flush high in his cheeks, and the way his free hand snakes down out of sight.

"Hang on." I narrow my eyes. "You *do* like it!"

Noah speaks slowly, finally meeting my gaze. "Are you seriously asking me if I like the idea of your lips around my dick?"

I grin and sit back. "Well, I know *I* do."

"Goddamn it," Noah groans. "Why are you always saying things like that? It's like I can't *not* be rock hard when it involves you."

"There's only one problem," I say, tapping one finger against my lips. "It's challenging for me to picture, since I haven't gotten a good view." I could certainly *feel* him the other night, but he keeps stopping short of letting me touch him, much less get him off, even with my hands let alone my mouth.

My mind races. What will it taste like? What will it feel like under my tongue?

Noah smiles, with his eyes slightly unfocused. "Are you asking me to show you the goods when I get home?"

"I suppose I can wait." All this talk is getting me hot and

bothered. I find myself glancing toward the top drawer of my nightstand. "But one way or another, Noah, I want you inside me next time we get together."

Noah's head rolls back against the pillows. His free arm twitches.

"Noah Abbott," I demand, "are you *touching* yourself right now?"

A moan as he shifts his weight. "Maybe."

I bite my bottom lip as my self-restraint crumbles and I reach for the drawer, producing the Rabbit from its hiding place. "Tell me more. Like, what you're thinking about."

Noah laughs but his eyelids have grown heavy and hooded. "I'm fucking my fist thinking about your tight pussy. Is that what you want to hear, Molly?"

"Yeah." I start the Rabbit, teasing my clit with its vibrating tip. My nightie is hiked up to my hips. "Keep going."

"The other night, you looked so good. You think I don't want you, Molly? You have no fucking clue." He looks almost pained; the camera sinks lower, allowing me a view of his exposed stomach. "I keep wondering if you'd take my dick as sweetly as you took that Rabbit. Inch by slow inch until I couldn't take that slick wet heat another second without ramming home all the way. If you'd squeal once I was balls deep. You'd like that, wouldn't you, dirty girl?"

Increasing the speed on my Rabbit, I whisper, "Why wouldn't I?"

"I'm bigger than your little toy that I know is in your hand right fucking now," he says, with only a trace of a smug smile. "Much bigger."

I open and close my mouth a few times before finally working up the courage to say, "Show me."

He only hesitates for a moment. Then he lowers the angle of

his phone until I can see his dick as well as his face. My eyes widen. He looks impossibly huge at this angle. I push my panties aside and press the Rabbit into me, gasping at how full it makes me feel. It's just a toy, though. Noah would be warm, and he would be... well, *Noah*. He'd be gentle if he was worried I was going to get hurt, and if I told him I wanted more, he'd give me everything he had. But never until I asked for it. Probably not until I begged.

I open my eyes and stare at his cock again, licking my lips and I thrust the Rabbit into me as far as it will go and flick it to high. "If you say I can take it," I tell him. "Then I can. I trust you to go very *slow* with me."

Noah's hand moves faster. "I bet you could, baby. I keep imagining what it would feel like to sink into you, as deep as you'd take me. I wonder if you'd moan. Thrash. Whisper my name."

I remember how open I felt the other night. How exposed. I wouldn't have thought that I would like to be at someone else's mercy like that, but it's different with Noah. I really do trust him.

"Remember... at the tantric love class..." I pant. "When I think about you... I imagine you... *ah!*... like that..."

"Yeah? That's what you like?" I've never seen Noah like this. Aroused, obviously, but also *open*. He's let down his guard for just a moment. For a split second, I can see the real man behind those haunted eyes.

At the sight, something splits wide open inside me too.

"I'd like—" I stop myself from telling him that *he's* been the focus of my fantasies lately. That's not what we're here for. "—that, yeah."

It sounds lame, but fortunately, Noah doesn't seem to be listening too closely. I watch in fascination as he grits his teeth and strokes again, sucking in a loud breath as his dick jerks in his hand, and he comes all over his taut belly in long ropes.

He lies there for a moment, breathing hard, mouth open and eyes closed. I try to chase that earlier feeling from just before I brought up that workshop, but it's gone. I turn off the rabbit and set it next to me on the bed, smoothing my nightie and fidgeting my underwear back into place.

"You okay, Molly?" he asks in a slurred voice.

"Yeah," I say, and it's the truth. This is strange, but I'm not sorry we did it. He just showed me more of himself in these past few minutes than he has since we met. And it had nothing to do with his body.

"I should probably wash up." He smiles at me sheepishly and lifts the camera until I can only see his face again. "We can make plans for... maybe the weekend?"

"Of course. Don't lose any more teeth until the next time I see you. That's what you say to hockey players, right?"

He chuckles as he sits up. "Close enough. But since I wear a goalie's mask, I still have all my teeth. I'll text when I'm back in Vegas."

We end the call, and I lie back on the bed, still feeling horny and confused. The words I almost said on the phone spin through my head.

I'd like anything, as long as you're involved.

I need to knock that crap off. Noah was clear about what he wanted. So was I.

I reach for my Rabbit again, telling myself that there's nothing wrong with a fantasy or finishing myself off. That's what this whole relationship is, after all. There's nothing wrong with getting to know my body—what turns it on and what doesn't. And there's nothing wrong with doing that with my friend Noah.

No, nothing wrong with that at all.

Still, as I wriggle out of my underwear altogether and use the toy the same way Noah used it on me the other night, I'm not thinking about his dick—at least, not in isolation—or some abstract fantasy. I'm remembering how it felt to sit in his lap and stare into his eyes, breathing in sync, until the whole world fell away around us.

And there *is* something wrong with that.

CHAPTER THIRTEEN

Noah

Viv holds my hand and skips at the same time, but with my long legs, I can keep up with her without following suit and losing my man card.

Her frilly dress floats around her chubby legs as she tugs on my fingers. According to Fran, Viv wanted to wear her pink tiara and go full princess glam for this date, but our nanny talked her out of it just in time. Although I wouldn't have minded. Viv's happiness means more than my being a little uncomfortable in public.

She shifts from one foot to the other. "Can I get more than one scoop, Unkie?"

"You can have as many scoops as you want, sweetie," I say, squeezing her tiny fingers within mine.

During the season, we don't get to spend as much one-on-one time together as I'd like. So when I have holes in my schedule, I always fill them with Unkie time. The entire team has a meeting with our owner later, but I have a few hours to spare right now for lunch and dessert with my best girl. We already went to have burgers and fries at the Rainforest Café. Of course, Viv had to pick out a new stuffie to add to her already overflowing collection. Between synthetic animals and garden gnomes, my house is being overrun with whimsy. I might even have to buy less books and start moving Viv's toys into my library.

And I wouldn't have it any other way.

I valeted the SUV and now we're headed toward Sloan's, Viv's favorite place for sweet treats. They serve these themed sundaes she loves—one of them even has a pail and a shovel like kids use when they're digging at the playground.

Since I worked out extra hard this week, I might indulge a little too. If you can't have a few extra calories now and then as a professional athlete, it's not even worth it to bust your ass on the ice and in the gym.

Once we approach the ice cream shop, Viv's eyes sparkle and she claps her hands together. The entire place looks like a Willy Wonka wonderland. The hot pink walls, candy-colored chandeliers, and walls of candies await my niece. Her shoulder-length blond curls bounce as she does a little dance on the toes of her shiny white shoes with the gold buckles that she loves. The swaying motion causes the tulle of her skirt to swirl, which just makes her keep doing it.

She points up at the menu board. "Oh, Unkie! Can I get the sundae with the sunglasses on it?"

"You can have whatever you want, sweetie," I soothe, rubbing my palm down along her riot of curls. She looks so much like Nat, sometimes staring at her hurts.

"And an umbrella too?"

I wink at her as I fish in my pocket for my wallet. "Ice cream isn't ice cream without an umbrella."

As we approach the high-top counter, she sighs. "You're so silly. Ice cream only comes with umbrellas at Sloan's. I love Sloan's."

With uplifted arms, Viv asks me to pick her up, and I oblige so she can tell the smiling teenager what she wants. Once we've ordered, we move toward the pickup counter. Before long, Viv has her sundae clasped tightly in her hands. I grab a few extra napkins just in case. There are a few tables outside Sloan's where you can stop and eat. I get Viv situated and then slide into the metal bistro type chair, hoping it doesn't collapse under my weight. Chairs never seem to be made for guys my size, and I always have to be worried about going splat on the concrete.

I pick up one of those little plastic spoons that always seems like it's going to snap in half. The first bite explodes across my tastebuds and I can't help but let out a little moan. I don't indulge often, so when I do, I try to enjoy every single mouthful.

Viv glances up at me, a dollop of whipped cream on her lips. I reach over and wipe it away with a napkin as she giggles.

"Unkie, can I ask you a question?" she says, swinging her legs back and forth.

I crumple up the napkin and toss it on the table. "Anything, sweetie. You know that."

She cocks her head to one side. "You see that lady over there?"

I turn my head slightly to see a very pregnant woman pushing a stroller with a toddler in it down the sidewalk. She's juggling packages, an oversized purse, and an iced coffee at the same time because her diaper bag overflows the storage beneath her stroller. God, I can't even imagine. Keeping up with Viv is hard enough. "Yeah, she's pretty."

Viv nods. "Yup. How did that baby get in there?"

White hot panic slices through me, settling into every single cell. Oh no. She's only four. It's too fucking soon for this conversation! With terror about to overtake me, I whip out my phone and pretend I have to answer a text. "Just one minute, sweetie, it's Coach. I have to answer him about the meeting later."

She nods as if she didn't just implode my world into Defcon 1 mode and slurps up more of her whipped cream like she doesn't have a care in the world.

When I damn well do.

I open a Safari page and type in how to talk about sex to four-year-olds as fast as my trembling fingers can fly. Clicking on the first thing that comes up, I scroll through and pray that I can find an answer before I slip into a full-blown panic attack. The article drones on and on about how it's important to talk about boundaries with kids who are 2-5 and you should bring up consent and make that your priority. Like how am I supposed to talk about consent with Vivian when we're talking about a pregnant stranger? When she doesn't even understand the concept? Damn the internet. This is going from bad to worse. There has to be a way to simplify things without lying outright. I want to call Fran so badly, but I also don't want Viv to think her question is wrong or bad in any way, or that I can't handle answering it. I want her to always feel that she can talk to me about anything—even uncomfortable topics.

Because the older she gets, the more challenging all the important conversations will become.

I decide to wing it but use honesty since it's the best policy. "Um... when two people love each other—a mommy and a daddy—they show their love with their bodies. And that love can make a baby inside the mommy."

I lean back in my chair. Not too bad if I do say so myself. I didn't make up a story like some people do about storks and tummies instead of uteruses, but I also kept it G-rated.

Really, Noah? Is that what you and Molly are doing? Keeping things G-rated? Sweeping away that mental image, I peer at Viv from over my sundae. Viv doesn't need to know about Molly and what we're doing or not doing.

Viv keeps eating and doesn't even look up at me as she asks,

"How?" around a mouthful of ice cream. "How do the mommy and daddy's bodies make a baby?"

My soul temporarily leaves my body. I pause. I stall. I clear my incredibly tight throat. In the end, I croak out, "Well, the mommy and daddy put their bodies together and the daddy's penis goes inside the mommy's vagina to make a beautiful child like you, or sometimes they get sperm and an egg from someone else and that works too."

She regards me. "When the pee stick goes in the virginia, does it make noise?"

Fuck me.

"Not usually."

"That's good." She twists her lips, and I can see her mind working. "Have you put your pee stick inside Molly's virginia?"

Every single muscle inside my body stiffens into a rigor mortis-like state. *I'm going to hell, I'm going to hell, I'm going to hell...* "Um... no."

She meets my gaze, engages it, and doesn't let it go. "So you don't love Princess Molly, Unkie?"

Is lying-not-lying like sorry-not-sorry? God, I hope so. "Molly and I are... friends."

We are so not friends. I can't believe I'm lying to Viv right now, but not about the sex part—about the emotions part. Oh, how the tables have turned.

"Oh. It would be nice to have a mommy again." She finally goes back to scooping up another bite of her whipped cream. "Does somebody know how to get the baby out of that lady?"

I finally exhale. This one I've got. "She has a special baby doctor called an Obstetrician, and he or she is an expert at getting babies born safely."

She stabs her spoon into her fudge sauce and licks. "Did an obstacle help me to get born?"

I nod. "He sure did. Your mommy had one of the best. He got you here safely, and I can still remember the first time I held you in the hospital. You were the most perfect baby ever. Before I even met you that day, I knew I loved you."

Viv rubs her tummy and says, "I love you too, Unkie. Can I be done now?"

I send up a solemn prayer to whoever is watching over the heavens today, because if I have to answer one more question about sex to a four-year-old, I might just die and join them.

* * *

Not one guy on the team likes the Venom owner, Dante Giovanetti. The guy's an asshat through and through, so when he calls a team meeting—off the ice, no less, 'cuz God forbid that the guy ever step out of his element and into ours—we all know it's going to be a hot mess. Anders and Latham's linemate, Cash—our resident man of few words, joins me, and the four of us catch a limo to the dude's gaudy casino, the Mona Lisa.

"Any idea what this is about?" Latham asks.

"It better be an announcement that we're bringing on a new winger," Anders grumbles. "I'm sick and tired of being double shifted."

Latham cocks his head. "You'd think Coach would tell us that, right? Dante's not supposed to be involved in player acquisitions."

"In any normal universe, yeah," I say. "But Dante's... Dante. That's all I'll say."

"As for why he's doing this?" Anders swivels his index finger around the group of sweaty guys trooping through the casino. "I bet you a hundred bucks Dante shows up wearing some fancy-ass designer suit, with his hair all slicked back, and gets a big ol' boner over the fact that we look like shit while he plays king of the jungle clad in Italian wool."

"No bet," Latham says at once. "We all know that much."

In general, Anders is a pretty easygoing guy, but Dante pushes every single one of his buttons. I get it. There's nothing Dante loves more than a power trip, especially if it means getting one over on somebody. I assume the attitude serves him well in business, but for us it means that we're constantly butting heads with the guy who signs our paychecks. Coach is pretty good about not letting on about how much Giovanetti grinds his gears, but Dante's ownership style is too hands-on for a guy who doesn't know his ass from his elbow when it comes to the game. He's the George Steinbrenner of hockey, minus the notoriety. Throw in the temper of Rocky Wirtz and you've got a five-alarm shitstorm almost every single day during the season.

Don't even get me started about the playoffs, which we've made the last five years. Three years ago, we won the cup and that got him off our backs for about all of five minutes. He acted like he had everything to do with it when we were only successful in spite of him, not because of him.

He busted a nut over all the glory that brought him and now he expects the same result every post season. It's a lot of pressure.

Sure enough, when we file into the meeting room, Dante's standing at the front wearing a dove-gray silk suit over a white shirt that's open at the collar perfect to show off his perpetual tan and polished black wingtips. His hair is slicked back, and a heavy gold chain supporting a horn pendant hangs around his neck. Designer shades are perched on top of his head. He looks like a 1930s gangster who's considering a hostile takeover of Vivid Entertainment.

Anders shrugs like, *What did I say?*, even though we all know the score. The guy's predictable if nothing else. I ignore the knot in my stomach threatening to bring back up the ice cream I just indulged in with Viv.

He keeps dicking around on his phone until we're all seated, not greeting anyone, not making the requisite small talk, relaying the clear message that we're not worth a single extra second of his time.

"You think he's doing something important, or is he just screwing with us?" Latham whispers.

"Farmville," Anders whispers back. "His carrots are ready for harvest."

One of the third line wingers in front of us overhears and lets out a bark of laughter. Dante's eyes immediately dart toward him. Our team owner turns off his phone and slips it into an inner pocket of his suitcoat before addressing Coach Brenig. "Is everyone here?"

"You'd know that if you paid any damn attention to your team," Anders mutters under his breath.

I elbow him in the ribs. I don't care how he feels about Dante, and most of us feel the same way. That doesn't mean I want him getting benched or traded over some smartass remark. Dante doesn't understand the team hierarchy. He treats his first line as shitty as he treats his fourth line. And being team captain earns Anders Beck exactly zero respect.

"All here." Coach leans against the wall with his arms crossed, staring at the floor. Whatever this is about, he already knows, and he doesn't want Dante to see how much he hates it. Which means we're gonna hate it too.

"Excellent." Dante turns to the rest of us and offers a humorless smile. "I wanted you all to know that we will be signing a new player. This acquisition will represent a shift in future player protocol."

Latham's eyebrows disappear into his hairline, and a few of us shift around in our seats. I don't know where Dante's going with this, but judging by Coach's body language, it's going to require a workaround.

"Your new defenseman will be a man named Marco Rossi." Dante's grin widens. "He'll be joining us from Italy, where he's spent two years—"

"*Italy?*" I'm not sure which of us said it, but Dante's eyes narrow to slits, and the room goes perfectly still as multiple mouths round into ovals.

"Yes," he says. "He's Italian. As will be all players we choose to bring on in the future. I am, in fact, full-blooded Italian. And the people I choose to surround myself with are as well. Do you have a motherfucking problem with that, Newberry?"

Coach's eyes widen into moons, and he gives an almost imperceptible shake of his head while Anders and I share a look of dismay. Italian players aren't known for being the best in the business, and something tells me that Dante hasn't picked this Rossi guy based on his skill at closing the gap. Judging by the look on Coach's face, he didn't get a say in this.

"If any of you are uncomfortable with this, please feel free to let me know. I'll be happy to make minor league accommodations for anyone who thinks that he knows how to run *my* team better than I do." Dante's eyes glint as he surveys the room.

We get his point loud and clear, because nobody in the room makes so much as a peep.

"I expect all of you to welcome Rossi with open arms. If you don't, I'll be the first to hear about it." Dante waves a hand. "That's all." Seconds later, his phone is right back in his palm. He's done with us.

Class dismissed.

Nobody says a word as we get up and troop out the door, although a few of the guys shoot Dante nasty glances that he pretends to ignore. He knows how we feel about him, and he doesn't give a damn.

I only hope the new defenseman has a better attitude than he does.

Anders, Cash, Latham, and me all stomp into a limo outside the Mona Lisa. Our silence lasts through the ride back to the arena, until we hit the gym, our safe haven away from Dante. The moment we're in the clear, everybody starts talking at once.

"What the literal fuck is his problem?" Anders demands, waving a hand in the general direction of the strip. "We train our asses off day in and day out so that he can sell merch with our names on it, and then he makes a decision like this, and we're just expected to lie down and take it?"

"If he was looking for good players, I wouldn't give a damn where he found them. But you can bet a dollar to a donut that the scouts weren't even involved in this." Latham slams his locker open. "Because I know for a fact that he's all about loyalty to the motherland or whatever. Now every time someone gets traded or injured, we're not gonna be looking for a player who matches our style of play—who will be a good fit and gel with the rest of the team—we're just gonna be looking at his passport. So we're just supposed to keep winning and winning without any help from the fucking front office? What the hell?"

"At least Dante knows your name," Anders gripes.

Cash lifts one eyebrow. "You want that?"

"For all we know, Rossi's actually good." I'm at least as annoyed as Anders, but yelling about it won't help, so I decide to play the peacekeeper for now. "Let's give him a shot. Like you said, Dante's all about making money, and assembling a shit team isn't going to do him any favors. He wants another cup just as much as we do."

"But not for the right reasons," Anders spits out. "And are you seriously taking his side?"

I grab some free weights from the shelf. "No. But I don't think that it makes any more sense for you to hate the guy for being Italian than it does for Dante to recruit him for the same reason. We know Dante's an ass, but we don't know about Rossi. At least not yet. Innocent until proven guilty."

"I'm not holding out much hope," Anders adds. "But I hear what you're saying."

Latham stabs his toe into the carpet. "I need someone to spot my bench presses. On her podcast yesterday, Scarlett Stone said I look so weak a Nerf gun could kill me. Then she said I couldn't lift an empty bag."

Cash obliges with a grunt. "No Scarlett Says."

As Anders joins the other guys heading toward the equipment, he blocks my path. "So...?"

"So what?"

My friend glances over his shoulder. "Don't make me beg for it."

My stomach clenches over how much to reveal because I already know where he's headed. "You're going to have to be more specific."

"The goss. The tea. The spicy deets about you and your sexy librarian." Anders waggles his eyebrows. "Was it good?"

I roll my eyes. I should never have told him about my foray into the world of... well, not dating, but whatever Molly and I are doing. "She's not a librarian. She's my little tater tot. And for the record, she owns a bookstore."

Anders nods. "Semantics. So, how's it going? Any *developments?*"

I appreciate the fact that my buddy cares about me, but I could do with him being a *little* bit less up in my business. "It's good."

"Good? That's all? Still no strings?" Anders mimes maneuvering a marionette.

"Not a one." I side-step, trying to get past him.

He moves to block me again. "See, here's the thing. Hotel walls are kinda thin, and you're not exactly a quiet guy. I may have been standing out in the hallway, sipping on my Cherry Coke that I had to go get so you could get rid of me, and I might have even heard you two talking and then *not...* talking."

"Anders, I didn't know that you were a pervy stalker." I hate to consider what he thinks he overheard, but I'll die before I ask.

His gleeful chuckle blisters my ears. "I'm just saying, it sounded like strings were forming. Or was that just the sound of your hand around your own dick?"

"You're totally mistaken. Thank you for your concern, but we're good. Now, are you going to let me wash the sweat off my balls or what?"

Anders lifts his hand in surrender and turns toward the showers. "Just looking out for you, man. Don't say I didn't warn ya."

I toss over my shoulder, "Maybe we need to find you a girlfriend so that you can start thinking about your own dick and spend less time worrying about what I do with mine."

Anders snorts. "It's not your dick that I'm worried about, Abbot. I'm worried that you're going to break that sweet little tater tot's heart unless you get your shit together and admit that you're into her. That there never was anything fake about your little arrangement."

"Even if I *was* into her, she's made her feelings clear," I point out even as my own heart squeezes inside my chest. Just the thought of Molly does something to me. That tiny woman makes me feel a certain kind of way. But only because we were friends before we were anything else. I like her.

Anders shakes his head. "You poor, sad man. You're blind to the truth. Don't worry, you'll catch up eventually."

It's a load of BS, of course. Anders doesn't know my feelings better than I do. Molly and I are just friends—for real.

Good friends.

With benefits.

I've got everything under control, so there's no reason to assume that there's any more to it than that.

CHAPTER FOURTEEN

Molly

"Hello, Earth to Molly." Mona waves one hand in front of my face. "Come in, please."

"Huh?" I snap back to reality. "Sorry, I was just, uh—"

There's no good way to end that sentence, because for about the hundredth time since our phone call the other day, I was fantasizing about Noah's dick. Watching him come all over his chiseled abs the other night definitely awakened something in me, something that even my obsession with Charlaine Harris, Laurell K. Hamilton, and the wide array of material on my AO3 account hasn't prepared me for, despite all the hours that I've spent pouring over them. Yes, the idea of being sandwiched between two horny, preternaturally pompous vampires has a certain appeal, but my ravenous pursuit of knowledge failed to enlighten me about one crucial fact.

Apparently, I have an oral fixation.

And that obsession has led to many fantasies that remain unfulfilled. My poor Rabbit has been struggling to keep up with my research. I always thought blowjobs were kind of degrading—like what kind of a man wants to shove his reproductive organ down a woman's throat to possibly choke her out—but now I can't stop watching bj after bj on PornHub and wondering what it would be like to *taste* Noah. Lick and sip his silky skin. Swallow that bead of pre cum after rolling it around on my tongue as every muscle he has tenses and flexes. On one hand, I can feel myself sliding into a sort of degenerate fugue state. On the other, I'm wet right now imagining what it would be like to suck Noah until he comes.

Just the thought of it makes me feel powerful beyond measure.

But I'd rather die than admit that to Mona. After all the time she's spent telling me that I need that, as she puts it, '*good D,*' she can never know the accuracy of all her teasing statements.

"I was thinking that we could redo the Halloween section into a—" Mona shudders. "A *Christmas* display. I feel dirty even suggesting it, but if you let me include that new furry series, *A Very Hairy Christmas,* I will volunteer as tribute."

"A *furry* series?" I raise an eyebrow at her.

"Yeah, it's Grade-A werewolf smut. I promise to label it M for mature and put it at the back where the kids can't reach it." Mona shrugs.

I open my mouth to argue, but my phone chimes before I can decide how to best address Mona's new scheme. It's a text from Noah.

🔨 *: Back in town. Are you free tonight for another lesson?* 😉

The winky face does me in. I shoot back a quick text while saying aloud, "Alright, Mona. If you think the people need werewolf smut, who am I to argue?"

Mona pumps one fist in delight. I can't even judge her this time—after all, I'm making plans for how I'm going to finally get my hands on Noah Abbot's naughty bits.

And not just my *hands*, either.

* * *

When Noah shows up at nine o'clock that night, I'm already tingling with anticipation. I keep remembering the little flashes of his dick I saw on the video chat the other night. Would it be wrong to ask him to drop his pants and skip the hellos?

"Hey." Noah's eyes sparkle as he kicks off his shoes. I get up from the couch and launch myself into his arms, practically crawling up his excessive height until I can reach his lips.

"This is the warmest welcome I've had in quite a long time," Noah says when I finally release him.

"I've been looking forward to this." I grab his hand and pull him back toward the bedroom. "I've been doing my homework."

"I take it that you have something specific in mind, then?" Noah teases.

I leave the bedroom door open even though it makes me feel more exposed, which is silly, because we're the only two people here. I'm full of nervous energy. Finally, *finally,* I get to be the one touching *him.* "I want to suck you off. Like right now."

Noah's eyes pop wide. "Molly, for fuck's sake!"

"I hope it will lead to fucking." I bite my lip as my eyes drift down toward his belt buckle. "So can I?"

"And what homework exactly goes into preparing to pop your blowjob cherry?" Noah asks. When he sees where I'm looking, he reaches down to rub his palm across his groin, which sends me into a tizzy.

My heart skips a beat. "I watched a DVD."

Noah stares at me as if I've grown a second head. "A *DVD?* You do know that porn exists, right? For free? On the internet?"

"I watched plenty of that, too. But you can't really see much, can you? I mean, the receiver opens their mouth and the penis goes in..." I make a circle with the thumb and forefinger of one hand, then insert my index finger into it. "I figured there had to be more to it than that, though, and I was right. It's called a blowjob, and people talk about getting sucked off, but those are both sort of misnomers. It's more than just letting a guy put his dick in your mouth, right? There's technique, and porn doesn't really show that. Porn's mainly for titillating men and not for learning and I'm a visual learner. Thus, a DVD."

Noah blinks a few times. "The receiver?" he echoes.

"Hello, Noah, it's the twenty-first century. Ladies aren't the only ones who suck dick."

Noah chokes on nothing and pounds his fist on his chest. "You certainly have a way with words..."

"Well, I said *receiver* the first time, which I thought was fairly descriptive." I cross my arms over my chest. "So are we doing this, or what?"

"I've had more romantic offers." Noah's eyes twinkle. "But I've never met a guy who would turn down head from a pretty girl, especially one who's done that much research on the subject."

"Surely you know at least one gay man, statistically speaking, but I get your point." I clear my throat and look around the room. "So, where do we start? Do you wanna lie down, or...?"

"Receiver's choice," Noah says with a wry smile.

"Maybe I should practice first." I turn toward the bedroom door, suddenly unsure of myself.

He chews on his lower lip. "Where are you going?"

"To the kitchen. I'm grabbing a banana." I gesture to the fruit bowl, which I can see from where I'm standing. "I figure I should warm up before the main event."

Noah shakes his head. "No need. My cock's right here. It's hard. It's aching. It's straining toward your full lips like a divining rod. You don't need a prop, and I promise that I'll appreciate it even if you're still just experimenting."

"But I'm trying to *learn*," I complain.

"I also promise to give you on-the-job feedback."

"Excellent. No banana required, then." I look around the room, then point to the wall beside the door. It's the only one that isn't completely taken up by bookshelves or the bed. "Stand there. Unless you're worried that your legs will give out?"

Noah chuckles. "Don't worry, I've got strong legs. Think about what I do for a living."

"Yeah, right. But when you made *me* come the other day, I was practically one of those single serving Jell-Os." I move in close to him, then get down on my knees so that I'm right at eye level with his groin.

"And what a sexy little Jell-O you were," he purrs. "Did your DVD teach you how to undo a belt buckle with your teeth?"

"Hell, no." I frown up at him. "I'm pretty sure that's not a thing, and I don't want to mess up my pearly whites."

"I love it when you talk dirty," Noah laughs. He rubs his palm across the bulge in his pants before undoing the buckle himself. He unzips slowly, then tugs his pants down so that his dick springs free.

He isn't fully hard yet, but even so, his penis looks *enormous* up close. For the first time since I started fantasizing, a little shiver of worry snakes up my spine. My eyes boggle at the sight. "I'm not sure I can fit the whole thing in my mouth at once. It's really long."

"That's exactly what every man wants to hear," Noah purrs.

"I get that, but I was being literal." I lick my lips and reach up to stroke his erection. When I do, his dick twitches. Fascinating.

"Is it okay if I say something?"

He glides a few fingers through my hair. "As long as it's positive."

I glance up at him and lift one eyebrow. "Thank you for

tidying up my workspace."

He sputters. "Seriously, Molly?"

Remembering the video's advice while admiring the manscaping, I wrap my hand loosely around him and stroke. Then I stick out my tongue and give the head an experimental lick.

"I don't understand that face that you're making right now," Noah comments, peeking down at me.

"It's weird, isn't it, to put someone else's organs in your mouth? Not *bad* weird, but confusing. Although, when you did it to *me* the other day..." I shiver at the memory.

"It's not weird at all," Noah insists. "It feels good for the receiver and powerful for the giver. Lovemaking is all about compromise."

Lovemaking? Is that what we're doing here? No, no, it's not.

Could it be? Ever?

Sweeping those pesky thoughts away, I raise one eyebrow. "How would you know? Have *you* ever sucked a dick? Because if you have, I'd want to hear details. That's kinda hot."

"In what universe would that be hot for a heterosexual man?"

I shrug. "You might be surprised. I read a lot of fanfiction."

"I just meant that I find pleasing my partner to be a huge turn-on," Noah clarifies.

"Speaking as your current partner, I'll admit that I find that terribly convenient. Okay, here goes." I open my mouth wider, lean in, and suck the tip of Noah's dick into my mouth. He groans immediately, and his cock twitches. The sensation is strange, but I find it satisfying. I look up to meet Noah's eyes as I work my hand around the base of his erection, sucking merrily away.

Just by watching Noah's expression, reading his bodily cues and listening to the way his breathing changes, I can tell what he likes, and what he likes *more*. The way his mouth drops open and his chest rises and falls as I caress him is even more thrilling than I imagined it could be. The heat builds between my thighs, and I adjust my posture a little.

I want this man inside me. I don't know what he's done to me, but I want to do every dirty thing that I've ever imagined, and I want to do them with him. There is absolutely no limit to the amount of filth I want to get up to with Noah Abbott before we're forced to part ways. I want the anal beads and the cock rings and the slaps across my asscheeks until they sting. The strength of my desire shocks me. I've never thought of myself as that kind of girl—not out of a judgment of anyone who is, but because I simply didn't think I was capable of this kind of lust. Of this kind of *wanting*. I swallow him so deeply that his cock nudges the back of my throat, bobbing my head, working my hand around him.

Dammit, I love doing this. I fucking love it. Throw one more sexual act into Molly's 'pro' column.

"Christ, Molly," Noah breathes. He reaches down to caress his balls. "If you keep that up, I'm not gonna last long. Forget how much I teased you earlier about DVDs and shit. You just keep on learning your way."

I practically glow with triumph. Noah Abbot, man of the world, is going to get off because of *me*. As the muscle in his jaw jumps, I moan onto him, and I feel how his weight shifts to lean more firmly against the wall.

"Molly—!" he croaks.

I pull back, still gripping him with one hand, and wait.

Nothing happens.

"Uh, Molly?" Noah's voice is strained and tight. "What are

135

you doing?"

The bolt of embarrassment that shoots through me kills the mood. "I thought you were about to come. Did I misunderstand that?"

Noah gestures to the extreme proximity between the tip of his dick and my mouth. His voice sounds more normal when he speaks again. "Yeah, but I'm not gonna come on your *face*."

I frown and tilt my head to one side. "Why not?"

"Is that what you were going for?" The heat of Noah's passion has visibly cooled, but I don't understand why.

I let my hand drop away from his softening cock. "The video made it seem like that was normal. I thought guys liked that."

Noah snorts and raises his shoulders toward his ears. "Fucking *video*," he mumbles. "I'm changing my opinion on that damn thing again. This... this is why sex shouldn't be learned from a manual."

"I did something wrong," I mutter, shrinking.

I would like very much to crawl under the nearest piece of furniture and hide until I'm alone. I feel stupid, but I don't understand *why*. I did what I was supposed to do. I followed the instructions. Where did I go wrong and why does he seem so put out by it?

Noah shimmies his pants back on. "I need a minute." He bolts for the bathroom.

I'm left kneeling there, wondering how I managed to fuck this up so badly. After a moment, I rise to my feet and head over to perch on the edge of the bed, trying to sort through my conflicting emotions. Just a few minutes ago, I felt like a sex goddess—strong and powerful and erotic.

Now I feel like I want to slip into the ugly cry.

Before I make much headway, Noah re-emerges. His face is damp, as if he's splashed water on it. He ambles over to sit down beside me, and the mattress gives slightly beneath his weight, tipping me slightly toward him.

"You didn't do anything wrong," he says. "I'm sorry if I made it seem like you did. It's just..." He rubs his hand over his eyes. "It's just disrespectful. I mean, it's *fine*, if the whole point is to feel good, but that's not really something most guys want to do with a woman they respect or care about. So it's not that guys don't like it or don't want it, but something like that always has to be negotiated in advance."

I puzzle over his words. I see what he means, but it's not his thesis that confuses me. "But that's what we're doing," I say, throwing my palms up. "We're a situationship. *Fuckbuddies?* Is that a thing? Isn't that all we are to each other? You're only with me to teach me the ins and outs of the fine art of boning. Right?"

Noah lets his hands fall to his lap and stares at me for a long moment without opening his mouth.

"Right," he says, but he doesn't sound sure of himself. "But I still like you. As a person, I mean. Shit, Molly. We've had in-depth conversations about Faulkner. I'm not going to blow my load on your face."

I don't get what's happening. I don't understand why he's acting so respectful and kind.

Unless he sees me as more than a sex partner, and he wants more from this than an emotionless booty call. That would go against everything he's said. Everything we agreed to. He can't change the rules in the middle of the game and neither can I.

But now, for the first time, I wonder if his body and his heart are in as much conflict as mine are. Because when I look into Noah's face, I see something more.

CHAPTER FIFTEEN

Noah

"Why the *fuck* does Dante think we're his chauffeurs?" Anders demands as I merge into traffic approaching the International passenger pickup at McCarron.

"Dante thinks that everyone should jump to do his bidding with a smile of gratitude that he asked," I retort. "And as the team captain, he wants *you* to roll out the welcome mat and play nice. But admit it—you're curious about this new defenseman."

"I just want reassurance that Dante's new pet isn't going to be deadweight," Anders grumbles. "That he's going to keep my head from getting separated from my body the next time I'm on a breakaway." He folds his arms over his chest. "By the way, what's with you today? You're in a weird mood."

"It's nothing," I say at once. He already knows too much about my relationship with Molly, and if I tell him how last night went down, he's going to laugh in my face. The *I-told-you-so's* will never stop. With my heart feeling more like mush than muscle and my mind racing with jumbled thoughts, the last thing I need is Anders hanging all over my back.

"I'm telling you, if this guy turns out to be as much of a dick as our boss, I'm out. A guy who doesn't know the first thing about hockey is the one responsible for signing new players? Since when is that a thing? He should just leave the important stuff to the scouts and the front office and stay in his lane owning casinos or decapitating horses or whatever the fuck they do."

I pull up to the curb and throw my SUV into park. "That's a bit savage. And are you gonna say that to his face, or just keep saying it to me? I recommend the latter unless you want to be fitted for a pair of concrete skates."

Anders gives me the finger before snatching up our little sign that says *Marco Rossi*. He rolls the window down and holds the sign out. "All I'm saying is, if the guy's too cheap to spring for a limo, he's not negotiating for good players. He's got something else up his sleeve. Like bonding before we're ready."

"Instead, he sprung for the rideshare," I point out. "Marco's gonna be sharing *our* ride."

"Har," Anders deadpans as I pull out my phone. "You and your dad jokes."

"According to the website, his flight's on schedule. And I allowed plenty of time for him to clear customs." I power my screen off and twist around in my seat, trying to get a good look at the terminal exits.

Among the milling crowd, a big, dark-haired guy stands with each hand on the collapsible handle of a giant suitcase. He has a cell phone propped between his ear and his shoulder. I've never seen him before, but he's wearing a Venom ballcap.

"I think that's the guy," I say. "It has to be. At least he's not diminutive. I mean, he looks like he fits."

I catch his eye and point to the sign. An immediate spark of recognition flashes across his face, and he grabs both bags and makes his way toward us.

I step out to help him get his bags loaded. The whole time, he doesn't stop shouting into the phone in Italian, except when he pauses his tirade to make eye contact with me and says, "*Grazie mille*," before picking up right where he left off. Even when he slides in the back seat, he doesn't even bother to greet Anders. As he buckles his seatbelt, he finally cuts off, but only because the guy on the other line starts yelling, also in Italian. I can't say for sure, but it sounds like he's talking to Dante.

"Trouble in paradise?" Anders murmurs, watching Rossi in the visor mirror. "I fucking knew it."

"Maybe you and the new guy will get along," I suggest. "Sounds like he butts heads with Dante as much as you do."

Anders chuckles, eyes still fixed on the mirror, watching our new teammate like a hawk. "Maybe. Hope he learns English fast enough. Because I am not learning one fucking word of Italian. Not even hello."

I don't envy Rossi trying to navigate joining a new team while living in a country that doesn't speak his language, but that's not my problem. Not that I plan on being mean to him or anything—more like he's not gonna be my focus. I'm more worried about what the hell I'm supposed to do about Molly.

"Hey." Anders prods my shoulder as I pull back out into traffic. "You've got that look on your face again and your head's not in the game. What's going on?"

I tug my lower lip between my teeth as I head toward the I15. "I'm just thinking."

"Yeah, I gathered, but it doesn't take a genius to figure out that they aren't *happy* thoughts. Come on, let me in." Anders prods me with one finger. "I'm your friend. I can help. Besides, I'm way better at handling women problems than you are. You're a little out of practice."

"What about Marco?" I asked, jerking my chin toward the back seat.

We pause for a moment; I can still hear Dante screaming in Italian on the line, and Marco's sulking in the back seat, staring out the window at the Las Vegas skyline like a lost puppy. He looks like he'd rather be anywhere else but here. Maybe we can take him over to the Venetian sometime and ease his homesickness by playing craps and ogling the cocktail waitresses. I already feel sorry for the poor sap. Not to mention they're shacking him up with Cash, whose words are few and far between.

"I think you're good," Anders says. "I haven't heard him utter a word of English."

"Okay, I'm gonna tell you something," I say to Anders. "But I need you to take it seriously."

Rossi starts talking again, waving one hand for emphasis. After a five-second outburst, Dante cuts him off again.

"I have a problem," I say in a low voice. "With my little tater tot."

"Did you accidentally propose during sex, or what?" Anders asks, rolling his eyes. "God, Abbott, you're so emotional."

"I, uh." I clear my throat and grip the steering wheel in a stranglehold. "I couldn't do... it."

"Couldn't get it up? There are pills for that." Anders shrugs. "It's not a big deal. Happens to the best of us. How's your cholesterol?"

My brow line lifts. "It's fine. That's not the problem. I couldn't finish."

Anders' eyebrows shoot up. "Oh, shit. There are no pills for that. You might want to see a doctor, buddy."

"It's not a physical thing. It's in my head." I lift one hand to tap my temple in irritation. "Like, I could have finished, things were going fine. But she wanted me to finish on her face."

Anders nods. "Aah. I see. I know why you couldn't."

"Well, then tell me, because I'm still at a loss. Like who doesn't pull the trigger when a hot as fuck woman sucks him off to perfection and ends with, 'Come on my face?'" As we approach a red light, I stomp the breaks a little too forcefully. "None of this makes any sense. It's like I lost my shit. I'm supposed to be the sexpert in this arrangement."

"You really have no idea what the problem was?" Anders asks in a sing-song voice that sets my teeth on edge.

My head shakes before I even pause to process. "It felt... rude."

His fingers tap the dash. "Because?"

"Because it's some cheap hooker shit!" I shake my head. "And that's not what I... that's not how we..."

"*Yeesss?*" Anders coaxes.

"Because she deserves better than that!" I can tell that I'm raising my voice, but I'm not sure why. Some defensive, animalistic part of my brain is still running through the basic math and coming up with the same wrong answer over and over again. *Molly + a faceful of cum = no can do.*

But she wanted it—she wanted to learn—hell, she even asked me to do it so she could experience something the way she wanted to. Full consent was freely given, so it should have been fine.

But she didn't *know better*, so I was right to call things off.

But now my balls are aching and my head feels like it's about to split open, and Molly thinks she did something wrong, and I still can't explain why I'm fighting this so hard. Maybe I should go over to her place tonight and give it another go. Maybe after thinking it through and talking it through, I'll be able to pull the trigger.

Only, if we try again, I'm just going to derail myself again. The facts are these: I don't *want* to finish on her face. Do I want to finish in her mouth? See that swan-like throat swallow my cum? Do I want to finish on her perfect tits? Her stomach? That delectable ass? Dammit all to hell! I don't fucking even know my own mind right now. That said, I can't figure out what I *do* want, and so I keep running the facts through my mind on an endless loop, and never getting any relief.

"Why did she want to do that, anyway?" Anders asks. "I mean... that's kind of odd for a girl who is so inexperienced she needs lessons in seduction. Did she say?"

"The instructional video. She watched some damn sex institute's instructional video, and they told her that was one of her options. Like choosing door number three or something."

A howl of laughter emits from the back seat, startling me so badly that I almost drive into the concrete barrier. Marco Rossi claps his hands with delight. Apparently, when I was focused on other *things*, he finished his call with Dante.

Anders shakes his head. "I have so many questions that I don't even know where to start." He twists around in his seat to look at Marco. "Let's start with you, new guy. How much of that did you catch?"

He juts his thumb toward the back of my seat. "Tall goalie love 'ejaculate on my face' tater tot. What eez tater tot? I hear in tone of voice woman eez his *amore*. And am eager to date zees passionate American women who actually let man come all over the face." Marco's Italian accent is so heavy that I have trouble making out some of the words, but clearly, he speaks a lot more English than we assumed.

"A tater tot is an American delicacy, kind of like a good pasta," Anders says, shooting me a devilish grin. "But in this case, Mr. Rossi, you have intuited correctly. My good friend Noah here has what we like to call a *friend with benefits,* but what he feels for her is more than friendship, to the point where he's having trouble cashing in on said benefits."

"The tater tot, she sound a-spicy. Women like zees not easy to find." Marco leans up between the seats and pats me on the shoulder. "So many girls, you must talk to, bring flowers, win affections, and woo, always with the woo woo, and still have so many rules man *no comprendere*. And you, my friend, have found a tater who zees desperate for your, how you say it? Your *sborra?*"

"His cum," Anders suggests.

"Ah, *si. Grazie, mio amico.*" Marco squeezes Anders' shoulder in one meaty hand.

I am going to die on the I15. This conversation is going to kill me.

I roll my eyes so hard I can see my brain.

"And yet, when she make zee simple request, you will not give *sborra* to her that way. Why zees, *mio amico?*" Marco holds up one finger and nods sagely. "Is zees because you want more than to have her in manner of zee sheep and be done? No, no, Americans say zees differently…" He thinks for a moment, then snaps his fingers. "Ah, *si, si*: to fuck like *cagna*? No, your *amore* like the moon, like the stars, like diamond. Tater precious to you. You reek of zees luck, *mio amico*. Not many man finds woman like zees in lifetime. Your amore should become your *moglie.*"

Having dispensed this sage romantic advice, Marco drops back into his seat with a whoosh.

"You're right, Noah." Anders raises his hand to Marco for a high-five. "I think the new guy and I will get along just fine."

"Whatever." I roll my eyes at them both. "So what do I do now?"

"Yeah, Marco, any advice?" Judging from his dancing eyes and upturned lips, Anders is enjoying the hell out of this. At least one of us is.

"Must make sure, *mio amico*." Marco's voice sinks low and serious. "If you cannot spill onto face while Tater suck, then make *amore*. If your *peesche* spills with passion at zees time, then you know."

This is definitely one of the top ten weirdest conversations I've ever had—with a stranger to boot—but as we drive Marco to his new residence in our gated community, rooming with our friend and teammate, Cash, I think over his advice. I'm pretty sure Marco just said I need to try lovemaking instead of just sex. And if I can come inside Molly without issue while we're connected in that way, then I'll know. Maybe he's right.

Only one way to find out.

CHAPTER SIXTEEN

Molly

The day after our failed lesson in all things head, I sulk around the bookstore all day. Noah was so bizarre last night, and I've spent the day torn between the memory of how his dick twitched any time he felt good—*yes, please*—and the confusion in his eyes when he tried to explain why he wanted to stop. He was the one who insisted that there could be no strings attached. My brain throbs with the confusion of trying to figure him out.

My situationship seems like it's failing. I almost feel like I've been sold a bill of goods.

After Mona leaves for the night, I close up the bookstore alone. I'm just locking up the register when my phone buzzes.

It's Noah, which is odd. He doesn't usually call me.

I answer and press the phone to my ear. "Hey, you," I say and then pause.

I'm still frustrated with him, and I'm not sure I'm ready to talk. He's being so damn confusing, and I can't seem to keep my head on straight. Isn't the man supposed to lead even in a situationship?

"Hey." The sound of his voice is enough to weaken my resolve. "I'm sorry about last night. I just want to reiterate that you didn't do anything wrong, and I probably didn't handle it the best. But I did some thinking today, and if you're open to it, I'd like to meet up tonight."

Even though the lights are out and the store is locked, I look around to make sure that I won't be overheard. "I don't know, Noah. I'm still not sure what happened yesterday. If I ask for something and give my full consent, how can granting that request be disrespectful?"

"It didn't feel right," he says. "And I'm still trying to figure out what was going on in my head. It might just be that we didn't negotiate it up front and it wasn't something you'd ever done before."

I tug at the hem of my skirt. "If we meet up for tonight, will it be for another lesson?"

"Yes."

I exhale sharply and close my eyes. "I'm not sure how to discuss boundaries if you can't explain what's going on in your head."

"We could discuss things ahead of time so that there are no surprises. Generally speaking, I mean." Noah swallows, and the sound echoes through our connection. "Is there something specific you want to do?"

"Well, I want to have sex with you." I spin a pen around on the countertop with one index finger. "Actual, honest-to-God, PIV, penetrative sex. But I get the impression that you're not comfortable with that, so..."

"Okay," he says.

I freeze. "What?"

"I think I'm ready," he says. "I can't promise that my brain won't freak out partway through, but that would be helpful, actually."

"*Helpful?*" I repeat.

"I have a question," he says, and doesn't elaborate.

"A question that can be answered through sex?"

"Pretty much."

I'm not sure what to make of that, but who am I to argue?

Maybe he'll tell me once he has the answer. "Can you be at my place around nine?"

"Yes," he says at once. "And I'll bring condoms."

Why does this situationship feel more stressful than running my store? "See you then, I guess."

After we hang up, I stare at my phone for a moment. Every time I've suggested actually fucking, Noah's pulled away. What's changed?

Not that it matters. Tonight, we're finally going to do something that I've fantasized about since day one. Having Noah in my mouth felt good, but I can only imagine that having him inside me is going to feel even better. Not only do I know from my experimentation with the Rabbit that I like the sensation of being filled, but it's *Noah*. He's big enough to pick me up like it's nothing, but gentle enough that I trust him not to take advantage of that. I wonder what sex with him will be like. Will he take charge? Will being stretched and full feel as good as I hope? Damn, if it doesn't live up to the hype, I'm going to be so disappointed.

And if penetrative sex with Noah Abbott doesn't feel good, how will I ever get up the desire or the nerve to try it again with someone I'm less attracted to?

I try to imagine what the evening might have in store, and my dirty brain supplies a vivid image of me bent over the bookstore counter with my skirt hiked up, panting and moaning as Noah stands behind me, thrusting into me, until I can't take any more. Then he reaches around my body with those huge mitts, tugs the top of my shirt down until my tits pop free of their lacy prison, and he pinches my nipples until I squeal.

God, I've got to stop this. I'm the only one in this twosome who seems so horned up by the prospect of what we're about to do.

Shouldn't that be a red flag?

With thoughts I'm somehow lacking meandering around inside my head, I immediately stand up and stuff my phone back into my pocket. Most of the porn I've watched for research purposes is somewhere reminiscent of the Anne Rice book we read for the October book group. The general implication seems to be that sex is somehow degrading to women, and that's... good? Forbidden fruit, and all that. But Noah doesn't seem to feel the same way, which leaves me wondering exactly what tonight has in store for me.

Only one way to find out. I finish locking up and set out for home.

* * *

I'm in bed, wearing a loose t-shirt, no bra, and pajama shorts, staring at the still-blank document that's supposed to be my new manuscript when Noah arrives. God, my agent's going to hate me.

I hear the door open, and then the sounds of Noah kicking off his shoes before his head appears in the doorway.

"Hey," he says. "Am I interrupting something important?"

I adjust my glasses and look up from the screen. "Nope. I just didn't know what to expect, so I figured I'd let you tell me what to do."

Noah lopes over to me and places one finger on top of the laptop shell. "Can I close this?"

I nod, and he pushes the lid shut, then removes the computer from my lap and sets it aside.

"So, what did you—?" I begin.

I don't get a chance to finish. Noah leans over me, planting a passionate kiss on my mouth. The fingers of one hand tangle with my hair, and the other caresses my cheek. I melt into him, and in our frenzy my glasses are knocked askew. Noah lifts himself onto the bed, pressing me back amongst the pillows. He's never kissed me like this, with so much feeling. As his weight settles over me, I grab his shirt and pull him closer still. Through the material of his shirt, I feel his rippled muscles and the frantic beat of his heart.

When he breaks this kiss, it's only to nuzzle against my jaw and nip at my throat. "I want to lick you and make sure you're ready for me. It would kill me if I hurt you."

Recalling the length and girth of his accouterments, I nod. "Okay. Just so long as we—*oh!*" He lifts my shirt and circles one nipple with his tongue. A moment later, one hand dips into the front of my sleep shorts and flicks across my clit. I cry out and arch against the bed.

"So wet already," Noah groans. "Do you want my dick that bad?"

"Yes." I dig my fingernails into his shoulders as his finger slips into me. "There's something to be said for the slow burn. I'm not proud here, Noah."

"Fuck, Molly, you're going to look so damn pretty with my dick in you. Think you can take it?" He drops kisses down my belly, pausing to punctuate his caresses with words that leave me shaking with anticipation. "It'll be a tight fit. You're so tiny... but you're also so damn wet."

I moan against the exquisite pressure. Noah's two fingers together are smaller than the Rabbit, but I'm pretty sure that his dick is bigger than the toy. He pulls my shorts lower, and when I flail my legs a little, he manages to get them off altogether.

The heat of his mouth leaves me sobbing with pleasure. I'm not even sure what he's doing down there; there's so much sensation at once, and my head spins as he fingers me, teasing my clit with his teeth and tongue. I run my fingers through his hair, pressing down without thinking at the same time that I lift my hips toward his mouth. The instant I realize what I'm doing, I release him.

"Why'd you stop?" he asks, taking a break from his oral efforts.

"Didn't wanna smother you," I mumble.

He kisses my inner thigh. "Ride my face, Molly. You're not gonna smother me, so take what you want." He keeps his eyes on mine as his mouth returns to its previous efforts, and the muscles in my thighs jump.

I close my eyes and lose myself in the rhythm of his movements. The smell of him surrounds me: fresh soap and pine shampoo and a deep, musky pheromone that makes my brain go haywire. This isn't enough. It feels good, but I need more.

Noah lifts his head again. "What do you want, Molly?"

"I need *you*," I gasp. "I need to feel you all hot and throbbing, stretching me as wide as I'll go. Please get up here and slide that huge dick inside me, Noah."

"Yeah?" He smiles and kisses my bare skin again. "I'll be there soon, baby. Tell me your fantasy. What's the ideal?" He gives me another lazy lick while he waits for an answer.

"Anything. Everything. I want to feel you come. Pulse. Jerk. The other night, whenever you felt good, your dick twitched, and..." I can't possibly say what I'm thinking. I wanted to be like the girl in the video, smiling up at her partner as his cock twitched over her, covering her in his semen. I want Noah to use the bondage kit again, to bend my knees, pull my legs wide apart and take me rough and hard until he comes inside me, leaving me dripping with evidence of how much he loved it.

Except, now I'm not sure. There's a fierce intensity to his

passion tonight. This feels less like a lesson or a game, and more... personal. Like the tantric love class, where I lost track of where we began and ended. That sounds even better than all the rest of it.

"I want to lose myself in you," I whimper. "And for you to lose yourself in me. Um... if that's okay."

Noah's fingers slide deeper than ever before, and his teeth graze my clit. All of a sudden, I come undone.

"That's right," Noah says, slowing the movement of his finger, spreading them apart to open me. "That's right, Molly. Stay with me."

Once upon a time, a single orgasm used to be plenty for me. Now I know that I'm capable of more, and even before the tide of my orgasm ebbs, I'm ready to move on to the main event.

Noah gets up to strip off his shirt and shimmy out of his pants. I should probably do something useful, but I just lie there and watch him as he undresses. When he catches me staring, his mouth turns up in a smile.

"What's so amusing?" I ask.

He slows his movements and flexes. "You."

"Am I not allowed to appreciate the landscape?" I ask.

Noah lets his pants drop, revealing the flushed curve of his cock, jutting up toward his stomach. I couldn't fit the full length of him in my mouth last night. Is it really going to fit *inside* me?

Noah retrieves a condom from his pants pocket, then climbs onto the bed, kneeling between my thighs. I watch in growing anticipation as he slides it on.

"What if I want you on top?" he asks. "That'll give you more control over how deep I go."

"Okay." I scramble to my knees, as Noah presses his back to the headboard. When he's settled, he pulls me into his lap.

"Are you ready?" he asks, palming my cheeks and sweeping

my hair away from my eyes. His expression is so affectionate, so gentle, that I almost think there might be more to this than mutual satisfaction, but I stop myself before I let that fantasy get the best of me.

As a glass half full kind of a girl, I'm just seeing what I want to see, not what's real.

"Yeah," I say. I spread my legs on either side of him and brace my hands against the headboard above his shoulders. "What should I do now?"

Noah places one hand on the back of my neck and reaches the other between us, adjusting the angle of his cock until the tip brushes against me.

"Take your time," he murmurs. "And if anything doesn't feel good, tell me right away."

I lower myself onto him and suck in a breath as he presses into me. *Fuck.* He's so thick, I'm not sure I can do this. With a mixture of pleasure at the fullness and pain at the stretch, I slide halfway down his length, but I can't make myself go any further. I squeeze my eyes shut as I try to adjust to the sensation of being entered like this. Maybe if I breathe through it, my internal muscles will relax enough to take all of him.

"Shh, shh." Noah lifts his other hand to the small of my back, cradling me against him. "No need to push yourself, baby girl. Just breathe and think about opening up. I'm not gonna move until you're ready, okay?"

I take a deep breath and do as he says, forcing my muscles to unclench. When I do, I'm able to lower myself the rest of the way, until every inch of him is inside me.

"Noah." I shiver. "Holy shit."

His brow creases, and his hands massage my waist. "Is that good or bad?"

I blow my bangs upward. "Good. It's just... a lot. I had no idea."

He fists my hair, then pulls my glasses free, setting them on the nightstand. Every move is careful and slow. He's serious about not pushing me and something unlocks inside of me at how tender this man is with me. Every move he makes says he cares.

I wish that my first time could have been like this, with someone so attentive and painstaking. Except, then I might not have felt like I needed lessons, and Noah and I would never have decided to give this a shot, and then I wouldn't be here—now—with this beautiful, big-hearted man who caresses my back while I try to relax on his dick.

"Hey." Noah kisses my neck. "When you're ready to start slow, can we try something? I keep thinking about that thing we did in the bookstore, with the eye contact and the tandem breathing. I'd like to try that with you tonight."

I run my hand over his ribcage. "Yeah. Okay. I'm ready."

His thumb swipes my cheek, and I lean into his touch. "You'll tell me if I do anything you don't like, right?"

"Totally." I turn my head to kiss his palm. "I promise." I focus on his eyes again. They're so familiar now, and the connection that we shared before returns in an instant, stronger than ever before.

It's like we spoke to each other with our eyes before our bodies.

Before our hearts.

Noah takes a deep breath. As he does, he lifts his hips. When he exhales, he drops back to the bed. It's a small movement, but the aftershocks go through me like an earthquake. I rest my hands on his shoulders and exhale along with him. With each inhalation, he thrusts into me. With each exhale, the pressure fades. He keeps our rhythm slow and steady, so that there are no surprises.

It doesn't take long for the warm heat of my own arousal to spread through my limbs. I breathe faster, and Noah's eyebrows climb. I nod slightly, and he increases the pace of his movements to match the new tempo of my breathing. Both hands slide down to my waist, holding me in place an inch or so above his hips to give him space to move. Each time he sinks deeper, I see stars. Each time he recedes, the friction sends my heart racing. My mouth drops open, and my eyelids flutter, but I never break eye contact.

I'm not sure which one of us changes tempo next. It seems to happen all at once, as if we're one being now with one shared thought. The world has narrowed to our points of connection, to the space inhabited by our own bodies. Noah groans with each breath, and I cry out at the exact same time. His pulse throbs against mine, and he maneuvers both of our bodies. When he first entered me, it almost hurt, but that sensation has disappeared entirely.

Now I no longer just feel full—I feel complete.

"Can you... come like... this?" he asks in between pants.

My little cries of ecstasy are the only answer I can give. He presses me to him, searching my eyes for an answer to that question. His own pleasure is obvious. He makes no move to disguise it. His pupils expand and his eyes gleam. I'm not just *making* this happen. We're on this journey together.

"Noah—!" I whimper. As he enters me, I break eye contact for the first time. My head rolls back as I come. It's a huge sensation, bigger than anything I've felt before. This isn't just a buzz through my clit—it takes over my entire body. Every cell explodes on a wave of pleasure so pure, I wonder if I'm imagining it.

Noah groans as my pussy flutters. My limbs tremble, and every time I clench around him, his body responds. He presses his forehead to my shoulder, losing the rhythm of our lovemaking and devolving into a frenzy of frantic thrusts. He finishes with a roar like that of a wounded animal, and his cock jumps inside me. Because of the condom, I don't get to feel him ejaculate like I want to, but maybe someday. My own orgasm fades a bit, but I clench again, tightening around him until he gives a little shiver. I stroke his hair and rest my head against his shoulder, resting against him.

I'm not ready to let go of this moment. Not yet. God, when this ends, it just might kill me.

We sit like that so long that I start to drift off. Then Noah stirs, and I look up into his flushed face.

"You okay, Molly?" he asks in a rough voice.

"I'm a Jell-O again," I tell him. "I don't think I can move. Ever. We're stuck like this."

He kisses my forehead. "Was that everything you'd hoped for?"

"Yes." I sit up, brushing my hair out of my face. "Did you get an answer to that impossible question bothering you?"

"Yeah. I think I did." Noah lifts me off of him, wincing as he slips out of me. "I'm sorry, I can't stay the night, since I need to get going early tomorrow." He sounds genuinely apologetic.

"Do sex friends usually stay the night?" I tease.

The same confused look from last night comes over his face. "I mean..."

"You can if you want," I say quickly. "Some other night, I mean." I like the idea of falling asleep next to him, never mind waking up next to him. Theoretically speaking, we could have sex twice in a row that way.

Settle down, Molly. One time, and you're already wondering how to make this happen again? You're going to become addicted to a man who's already made it clear he's not available in that way.

The thought makes me smile, and Noah answers with a smile of his own.

"We'll talk about it. Want to take a shower before I go?"

"Like, together?" I sit up, instantly rejuvenated by his offer. "Is this an opportunity for another lesson?"

Noah gets out of bed before sweeping me up in his arms. "Could be. Or we could just shower. I don't want to re-Jell-O-fy you in the shower. That's how people get hurt."

"Seems like you have no problem holding me up." I bat my eyelashes at him. "You're pretty big and strong."

Noah laughs as he carries me into the bathroom. "You make a valid point."

In the end, it turns out to be a PG-13-rated shower at best. Noah shampoos my hair and rubs my scalp while I return the favor, but it makes me strangely happy that Noah didn't just finish and leave. This feels... coupley.

And I like it far more than I have any right to.

CHAPTER SEVENTEEN

Noah

Despite Marco's predictions, it seems extreme to suggest that I love Molly. I hardly know Molly. We haven't gone on a single proper date, one where we talk about our feelings and our memories and our values and what we like and don't like— other than that very first day when we went to the bar, but that doesn't count. I wasn't *courting* her then. I have no idea what she wants out of life. I know more about her sexual preferences than her personal thoughts, and I've explored her body more than I've explored her mind.

So I can't be in love with her.

That said, I don't know what else to call the tight band that compresses around my chest every time that I think about her. How the thought of her washes over me like sunshine, chasing away all of the remnants of pain that still linger after Nat's death. How our souls seem to intertwine, swelling into something bigger and stronger than both of us alone.

"Stop looking sad, Unkie," Viv commands as she watches me bustle around the house getting ready for my game tonight. She points one little finger across the table at me as if she's waving a magic wand. "Nanny Frannie says to turn frowns upside-down." She digs her index finger into the sides of her mouth and forces them upward. "'ike thiff."

"Nanny Frannie?" I repeat. "Is that what we're calling her now?"

"It rhymes, dear." Francine pops one of Viv's Skittles into

her mouth and chews. "And I'm inclined to agree. You seem quite gloomy today."

"Is it because of Princess Molly?" Viv asks. "Did she lose her crown?"

I whip back around to face her. In the booster seat she's perched upon, Viv looks larger than she is, and she's clearly enjoying her newfound height.

"Um." I take a hasty sip of my bottled water, stalling for time, but I'm unable to come up with a suitable answer in the allotted time. "Why do you ask?"

"Because you like her." Viv lowers her voice into what's supposed to be a whisper, although she still manages to be almost as loud as she was at full volume. "I like her, too, Unkie."

"Well, I. That is, um. I guess that's why she's coming to my game tonight. To support the, um, team and all." I wasn't prepared for this. Half the reason I agreed to start seeing Molly in the first place was that we planned to keep our lives separate from our relationship. If Viv's aware that we're dating—and is *okay* with that and encouraging it even—then who am I really protecting?

"That's good. I hope you gave her a jersey to wear. But not a smelly one." Viv nods like all the wisest preschoolers do. "I'm sure she likes you, even though you're a big stinky boy."

I sputter, and Francine quickly grabs a dish towel to hide her face.

"What?" Viv looks back and forth between us. "Well, he *is*, but we love him anyway. Don't we, Nanny Frannie?"

"We certainly do." Francine regains her composure.

"Oooh." Viv's eyes widen. "Can Molly come to the Barbie-cue? She can borrow one of my crowns. We can be twin princesses!"

It hadn't occurred to me to invite Molly to the cookout next week I'm hosting to welcome Marco. It's mostly going to be guys from the team... but maybe I should. After all, they'll see her at the game tonight and make their own assumptions. Inviting her would mean that we'll have to change the terms of our situationship, but after the other night, I need to admit to myself that it's what I want. It's one thing to take relationship advice from the new guy, but when my four-year-old niece is more attuned to my relationship than I am, we have a problem.

"I'll ask her," I say.

Viv claps her little hands, and Francine's eyes linger on me as she takes another handful of candy.

"What?" I ask, narrowing my eyes at her.

"Nothing." She gives an offhand flick of her wrist. "I didn't say a word."

She didn't have to. Her eyes gleam with triumph, most likely because she had a hand in orchestrating this new development in my love life. I'd be exasperated, but to be honest, it's nice to have someone in my life who's on my side. Francine just wants me to be happy.

After grabbing my stuff, I load my SUV and head to the Venom arena more excited than anxious about the night ahead. This is the first time in my NHL career that I'm going to have a woman who's important to me in the stands.

After what feels like an eternity, it seems I've found my true north.

* * *

Skating onto home ice never gets old. The arena's electric, a hive of buzzing fans wearing Venom neon green. Under the huge spotlights, camera flashes catch my eye as I glide to the net, the cage where I'll be king for the night.

"Let's kill it tonight, boys!" Anders, our captain, shouts, his voice a war cry over the roar of the crowd.

"Born ready," Latham quips, stick-handling a puck with a showy flair.

I catch Cash's eye. "Big game tonight. The Thunderhawks are tough this year."

He grunts in agreement. "Damn straight."

But it's not just another game. Not tonight. My eyes scan the friends and family section, landing on my little tater tot. She's wearing my jersey, and God, she's never looked more beautiful. It's like she's my personal good luck charm, an angel in team colors. And just like that, the stakes shoot through the roof.

I almost can't believe she's here.

For me.

The guys hit their groove one by one, circling the ice in fluid motions. Anders and Latham take turns passing to each other. Cash skates laps, a solitary figure lost in his own world. I swear that man even thinks in three-word sentences. Marco's at the blue line, practicing slap shots and muttering Italian curses when they go awry.

But me? I'm in my crease, deflecting pucks, feeling the weight of my pads and the flex of my stick. Each save hones my focus, like a blacksmith tempering steel. I'm getting in the zone, that mental space where everything fades but the puck and the play.

"Hey, Abbott! Ready for some heat?" Latham calls out, circling closer to my net. His grin is all mischief, like a kid who's just stolen a cookie.

I chuckle. "You're more like the flame on a Bunsen burner."

Latham skates up, lining himself for the shot. "Prepare to get schooled, Dad."

I smirk. "Teach me, Professor Newberry." Even though Latham can't see my eyeroll from behind my mask, I still do it.

The guys on the team call me 'Dad' for my sage advice and epic dad jokes. Yeah, I'm the Aristotle of locker room wisdom—now let's see if Latham's got anything on Socrates. "And make it quick—I've got a dad joke that needs delivering."

He winds up and fires, a missile aimed straight for the top corner. But I've got it easily since I know his tells better than most—my glove snaps out, snatching the puck from the air.

As the small crowd down by the glass cheers and pounds their fists, I skate toward them, locking eyes with Molly. I blow her a kiss and tap my jersey—number 30, the same one she's wearing. It's like marking my territory, only sweeter.

As my girl beams down at me from above, she gives me a fist pump, the puck bunnies scowl.

But the guys... they burst into laughter.

"Did you just... caress your jersey over a fucking warm-up save?" Anders chuckles, shaking his head. "Scarlett Says is gonna have a field day with this. And the blogs too. I can almost see the headlines."

"Don't encourage *her*," Latham groans. "That woman already thinks I'm a walking meme."

Marco skates over, his eyes shining with a mix of victory and sentiment. "Ah, Noah, you catch the puck and her heart, *sì*? Truly, you are the Casanova of the crease!"

Cash simply says, "Christ almighty."

I grin, skating back to my net. "What can I say? I *am* the Casanova of the crease."

The final horn for warm-ups blares, signaling it's time to get serious. We skate back to the bench, the atmosphere thick with a mix of sweat and anticipation. As we line up, I catch a glimpse of Coach Brenig, his face stern but eyes twinkling—tonight's a big one, and he knows it. He gives us his usual lecture disguised as a pep talk.

The PA system springs to life, echoing with the voice of the announcer notifying everyone of each teams' starting lineup.

I tap my stick against the boards, a goalie's applause for my crew. The rink lights dim momentarily, only to flare back up as the crowd roars in approval.

"And in goal, the man between the pipes, Noah Abbott!" the announcer blares.

That's my cue. I skate out to my crease, the cage where the magic will happen. The crowd's chanting, a rhythmic mantra that pumps through my veins like adrenaline.

The announcer's voice booms through the arena again. "And now, facing off for the Vegas Venom, Latham Newberry!"

Across from him stands Dan Martin of the Seattle Thunderhawks. All six foot four and two hundred twenty pounds of him. Dude's like a brick wall. The tension's as thick as molasses as they hover over the face-off circle.

"Let's make Scarlett proud," Anders says with a wink, lining up next to Latham, his eyes locked on the puck.

Cash takes his spot on the opposite wing, stick at the ready. "Time to shine."

The ref drops the puck, and like a magician pulling a rabbit out of a hat, Latham swipes it back to Marco. Ah, Marco, still getting the hang of American hockey. He fumbles for a second but gains control, passing it up to Anders.

"Is *buono*, *si*?" Marco calls out, a little too loudly.

"*Perfetto*, Marco," I shout back, guarding my net as if it's a vault and I'm the only one who knows the combination.

Anders takes Marco's pass like he's been handed a golden ticket, skating full-tilt into the Thunderhawks' zone. He dekes left, then right, finally firing a shot that the opposing goalie barely deflects.

"Nice try, Cap!" Latham yells, already on the rebound like a moth to a flame.

Cash, the silent enforcer, lays a body check on a Thunderhawk that's so loud, I swear I can hear it through my facemask. "Sit down," he growls, a man of succinct eloquence.

The puck ricochets back to Marco, who doesn't hesitate this time. "Got it!" he yells and slaps a shot that misses the net but crashes spectacularly into the boards.

"Close enough, Marco," I call out, suppressing a laugh. "You'll get 'em next time."

The crowd roars, their energy a tangible force, a sixth player on the ice. I'm in my zone, but my mind keeps drifting back to her. Molly. My nerdy, beautiful, jersey-wearing little tater tot. And what I want to do to her the next time I see her. Too bad we're getting on the plane for a road trip right after we shower tonight so that will have to wait.

I watch the clock ticking down—less than five minutes in the third period. My team's still clinging to that 3-2 lead. Every tick echoes in my helmet like a metronome set to 'heart attack'. Anders and Latham are up front, doing their best to keep the puck in the Thunderhawks' zone. Cash, the man of action, body-checks another opponent in open ice like a steamroller, earning a collective "Ooh" from the crowd.

"Dude was toast," he says, skating back into position.

Marco circles near the blue line, his eyes wide but focused. He looks like he's finally catching his American hockey stride. "Is intense, *non*?" he shouts over in my general direction. I can't help but chuckle. "Welcome to the NHL, buddy."

A Thunderhawk breaks away, the puck on his stick like it's glued. My pulse spikes, but I'm ready—legs tense, glove hand twitching for action. He shoots. I save. The crowd erupts, and for a split second, my eyes find my girl in the crowd. It's like she's my North Star, guiding me through the most nerve-wracking moments. If I had known how amazing it would feel to have someone in the stands just for me, I might not have been so closed off to a relationship.

Serrano bursts through our defense, a streak of menace on a breakaway. My every sense hones in on him, adrenaline pumping like jet fuel. Just as he crosses our blue line, Marco lunges in a last-ditch effort to stop him—and takes him down with an egregious trip. The ref's whistle slices through the arena, harsh and immediate. A penalty shot is awarded to the Thunderhawks' star forward, Alex 'The Surge' Serrano. My heart turns into a drumline in my chest, each beat echoing, *this is it, this is it.*

"Penalty shot," Cash states, skating past me. "Big moment."

Anders shoots me a look, his eyes saying what we're all thinking. Serrano's success against me could tie the game.

The Jumbotron replays the trip, and the crowd's reaction is a mixed bag of cheers and jeers. But in my cage, it's just me and the puck. The world narrows, the noise fades, and my gaze locks onto that little black disc that's about to become my dance partner—or my doom.

I unclasp my facemask, pulling it off as if I'm unveiling a secret. My hair's a sweaty mess, but I don't care. I shake it out, feeling every strand break free, like unshackling a part of my soul. The crowd notices, and the arena goes berserk as I prepare for the battle ahead. Whistles, cheers, shouts—it's a cacophony of raw emotion.

Then, my eyes find hers. Molly. She's on her feet, her hands clenched in front of her like she's praying for a miracle—or maybe she is the miracle. Our eyes lock and hold, and it's like an electric charge zaps straight through me. I can't look away. I don't want to look away. The world blurs around her, and I drink her in like she's the anchor I didn't know I needed.

Latham's voice yanks me back to reality. "Dude, if you're done making us all witness the pathetic expression of a pussy-whipped man, maybe win this one for the team?"

The smirk on his face says it all, but he's right. I need to seal this win. I grab my water bottle, squirt a jet into my mouth, and replace my facemask. As it clicks into place, it's like I've locked in a piece of her strength, her essence.

The ref signals for the ice to be cleared, and my teammates reluctantly skate off, leaving just me and Serrano in this gladiatorial showdown. As they clear, Marco shoots me a quick, chagrined glance.

"You've got this, Casanova!" he calls out, his words a rapid-fire burst as he reaches the bench.

I chuckle, even as I steel myself for what's coming. "You know it, Rossi. And if you trip somebody again, do it more quietly!"

Alex 'The Surge' Serrano picks up the puck at center ice, his skates a blur as he rockets toward me. Every muscle in my body tenses, every sense heightens. The crowd is a deafening roar, but in my ears, it's just white noise. All I can think of is her. Molly. My Tater Tot.

She's watching me. *Supporting* me.

Serrano fakes left, then shoots right. My heart's in my throat, but my glove is faster. With a leap that feels like I'm defying gravity, I snag the puck out of the air. Time freezes. The arena goes silent, then erupts into pandemonium. I'm pretty sure even Dante's on his feet.

The guys jump the half wall so they can swarm me, their cheers a symphony of triumph. Latham whoops like a man possessed, Anders shouts something about making history, and Marco... well, Marco's getting emotional like he's just won an Oscar. Mainly because I just saved his ass.

"Ah, is *bellissima!*" he cries out.

But my eyes find her. Molly. She's leaping, screaming, celebrating—just like everyone else, but also like no one else. Because this save, this moment, this win—it's all for her.

As the final horn blares, sealing our victory, the stadium turns into a madhouse of elation. Confetti cannons explode, dousing us in a shower of neon green and black. But the best part comes next.

"And the first star of the game, with the save of the season, Noah Abbott!"

The crowd roars, but her cheer pierces through them all. Molly's on her feet, clapping, yelling, being my one-woman fan club. And that's when I know for sure that things have changed between us. I have a question to ask her. An important one.

I skate out to center ice, my stick raised in a salute to the crowd, but really she's the only one I care about impressing. Cameras swarm me, microphones are shoved in my face, and I answer each question with practiced ease.

As I skate off the ice, a tunnel of high-fives and backslaps from my teammates guides me toward something even more real—my feelings. I've made saves before, but now I realize I've caught something I can't—and won't—let go of. Every cheer, every slap on the back, they're not just for the game.

They're for her.

My little Tater Tot.

* * *

Molly and I agree to a phone chat on Thursday night, since I'm on the road again. But now that I've made up my mind, I don't want to put off this conversation. Just a few hours ago, I helped the Venom put another tick in the W column, and a sense of calm washes over me. We're at the top of our division, and there's nothing like being bone tired after a hard-fought game where you come out the victors. I cling to that natural high as I run through what I want to say to Molly.

This isn't a lesson, I clarify to her. *I just want to see your face. I miss you.*

She replies with a blushing emoji, and it's all too easy to picture her heart-shaped face going pink around the edges.

Jostling my body around to get comfortable in the bed that night, I'm already wearing my PJs. My hair is still damp from the shower, and I feel strangely self-conscious about my appearance. When she looks at me, I want her to feel something—I want her to like me as much as I like her, dammit. I want her to feel, as Marco put it, that I'm precious to her.

Like diamond.

As soon as the bathroom door closes behind Anders with a mumbled warning to 'keep my dick in my pants,' I push the button in my contacts. Her face pops up on the screen, and my heart clenches. If there was any doubt at all in my mind, this resolves it ten times over. I feel something for her. Love? I don't know about that yet, but it's definitely in the neighborhood.

"Hey, beautiful," I murmur.

Molly's face goes as pink as the emoji. "Hey, yourself. What's going on?"

"I have something to tell you. Well, something to ask you." Dammit, why is it so much easier to flirt when there are no stakes?

"Okaaay…" Molly drags the word out as she settles on her couch. Her blond hair is pulled up in a messy bun on top of her head, and she's wearing an oversized t-shirt that says *I Like Big Books And I Cannot Lie.* "Hit me."

"I don't think I want this to be a situationship anymore." Her look of confused alarm hits me like a slap. "I'm not saying that we should call things off, but, oh, hell. Molly, will you be my *real* girlfriend?"

"Oh!" The smile that spreads across her face is a huge relief. "Are you serious? What changed?"

"You know how I said that I wanted to test a theory the other night?"

Molly nods as her eyes gloss over. "Vividly."

"I wasn't sure if I couldn't finish that one night because of my own hang-ups, or because I wanted to do something more meaningful with you. I guess we know now."

"We certainly do. What happens if I say yes? What changes? Do our lessons stop?" She cocks her head and frowns at something off-camera. "I haven't had a boyfriend since high school, and I'm not sure what's involved."

"I'd treat you the way I'd treat any woman I cared about. We could still have 'lessons,' but I'd like to be more, hmm... emotional? And I don't wanna do anything that's disrespectful to you."

Molly considers this. "I'm still not sure that something is 'disrespectful' if I'm the one requesting it, but I understand that you have your own boundaries. So can we still keep learning while we're respecting each other?"

I love the way her mind works, so much like mine. "Of course."

"What does that leave on the table?" Molly asks. "Breast play? Butt stuff?"

I choke on nothing. She has a gift for saying the last thing I expect. "If you want?"

"That was mostly a rhetorical question." Her lips curl into that familiar wicked grin. This woman loves pushing my buttons in the best ways. Since I met her, I feel less like a man carrying around bucketfuls of pain about the past and worry over the future and more like myself. "Yes, Noah, I would be happy to try being your *girlfriend*. I like you, too. And I trust you. I want to spend more time with you and get to know your really big... brain." Her brows pull sharply together. "What does this mean for keeping our personal lives separate from our relationship?"

My fingers flick at a piece of lint on the bedspread. "Actually, I was going to ask if you'd be interested in coming over next week for a barbeque. It'll be mostly guys from the team and some of their wives and girlfriends, but Fran and Viv will be there, too." Anders is going to shit a brick when he finally meets my 'tater tot,' and if Marco doesn't understand plain English, I'm going to have some choice words with him beforehand about the US version of the bro code.

"That sounds nice. I've never been to your place before." Molly grins, her childlike glee matching the sort of wild delight I'd usually expect from Viv.

The prospect of three elements of my life colliding in one event is a little bit terrifying, but it's also a thrill. Vivian, Fran, and Molly already get along, and I know for a fact that my girls would be thrilled to spend more time with my girlfriend.

My *girlfriend*.

Instead of placing a weight on my shoulders, the word does the opposite. I feel lighter when I say it.

I grin at Molly like the fool I am. "I'll text you the details. I'm going to be pretty busy this week since we have a homestand, but it'll be nice to have you over to the house. Viv can introduce you to the Gnome Gloam."

"Hang on, the Gnome Gloam is a real *place*?" Molly lets out a delighted laugh. "Amazing. I can't wait."

I settle back against the pillows. "So, *girlfriend,* tell me about your day."

The night tragedy struck, I stopped believing that I was capable of unfettered happiness. Turns out, I was wrong. As Molly tells me the story of a man who came in to special order a book that he couldn't remember the title, author, or subject of, I'm filled with nothing but hope and contentment.

If nothing else, we have a crazy physical chemistry in common. We have a crazy love of books in common. We share a sense of wonder and a sense of humor. We both lack drama and we're willing to communicate even over the tough topics.

Similar values.

There have to be many other things we'll find we have in common.

I'm not broken. Molly's giving me a chance to start over, and damned if I'm not going to grab that opportunity with both hands.

CHAPTER EIGHTEEN

Molly

When Noah texted me his address, he failed to mention that he lived in a goddamn mansion. Not that I'm poor by any means, but this is on a whole other level. The NHL must pay well.

As I get out of my car, I stare up at the enormous house, pushing my sunglasses up on top of my head. I wore a pink sundress over my yellow bikini, my favorite pair of strappy sandals that feel like something a Greek goddess would wear, and I have my magic wand in tow—when a princess visits another kingdom, she has to be prepared.

Before I left my townhouse, I thought that I looked cute, but now I feel massively underdressed.

Relax, it's just Noah's house. He likes you just as you are. There's no need to be nervous.

A paper sign taped to the garage points guests to a gate in the fence. Music streams from hanging speakers in the backyard, and vehicles fill the driveway and overflow all along the street.

"A princess is a princess wherever she goes," I remind myself, and lift my chin high before stepping through the gate.

The party is in full swing, and I stop at the corner of the house, gripping my wand in both hands as I take it all in. At least fifteen other people mill around, eating and drinking, none of whom I know or even recognize. A huge portion of the backyard is landscaped, and a big chunk of *that* is taken up by a pool. A few people are already lounging in the water, beers in hand; others are grouped around the grill, where Noah and two other guys are talking while Noah flips burgers. I don't see Francine or Viv, and nobody else is familiar.

I'm still frozen in place when a handsome, bearded, black-haired man in a t-shirt and board shorts notices me. He strides over and opens his arms, grinning from ear to ear.

"Tater Tot!" he exclaims. "Great to meet you. I'm Anders."

"Uh, hi?" I try for a smile, although I have no clue who this guy is or why he's calling me a carbohydrate.

"Anders? Noah's best friend, giver of excellent advice?" At my blank stare, Anders shakes his head and turns toward the grill. "What the hell, Noah, you didn't tell Molly about me? What the actual fuck?"

"Language," Noah calls back. "This is a family-friendly event."

"Unbelievable," Anders mutters, but I can tell from his tone that this is just banter. "That guy doesn't appreciate me enough. Well, never mind." He returns his attention to me and holds out a huge hand. "I'm the team captain—arguably the best Venom player. And *you're* the bookworm who's got my buddy's head turned inside-out. I'm super excited to get to know you better."

"Noah talks about me?" I ask, brightening at this news as I clasp his palm and shake.

"Frankly, he won't shut up about you." Anders winks. "It's exhausting. Do you want a drink? The food isn't ready yet, because *somebody keeps getting distracted!*" He shouts these last words toward Noah.

"Only because some ding-dong keeps distracting me," Noah calls back. "Stop harassing my girlfriend, Anders. Molly, feel free to toss him in the pool if he gets annoying."

The fact that Noah feels comfortable calling me his girlfriend in this public space, around his teammates, gives me a sensation. Yeah, butterflies taking flight.

"As if she could toss me," Anders scoffs.

I tap him lightly on the chest with my sparkly pink wand. "Never doubt my princess powers, sir."

Anders lifts his hands in the air, still clutching his beer. "Whoa, careful where you point that thing."

I laugh and let Anders lead me over to a cooler, where I fish out a hard cider. I'm about to head over to the grill when a high-pitched voice cries, "Princess Molly! You brought your *wand!*"

I turn to greet Vivian and am immediately bowled over by a giant black-and-pink monstrosity. My butt hits the ground before I know what's happening, and something wet swipes the side of my face from my chin to my temple.

"No! Bad dog!" Viv cries.

It takes me a moment to realize that the larger-than-life creature standing next to me is some kind of guard dog wearing a pink tulle cape and a pointed princess hat. She licks my face a few more times before bounding over to Noah.

Vivian comes running over and crouches down beside me until her ringlets fall across her cherubic face. "Did she hurt you, Princess Molly? Biscuit, come back here! Naughty, naughty, Biscuit!"

The huge dog frolics back toward us, plants her butt on the ground beside Vivian, and wags her stumpy tail so hard that her whole body shakes.

"So rude," Vivian complains. "We need to have a talk." She straightens up and crosses her arms so that she's eye to eye with the giant dog. Then she stabs her pointer finger in my direction. "Say you're sorry."

Biscuit hangs her head and looks up at Vivian with tragic eyes.

"Not to me." Viv points at me. "Apologize to *Molly*."

Biscuit turns to me and gives me the same look. Her tail twitches once.

It's hard to take a dog in a princess hat seriously, and other than the surprise of being knocked over, there's no harm done. I get back to my feet and dust myself off. "You're forgiven, Princess Biscuit," I say.

"Biscuit! Come!" Francine appears in the doorway. The dog goes loping back to her, and Francine leads her inside, clicking her tongue.

Viv lets out a long-suffering sigh. "No manners. No manners at all." She bends down to collect my wand from the dirt, and I grab my unopened cider. After a moment's consideration, I set it aside, figuring that it will probably fizz all over the place if I open it now.

"She seems like a nice dog," I say. "I don't think she meant any harm. Say, Vivian..." I lower my voice and crouch down to her level. "Any chance I could see the Gnome Gloam?"

"*Yes, Princess Molly!*" Vivian grabs my arm in both hands. "Come with me!" She drags me off toward the back of the yard. "I'm gonna show you my favorites!"

"See you later, Anders!" I call, waving my wand at him as I go.

It's been a while since I had a backyard; the townhouse where I live has a swing set and playground for the kids as communal space and a shared pool, but there's only a small patio to go to and relax outside that's private and just for me. Besides, this is Vegas. Most days it's too damn hot to be outside anyway. But hockey season is during some of the desert's mildest weather. Noah and his family have made excellent use of his huge outdoor space, and he has those floor-to-ceiling, paneled glass doors that create that indoor/outdoor illusion.

Most Vegas yards rely on cacti and hardscaping, but they've taken it a step further.

"Wow," I gasp. "Look at all of your subjects, Princess Vivian!"

Viv plants her little fists on her hips and surveys her empire. "Yup!"

My gaze sweeps the yard a bit overwhelmed. "How many are there?"

"Nanny Frannie says sixty-three now."

I whistle. "That's a lot. Do they all have names?"

When she nods, her platinum-blond curls bounce around her neck. "Most of them."

Making a sweeping gesture, I ask, "Is there anyone special I should meet?"

Viv points to a little female gnome dressed in a green tunic and stripey socks. "That's Miss Buttercup. The one with the big glasses is Merlin. The one riding the snail is Spoons, and that one there, the little one, see him? That's Zach."

"Ah." I bite back a smile and dip into a curtsy instead. "How do you do, Zach?"

Vivian leads me to a bench at the back of the garden, far away from the rest of the group. As I sit down, Francine reappears at the back door. She scans the crowd, probably looking for Vivian, and smiles when she sees us sitting together. I toss her a little wave to let her know we're okay and settle in beside the girl.

Vivian swings her feet off the edge of the bench. "Molly, do you like Unkie?"

"I do," I tell her. "Very much." Noah is still standing by the grill, watching us with a creased brow. When he catches my eye, he smiles at me and lifts his beer.

"Good. He's stinky, but I like him, too." Vivian scoots closer until her arm touches mine. "Do you *looove* him?"

I take a breath and pause. With little kids, I've learned that honesty is the best policy. "I'm still figuring that out. We haven't known each other long enough to say for sure."

Vivian pulls her mouth to one side as she considers this. "How long does it usually take?"

"It depends on the person. Sometimes it can take years, but..." I smile at Noah's broad back. "I don't think it will take me that long. Not with him."

"So you'll know soon? Good." Vivian nods. "Please love him a lot. He needs it. Ever since I've known him, he's been so sad. He makes more pouty faces than I do."

I twist toward Vivian. "What do you mean?"

"He frowns and stares with his googly eyes. He doesn't go outside with Biscuit. He doesn't play with me. You know when you fall and get an owie on your knee, and it takes a long, long time not to be purple anymore? Fran says that Unkie Noah's heart is like that. When Mommy and Daddy died, he got hurt, and his heart is still purple."

"Ah." I nod. "I see. That happens sometimes. It can take a long time for that purple part to fade away."

"When you fall in love with Unkie, are you gonna live here with me and help me build my kingdom?"

"I don't know." I swing my feet, imitating Viv's movements. "We haven't talked about it yet. What would you want?"

"I want you to come here and be my mommy," Viv says at once. "I don't remember my old one. Fran has pictures, but that's all. She was really pretty, but you're pretty too. I miss having a mommy."

My heart breaks for her. "How does that make you feel?"

Viv sticks out her bottom lip while she thinks about this. "Um. Sad, maybe? I think Unkie wants me to remember, so I can be sad with him, but I was too small when my mommy and daddy went to heaven."

"Thank you for telling me," I say. "I don't know if I'll come live here, but if I don't, it will be because Noah and I decide that we don't want to live together. It won't be because of you. You will always be welcome in the store and you and I will always be friends, okay?"

Noah's worried about hurting Vivian by introducing someone who might not stay, and I want to honor those concerns. Vivian is a sweet little girl—so innocent despite such tragedy and so pure of heart— that the idea of spending more time with her softens me, but I don't want to make promises I can't keep.

Even if the idea of moving in is more appealing than it should be.

You've only been officially dating for a few days, and you haven't spent any time with him. Just because you're compatible in the bedroom doesn't mean you'll make a good couple. Still, knowing that his little family would welcome me is a huge relief.

Vivian and I talk a little longer, mostly about gnomes and something called a Closet Hobbit, until Noah announces that the burgers and hot dogs are done, and everyone grabs a paper plate and side dishes from a communal table and then congregates around the grill.

I brave my cider, which has warmed up but thankfully doesn't explode when I pop the tab. Noah, Viv, Anders, and I all eat together, while their new teammate—a guy that Anders introduces as New Guy Marco—regales us with stories in broken English about life in the Italian countryside.

After we've eaten and chatted for a while, we migrate to the pool. A few people leave, and the sparser the party gets, the more relaxed I feel. I hover at the edges of the party, people-watching, but mostly focused on observing Noah and Vivian splashing around in the pool, while I dangle my bare feet in the water.

Eventually, Fran comes over to join me. "Did you and Vivian have a nice talk?"

"We did. She's an angel, and she and Noah are adorable together." At the moment, Vivian is hoisted on Noah's shoulders, ordering him to march around in the pool. Noah says something and starts to crouch down so that Viv's feet approach the water, and she shrieks in a mixture of alarm and delight. This is a side of Noah I haven't gotten to see before, and I adore it. When a man treats a child with such loving care—prioritizing that child's needs before his own—he starts to look like forever.

"Yes." Fran elbows me slightly. "He makes an excellent father, doesn't he?"

"You're not being very subtle," I point out.

Fran shrugs. "Who needs subtlety? It's the truth. Noah's a darling. And if he wasn't, I'd tell you."

I trail my fingertips through the warm water. "I'm pretty fond of him myself."

"Good." Fran leans back on her palms and splashes her feet a little. "You should come over for dinner sometime."

Noah appears next to us, with Vivian still held aloft. "Don't worry, I'll order takeout. Francine's cooking might be a little *too* exciting. And I can't even boil water."

"Hey." Viv taps the top of Noah's head with one finger until he looks up. "Be nice to Nanny Frannie." She looks up at me. "When can you come over, Princess Molly? Can we have a tea party? Can it be tomorrow?"

"Not tomorrow," Noah and I say at the same time. I don't

know what Noah has planned, but I have a standing date tomorrow, and I can't miss it, not even for something that makes me feel so warm and tingly inside.

So whole.

"How about next week?" Noah suggests. "Tuesdays are spoken for, and we have a game on Wednesday, so... Thursday? Friday?" He lifts one eyebrow. "We could have a sleepover."

"*Yes! A sleepover!*" Viv pumps her arms in the air, and Fran coughs to cover a laugh. "We can make a fort! We can eat popcorn and watch *Frozen* and play Candyland! And I can sleep in the big bed with you, Unkie, and Princess Molly!"

"I could even read you a bedtime story," I offer, not quite sure what to make of the fact that Vivian thinks it would be okay if Noah and I slept in the same bed. "I'll see if Mona can open for me on Saturday."

Noah's smile is as open and genuine as I've ever seen it. Maybe it's the fact that he's in his element, or maybe making our relationship official is part of a bigger change in his mental landscape.

This all feels so cozy. So comfortable. So *easy*. If someone had asked me to describe my ideal man, the likes of Noah Abbot wouldn't have sprung to mind, but now that he's in my life, he's everything I never even knew I wanted.

"Plus, I'll be able to show you my library," he says.

I snap my fingers. "Oh, shoot! I never did get your book in. I guess I've been a little distracted. But I'll get on top of it."

Noah walks backward through the water. "No rush," he says. Then he leans in to whisper so only I can hear, "I'd rather you get on top of me."

As he chuckles and moves away, he dips his head below the water, while Viv squeals and squirms as the water rushes up to her waist—and no higher. Noah waits there a moment before standing up again, and the whole of them howl with laughter.

I laugh with them because Noah's right. There is no rush. We have all the time in the world.

CHAPTER NINETEEN

Noah

The Sunday after the barbecue, I wake with the heaviness of a lead weight in my stomach. Not even thoughts of my first official sleepover with Molly and Viv can brighten my mood. I think of my childhood. I think of me and Nat playing tag, riding our bikes until dusk, eating bomb pops until we got head freezes.

Fighting.

Making Up.

Fighting again.

Today... today marks the anniversary I'd rather forget.

Three years ago today, Natalie and Steve died. I lost one of my best friends and Viv lost everything. Every day, Viv gets bigger and brighter and more outgoing, and my sister will never know what a lovely, brilliant, imperious little girl she created, full to the brim with all the best parts of her. I mean, she *knew*, but she'll never get to experience the gradual progression of Viv's childhood. Never get to see her turn into a beautiful and vibrant young woman.

Most days, that knowledge sucks. On the anniversary, it guts me.

After a few moments of lying in bed, I head downstairs. Francine has breakfast going—something she can actually make without incinerating it—toaster waffles, whipped cream, and fresh fruit. Viv's doodling on a notepad with a pile of crayons; when she sees me, her face lights up.

"Unkie! Look what I made!" She drops the crayon and holds up a piece of paper. Three stick figures stand in front of a house. The one in the middle is obviously Viv, based on the pink princess dress and tiara she's wearing. Two smiling adults hold her hands, a man with shaggy blue hair, and a woman in a yellow dress with blond hair.

"Nice." I move around to sit beside her, wrapping one arm around her tiny shoulders. "That's good, honey. Is that your mom and dad?"

"Nope." Viv points to the man who I now realize is wearing the Venom colors. "That's you, and that's Molly. I asked her if she was gonna be my new Mommy since I don't have one anymore."

My throat constricts at the casual way my niece discusses her parents' absence. There's no reason for her to feel differently, I suppose, and I'm glad that she doesn't yet understand how much she's lost. This is the only life she remembers.

I hope that's enough.

For her, the majority of the pain will come later once she understands what loss means.

"Isn't that sweet?" Fran asks. She catches my eye and gives her head a tiny shake. She knows exactly what today is. "And what did Molly say?"

"That she isn't sure about you yet, Unkie, but we can still be friends even if she can't be my mommy. Is she not sure because you're stinky?" Viv points to the house in her drawing, where a smiling oval face stares out of the window alongside a four-legged black smudge. "I drew you, too, Fran, inside with Biscuit. If Molly comes to live here, will you still be my nanny?"

"Viv, sweetheart." Fran pops the last of the frozen waffles out of the toaster and comes around to the other side of Vivian's chair. "Today isn't a good day to talk about this. Uncle Noah is feeling sad today. Do you remember why?"

Vivian frowns at me, then shakes her head. "Why should he be sad when Princess Molly was just here to make him smile?"

Fran scoops some waffles onto a platter. "Do you remember how we celebrated Biscuit's birthday this summer?"

Vivian nods. "Yes, and it's going to be my birthday soon!"

"That's right, my darling." Fran pats the top of Viv's head. "We celebrate birthdays because we want to remember when our favorite people came into the world and make them feel special. Today's a sad day for Unkie, though, because some people he loves very much had to leave the world."

"Oooh." Vivian's eyes widen, and she stares down at her drawing. "Is today the day my first mommy and daddy died?"

"That's right." Fran kisses her temple. "So we're going to let Noah feel his sad feelings and not ask him too many questions, alright?"

Vivian whips around toward me and wraps her arms as far around me as they'll go. "I'm sorry you feel bad, Unkie. If I could bring back your smile, I would."

I hug her close. On days like this, I don't know what I'd do without Fran. It's hard enough to unpack my own feelings, much less explain them in a healthy way—one that won't make Viv scarred for life.

My precious niece tips her face up to look at me without letting go. "Should I be sad today, too? We could be sad together."

"It's okay, kiddo." I sigh heavily. "I'm going to go be alone with my sad feelings for a little bit, and when I come back, I'm going to try my hardest to let that go and the three of us can do whatever you want to do."

Fran taps my niece's shoulder. "Today is hard for Noah, but do you remember what your book says?"

Viv's brow wrinkles as she finally lets go of me. I know which book Fran's talking about. It's the picture book about grief and loss that Fran bought to help Vivian explain why I get sad when I think about her parents.

"Sad feelings aren't for the people who went away," Viv says slowly. "They would want us to be happy. So Unkie is just sad because he misses people?"

"That's right," Fran says. "You know how sad you sometimes get when Unkie's away for work? It feels like that, but for a long, long time."

"Forever," Viv murmurs. She leans her head against my arm, and I wonder if I should say something to redirect the conversation, but before I can, Viv points to the waffles. "I'm hungry, Nanny Frannie. Can we eat now?"

"Of course!" Fran smiles as she gets up from the table. Viv's ability to bounce back from tough subjects astonishes me, and I wonder if that's because she runs out of questions, or because she understands how hard this is for me with that pure wisdom that only kids seem to have when it comes to the most difficult topics.

As we eat our breakfast, Fran and Vivian talk about other things, and I chime in occasionally. I wish that Vivian had memories of her parents, but maybe that's selfish. She's happy now, and any sadness she feels about them at this point in her life is limited to her desire for *a* mother, not *her* mother specifically. When I help myself to another waffle, my eyes drift to Vivian's drawing of the happy family she craves.

Why the hell have I been fighting this so hard? Molly's perfect, not just for me but for Vivian as well. That's one reason this anniversary feels different than in years past.

This year, for the first time, I have hope that things will get better for both of us. That we can come out the other side stronger.

Better even.

After conscientiously moving through all the stages of grief, I'm giving myself permission to be happy.

* * *

Vivian stays behind with Francine when I leave for the cemetery. I stop at a nearby shop to pick up a bouquet, then make the drive out toward Henderson where my sister and brother-in-law are interred. I spend the drive grappling with the urge to call Molly. It would be nice to have her here with me today. I think I might be ready to open up to her about how hard things have been for me, and I wouldn't mind lying in her bed for a while and just... breathing.

Becoming comfortable with things feeling normal again.

Just sharing air with someone I care about, who's still here. Someone who wants to support me through good times and bad. Someone who wants to honor my darkness while also filling it with light.

I tap the car's Bluetooth system before I remember that Molly said she wasn't going to be around today since she had some kind of standing appointment. That's fine—just knowing that she's out there in the world and caring about me, her boyfriend, is good enough. I promise myself to bring this up next time. Maybe I'll even mention it in grief counseling.

Maybe—and here's a crazy thought—I'll finally be able to stop going one of these days. Moving on from my sister's death always sounded like I was just supposed to get over it, but I'm finally seeing that the end goal is to stop focusing on what's gone and start rebuilding my own life. And now with Molly in it, I'm well on the way.

It's a warm fall day, but not too hot. The full sun kisses my skin even through my tinted windows, and I push my shades further up my nose. Once I find a spot, I park and make my way over to Natalie and Steve's shared headstone, relieved that the flowers might last a day or two this time before they wilt in the sun. A few other people mill around praying and weeding and putting flowers in pots and metal vases stuck in the earth, but we end up averting our eyes from one another. In this space, the pain of our loss is sacred. We let one another go about handling our grief as best we can without interfering, even with eye contact.

I'm sure when other mourners pass by Nat and Steve, they shake their heads over the waste of a young couple gone far before their time. I imagine they wonder about how Nat and Steve died.

Together.

Forever frozen in death.

I know the way to the grave by heart, and my feet automatically carry me to the site. My own pain bubbles up, but I numb it out a bit and don't let it overflow. Today, I'm running on autopilot, muscle memory but the usual sharp pain has faded somewhat, blunted by time and intervening good memories. I lost my sister and brother-in-law, but I gained a daughter. It was a terrible price to pay, but there's only so long that I can cling to all my darker emotions before the illuminations cast by Vivian and Molly dispel the shadows.

The phoenix rises from the ashes, which means something has to burn to the ground before that bird can spread its wings and fly. That imagery hits home now more than ever.

"Hey, Nat." I speak the words aloud before I even reach my destination, as if I've spotted my sister among a crowd and want to get her attention. "I miss you, sis."

Her headstone gleams in the sun, polished black granite that bears two names and four dates. Before I can stop it, my hand reaches out to caress the smooth surface and it feels cool underneath my fingertips.

I don't think that my sister's here. Vivian's book tells her that the ones we've lost are all around us, in the flowers and the wind and the blue summer sky, little fragments of love scattered wherever we go. I don't believe that, either. I carry my sister with me in my heart. She's in every breath I breathe and every word I speak. Whatever parts of her still exist are rooted in my memory: our pillow fights when we were kids; the time she told my parents I'd snuck out after dark to kiss a girl for the first time and got me grounded; the way she used to tackle me and hold me down so that she could put my hair in pigtails and paint my face with makeup 'to make me pretty' even though I tried to fight back; how she cried when her high school sweetheart dumped her for her best friend; the love in her eyes when she looked at Steve on their wedding day; the tears that spilled down her cheeks when she held Vivian for the first time and asked us, *Isn't she perfect?*

For all the things I remember and all the things I don't, I carry her with me. I'm the only thing keeping her alive, and each memory that slips away from me is another little piece of her gone forever.

Until recently, I was afraid of what would happen if I let her go. Now, I wonder how she would feel about how tightly I've clung to my grief.

Doing nothing but holding on.

Sad feelings aren't for the people who went away, Viv said this morning. They would want us to be happy, Unkie.

Grief is for the people who are left behind.

I lay the flowers on Natalie's grave and stand over her. "Hey, sis. Hey, Steve-o. I'm sorry it's been so long since I've been here. I should probably come more than once a year. Someday, maybe I'll bring Viv along. I wish you could see what a little diva your daughter has grown into." I laugh aloud and shove my hands into my pockets. "She's a lot like you, Nat, but you were never as girly as she is. I don't know where she got that from. She's putting me through it though. You should see her Gnome Gloam. Don't even get me started on what she's done to Biscuit. And having an entire collection of tiaras? Yeah, I guess that's a thing."

Usually, I just come here and cry. I'm not sure what to say now, so I kick around a pebble in the walkway. A sliver of hope cracks my heart open a bit and the words slowly come.

"I met someone, Nat," I murmur. "A girl. Well, a woman. I know you always hated when people talked about grown-ass adults like they were still little kids, but in this case, I don't think she'd mind. She's a kid at heart. Viv wants a new mom, and as much as I hate the idea of anyone replacing you, I think this woman would be a good fit for us. You'd get a kick out of her. I think, um. I think she might be the one." I swallow hard, ignoring the knot of pain gaining size in my stomach the longer I stand here. "It's too early to tell yet, but I figured that if I didn't tell you, you'd kick my ass for keeping secrets." I chuckle again and drag my hand across my face. "God, this feels weird."

I turn away from the headstone, wondering what else to say. Everything I can think of seems so trite.

"I feel like I'm coming to life again, Nat. Like I've been sleepwalking, and I'm finally waking up. And it's all thanks to… to… Molly?" I squint across the sloping cemetery to a small blonde figure clutching a bouquet of lilies.

That figure—I'd know it anywhere.

What the hell is she doing at my cemetery?

I shield my eyes from the sun since I took my sunglasses off out of respect but sure enough, it's Molly, reaching beneath her glasses to wipe tears from her eyes. I can't see her expression from my vantage point so far away, but I recognize that sag of shoulders, that hunch of back.

Because I've been there myself.

Pain does something to the body—shrinking it as it makes its presence known.

"I love you, sis." I kiss the tips of two fingers and brush them across the headstone. "But right now, I've got to figure something out. I'll let you know how it goes." Then I set off down the path that winds between the plots.

Molly's face is puffy and red as I approach, her beautiful features twisted into a mask of grief. Seeing her like this only causes my own to rear back up and threaten to overtake me. I want to reach out to her. I want to hug her and hold her close and take every uncomfortable emotion she's ever felt away. But then it occurs to me that our relationship is so new and I shouldn't intrude on her mourning, so I stop before I reach her, out of earshot in case she has anything to say to her loved one. She's still clutching the flowers when she spots me, and she smiles through her tears.

"Noah?" she asks. "What are you doing here?"

I shove my sunglasses back on my face. "I came here to pay my respects. Do you mind if I...?"

She waves me closer. "Of course. I'm here for my Uncle Arthur."

"Yeah? The one who left you the bookshop?" I slip my arm around Molly's waist and nod to the headstone, feeling like I should say something. "For what it's worth, Uncle Arthur, your niece is doing a great job turning your legacy into something even greater than it was when you left it."

Molly laughs and sniffs at the same time, choking on her tears. "Sorry, sorry. I didn't think that this would still be so hard. It's been *years*, you would think that it would get easier. I just feel like he missed out on so much. He was my godfather, you know. We were very, very close. There were things I couldn't say to my dad, but Uncle Arthur was always there to lend an ear. If it weren't for him, I never would have been able to indulge in my love of books. It was something we shared."

I squeeze her gently and kiss the top of her head. "I'm here for Viv's parents. I know how tough it is. Do you want to talk about it?"

Molly bends down to place the lilies in a green vase in front of Arthur's grave, then takes my hand so that I can help her get back to her feet. "It was just so *senseless*. He should have been *fine*. The last three years have been so hard."

My fingers tighten on hers as my eyes scan the headstone. Uncle Arthur's stone is etched with the exact same date as Nat and Steve's. "Three years today?" My mind races as my heart rate picks up. That's an odd coincidence. Then again, Las Vegas is a huge city. Multiple people die every single day. "You said he died from natural causes, right?"

"Y... yes." Molly shivers and wipes at her tears again. "God, it was so damn tragic. There weren't any signs or symptoms. Nothing. I've never known anyone as healthy as my Uncle Arthur. But he went into cardiac arrest and passed out on the highway, losing control of the car and swerved into oncoming traffic, and—"

I see stars as all the breath whooshes from my body, leaving me empty.

As empty as the night I lost Nat.

No.

No.

No.

"Noah?" Molly looks up at me as I stumble back, putting my

palms up between us.

"You're fucking kidding me," I mutter, eyes wide and unseeing. "Are you serious? Did you *know* about this? Did you fuck with me on purpose? Is this some kind of sick joke?"

"Know what?" Molly reaches for me, but I slap her hands away and step backward. "Fuck with you? Noah, are you okay?"

"No, I'm not okay." I jab one finger at the tombstone as the floodgates of all the emotions I thought I'd worked through already come rushing back in like they were being held back by the Hoover Dam. My eyes focus on Molly, but they don't see her. "Your Uncle Arthur is a goddamn murderer."

This isn't happening. It can't be. It has to be a bad dream and I'll snap awake in a pool of my own sweat any second now. Everything is just a trick of my mind: the sunlight on my skin, the warm breeze ruffling my hair, the smell of flowers and earth, even the distant hum of traffic. It's fake, because this is impossible. Because if it's not impossible, then the pain I'm feeling right now is my heart being ripped from my chest cavity and shredded without the benefit of anesthesia.

"Noah, what's wrong with you?" Molly rocks back on her heels, and her face falls. "You're scaring me."

As my whole body trembles, I inhale and loom over her, unleashing my rage. Unleashing all of it—every last sliver of agony I've ever felt and then some. For Viv. For me. For every motherfucking memory I deserve to make with my family that's no longer possible. "He killed my beautiful, special, perfect sister. He killed Natalie. And Steve—and he almost got Viv, too. It's a miracle he didn't. But he left that little girl an orphan even while God spared her precious life!" Every wall in my heart that I've spent years trying to pull down rebuilds in a flash of disbelief and then anguish. "Do you know what they called my sister in the hospital, Molly? Well, I'll tell you. They called her a body. And I couldn't even see her to say goodbye, because that body was in parts. How can you cry over the man who did that? How can you sit there and pretend like that's okay?"

"Your sister? And Vivian?" Molly's face pinches in confusion. "Noah, I'm not sure what you're talking about."

"Yeah, my sister." I thump my fist against my chest. I want to hit something, to flip something, to throw down with this Uncle Arthur fucker the way some guys throw down on the ice. I want to grab a shovel and dig up his carcass just so I can spit on it. I want to hurt him as badly as he hurt me. As badly as he hurt *Viv*. "My sister, whose only crime was being in oncoming traffic when he lost control of his car."

Molly takes a moment to process this, but instead of acknowledging what her uncle did, she takes his side. I can't even believe what's happening right now. "He had a fatal heart attack," she whispers, eyes wide as moons while backing toward his headstone. Other mourners stare at us with pity, but I don't give a damn. "He died instantly, Noah. It wasn't his fault. Tragic accidents are just that. Accidents."

"Well, he could have had the common fucking decency to die alone of his *natural* causes, where he couldn't hurt anyone." I'm dimly aware of how childish and irrational I'm being, but my pain overrides everything else, and after three years, I finally have the name of the monster who's to blame for imploding my life and Viv's.

And I want a pound of his flesh right along with the new plate of sorrow I've just been served.

Back at the time, I deliberately put the name of the *driver* out of my mind, letting my agent handle all the legalities, so I never made the connection. I only heard his name once by accident, since I avoided the papers and the news. Art Palmer. Uncle Arthur. But damn it if I'm not connecting every single dot right now.

Molly chokes on a sob, but I glare daggers at her pain, only concerned with my own and how it's now rolling down the tracks like a runaway train, imploding everything in its destructive path. Everything else is far away. The only things that are real to me right now are my torment, my loss, my fury, and my despair.

A voice that sounds a lot like Fran's echoes through my head. *Molly's got her own sad feelings, Noah. It's not fair to blame her for everything you feel.*

You know what, Fran? Fuck you!

I can't let myself feel anything more. I have to dial this shit back before it overtakes me. I can't let my emotions ride me like this. If I do, I'll end up back in that hole where I spent the first year after Natalie's death. It might kill me.

The only safe thing to do is shut down. Turn off my emotions, even the ones that have to do with Molly.

And build my walls bigger and stronger than before.

Glaring at her, I grit out, "When you can take accountability for what that monster did, we can talk, but not one fucking minute before that time."

I pull myself together and turn on my heel, leaving Molly in a heap on the grass, sobbing behind me.

I keep myself steady the whole drive back home. I don't think about the hurtful words that spilled so easily from my mouth, or how Molly reacted. I don't care one whit about her pain over a man who doesn't deserve it. I don't acknowledge the sense of betrayal that fills me right to the brim. I make myself drive like a rational human being, keeping everything pushed down deep.

Because Nat and Steve left Viv behind. She lived. God decided to save her and now her future happiness is up to me.

I never loved Molly, I didn't. I just thought I did because I let myself feel again in a moment of weakness. It won't happen again.

Fran and Vivian are outside playing with gnomes when I return. Viv's back is to me, but Fran sees my face as I push through the front door. Her concern is obvious, but I've got a ticking time bomb inside me, and I can't let Viv see me go off. I have to be strong for her, and to be frank, I don't know how much strength I have left. Waving Fran away, I stalk past them.

Biscuit is sleeping on my bed, and she lifts her head when I slam the door, kick off my shoes, and collapse beside her.

"Hey, girl," I say. The words barely make it out before I have to bury my face in my pillow. Only then, when my voice is muffled, do I let myself burst into tears. My pain flows out of my body and onto my dog like a river.

Minutes pass. Maybe hours. All I know is it feels like days. Biscuit finally licks the moisture off my face, and I inhale a shuddering breath, not sure if the tears are going to start again or if they're all dried up.

I hate Arthur. I fucking hate him. Because not only did he take Natalie and Steve out of our lives, but now he's taken Molly, too. How can I be with someone who's carrying the ghost of that bastard around in her heart the same way I'm carrying my sister?

But Nat... she *deserves* to be carried forever. She deserves to be remembered and loved and treasured.

Biscuit licks the back of my head and leans her muscular ribcage against my side, eventually letting her head settle on my back. I want to comfort her, to tell her I'll be fine.

The thing is, I'm pretty sure I'd be lying.

Every cell in my body is screaming that I'll never be fine again.

CHAPTER TWENTY

Molly

When I show up for work the next morning, Mona takes one look at me and drops her entire armload of books.

"By the tentacles of the Flying Spaghetti Monster, Molly. You look like *shit*. What's wrong?"

I swallow hard. "Didn't sleep."

"I mean, duh." Mona takes a tentative step closer. "But, like, *why?* You look like you got punched in both eyes. Have you been crying?"

"Your bedside manners leave something to be desired," I croak.

I have to be honest with myself because I feel like an old sponge that's been left out in the sun. The only reason I'm not crying right now is that I'm too dehydrated to keep it up. And I refuse to drink any water. I want to die a slow death.

Mona's gaze sweeps my body. "Seriously, Molly. What's going on?"

I crouch down to collect the books she's dropped. "Noah and I broke up."

Mona sucks in a breath. "Wait, you two were *dating?*"

So many emotions have been banging around my body since the cemetery, I never know which one is going to land. "Yes. Past tense."

"Wow." Mona shakes her head. "I assumed that you two were just playing hide the sausage. You know, spearing the ol' clam. Slapping uglies."

"*Mona*. I get it." I stand upright and go back to working on the display. "Yes, we fucked. I guess he caught feelings because he asked me to be his girlfriend. I even met his family. Then we dated like a normal couple for a hot second. But he's not who I thought he was. Not by a longshot. Now our next date is off. The sex is off. The feelings are *definitely* off."

"Oh." Mona leans back against the counter and crosses her arms. "What did he do?"

"How do you know it was him?" I ask.

Mona waves a hand. "Oh, please, it's obvious. You're a literal unicorn-slash-fairy-princess-slash-mermaid. You're so sweet it gives me cavities. If *you'd* done something, you'd be crying into a rainbow Frappuccino and asking me how to make things right. It's *obviously* Noah's fault. Also, he's a man, and men are dicks. Sometimes they intend to be and sometimes they're just dumb. Which is it in this case?"

Usually I'd argue against sweeping statements like this, but all I say is, "Damn right, they're dicks."

She nods and twists her lips. "See? So why don't you tell me what's going on?"

My hand trembles so badly that when I go to stand the next book upright, I immediately knock it over. Mona darts over to help.

I suck in an inhale that barely fills my lungs. "He blames me for his sister's death."

Mona gasps and clutches the book to her chest. "Holy shit. Are you a closet member of the mob? Are we laundering money through the store? Why the hell didn't you tell me so I could make it out alive?"

"Of course not," I snap, tugging the book out of her hands and putting it back where it belongs. "When Uncle Arthur died, he lost control of the car..."

"I remember you telling me about that." Mona frowns, but for once she lets me keep going without saying anything. Almost like she understands the strength of my emotion and has decided to respect it.

My stomach plummets before I even say the words aloud. "I knew that he hit a car in the opposing lane and there were fatalities, but I didn't know who. There was an investigation and they keep that stuff under wraps until they decide if criminal charges are going to be filed. I hired a personal injury lawyer to handle all of it, because I just... couldn't. Then I was dealing with the bookstore and the insurance companies... and there are privacy laws because Steve, Noah's brother-in-law, worked for the federal government." I let out a shaking breath that almost sends me over the edge again. "Natalie and Steve were in the other car. And maybe their daughter, too, I wasn't entirely clear on that when Noah was losing his shit."

"Hang on, you mean Vivian?" Mona holds her hand up to her waist. "This tall, incredibly pink? She was in the car Arthur hit? Her parents died and she lived? Goddamn, no wonder Noah freaked out. Not that it's any excuse, but... holy shit. That's a lot."

I whirl to face her. "Don't you *dare* blame Arthur for that."

She lifts her hands in surrender. "Not on purpose, obviously. I'm not saying that it's right for Noah to blame him, just that I can see why that would throw him for a loop, and men aren't good at handling strong emotions that come out of nowhere. They're not as emotionally intelligent as women. They tend to think the worst. And as a professional athlete with an extremely demanding career, he still had to step up and become a father to a baby. His choice about starting a family was taken away from him. I can't even imagine what he went through—what he's still going through. I'm just saying I can see both sides,

Molly. Maybe it's my understanding of how the human mind works. I see why he would question you about the coincidence of it. Why he might think that you knew about it and withheld that information. He's probably harbored a lot of unresolved resentment since losing his sister, and since he didn't have anyone to blame at the time, he's blaming Art and taking it out on you now that he's finally putting a human face to the tragedy."

I stare at Mona, open-mouthed. "Are you kidding me?"

"Sorry," she says, lowering her hands. "Psych degree. I can't help it if I'm smart sometimes. I can hardly hold that information back—even though I know you don't want to hear it. So, what am I supposed to do now?"

"I don't know." I flap my hand at the POS system. "Inventory until opening time?"

She leans in and gives me an almost hug. "No, I mean for *you*. You're sad. I'm the sad one. We can't both be sad. You're not playing your role correctly."

"Then I guess it's your turn to be the happy one." I don't know how to fake my way through functionality this time around. I'm a mess, and I don't have the will to haul myself up by my bootstraps and pretend I'm all good.

"Happy isn't my thing," Mona says. "We need to fix you instead."

I shake my head so hard a stabbing pain hits my temple. "I don't think this can be fixed."

"Ah, ah, ah." Mona wags her finger at me. "Hold on there, boss. Hear me out. I'm not saying that we need to fix things between you and Noah. He's the one who acted out, so that's on him, and if he *does* get his shit together, it's up to you whether you want to forgive him for letting his grief and pain overwhelm him. To even get considered for a second chance, he'll need to grovel and grovel hard. I'm asking what we can do about *this*." She circles my face with her finger. "What do we need? Wine? Chocolate? Ice cream? Chick flicks? A spa day?" She shudders. "God, I hope it's not a spa day, but if I have to get my face exfoliated with cucumber pulp and have a stranger massage my feet while she speaks ill of me in Mandarin, I will endure it. For *you*. You're not at fault here, but something tells me that you feel like you should have done something differently. Forget that. I want you to take care of *you*."

"Aww." I shuffle over and stand on my tiptoes to kiss her forehead. "You're a sweetie."

Mona sticks out her tongue. "I'm a scion of night, actually, but your point is made. You need some self-care. What do normal women do for self-care? Something with aromatherapy candles, probably. And toenail polish. It's always about the toes."

I crack a genuine smile. "What do *you* do to make yourself feel better?"

Her response is immediate. "I spend the evening doing tarot readings and making adorable voodoo dolls of my enemies. Then I fetch my extra-long stickpins, uncork a bottle of Merlot that's red like blood, and see where the night takes me."

"Maybe we could split the difference," I suggest, raising my eyebrows. "Tarot and a board game? I don't particularly want to hex anyone."

Noah's suffered enough. I don't want him to hurt. I want him to see reason. I want him to *apologize*. Even if Mona's right about his feelings, that doesn't excuse the things he said to me in the cemetery. I know enough about grief, however, to realize that people make mistakes when their emotions steal away their better judgment.

"Ooh, or I could teach you to play the new video game I just got into." Mona rubs her hands together. "Do you really wanna do something after work?"

"Sure. We haven't hung out much lately. Are you sure you're free? I don't want your grades messed up."

"Impossible," Mona assures me.

I'm not sure if she means that her grades are impeccable, or if they're so terrible that they're beyond saving, and I don't ask. I assume the former, given how much she studies. Despite her goth act, she's nowhere near as much of a nihilist as she pretends to be.

"Then I'll text you when I close up, and we'll figure out dinner plans." I rub my aching eyes. "Thanks, Mona."

"Anytime." Mona gives me a thumbs-up. After a moment's consideration, she crab-walks toward me, arms outstretched and a pained smile on her face.

"Everything okay?"

"I'm hugging you," she says. "For reals this time. But hugs are weird, so please accept that this is going to be awkward."

I throw my arms around her and squeeze her close, while she pats my back.

"Feel better?" she asks.

I smile against her shoulder. "A little."

"Oh, thank God." She squirms until I let go of her. "Alright, that's all the touchy-feeliness I can stand for the day. I'm gonna get to work now."

"I'll be back in the office for a bit doing inventory," I tell her. "A new shipment just came in. Oh, and Mona?"

She bows. "Yes, my liege?"

I exhale as I drink in the empathy on my friend's face. "Thanks for being so nice to me."

Mona hisses. "I'm not *nice*. I'm more like apathetic."

"I'm gonna have to disagree on that front." I wink and turn

back to the office, where our Monday shipment is waiting to be unpacked, re-counted, and entered into the database.

As I work, my sadness returns, but as long as I can keep busy, I'm alright. The real kick in the pants comes when I pull out an old hardback copy of *The Quest of the Silver Fleece*, on special order for Noah Abbot. It finally came in.

No rush, he'd said when I mentioned it. Was that conversation only on Saturday? It feels like a lifetime ago, but it's been less than forty-eight hours.

I set the book aside, remembering what Mona said about the onus of repair. It's not my job to reach out to Noah and try to fix things. He's the one who hurt *me*, which means that it's on him to contact me if and when he's ready.

And if he doesn't, then I'll have to be prepared to forgive him for my sake and move on.

Alone.

CHAPTER TWENTY-ONE

Noah

I'm dragging my ass at morning skate, letting a couple of normally easy saves hit the back of the net. Even Anders shakes his head. But nobody's in the mood to practice. It's Monday. It's abnormally gloomy outside the arena. I'm depressed as hell, and I can't get my head in the game. Marco just one-timed me from the point with a rocket. Despite being Italian, he's not as bad as he could be. And he's big—which is important for a defenseman in the NHL. There might be hope for the guy.

"Abbot! Stop moping around and get your shit together!" Coach Brenig calls. "So many pucks have blown by your head today, you're gonna need a new facemask."

I nod, but my attention span is shot. I didn't sleep for crap last night, and I feel like a dick for ducking out and leaving Fran to explain to Vivian that I wasn't feeling well, but I didn't tell her what was wrong. I barely grunted when she knocked on the door. I couldn't face them, because what was I supposed to say? *Sorry, Viv, but the woman you want as your new mommy is related to the man who took your real mommy away.*

Fuck that. For one thing, it doesn't make sense. After I expelled every single tear that had been marinating behind my eyeballs, I came to a realization. It's not Molly's fault. I genuinely believe that she didn't know, because no one could fake that shock and surprise in the middle of a damn cemetery, but the fact that she *defended* the man who took my sister away? That part's bullshit. There's no way I'd be able to kiss her again without that fact running through my mind.

So because of the tragic circumstances around a senseless tragedy, I've lost Molly. Good thing this happened before things really got going. What would have happened if I'd found this out months or even years down the line? Better to cut the cord now when it doesn't hurt as bad. So long as Viv doesn't know the truth, they can still be friends, and I won't have to feel guilty for excising another mother figure from her life.

Doesn't hurt as bad? Who the hell am I kidding?

I don't realize that I've bellyflopped down on the ice until Latham shoots another rifle that hits my mask and rings my bell.

"Yo, dude, what the hell?" he asks, skating closer to loom over me. "You're gonna get yourself straight into concussion protocol over a practice! Pull your head out of your asshole."

"Sorry." I rest my stick up to my shoulder and struggle to my skates. "I feel like crap today. Gonna sit this one out. Let my backup take some shots."

Coach comes over to read me the riot act and tell me to get my ass back in the net, but before he can get his bluster on, I say, "It was the anniversary yesterday."

"The anniversary of what?" he demands. Then his eyes widen. "Oh, hell. Alright, ride the bench and get your bearings while the rest finish up. And have Brett check your head."

I slouch over, letting my elbows rest on my knees as the other guys zip around the ice, shooting me curious looks. Brett, one of the trainers, looks at my pupils with one of those tiny pen lights and gives me the all clear. It's been a while since I did something like this. Usually, staying focused on the game I love with all my heart keeps my mind off of things, but not today.

When we hit the locker room, Latham and Anders corner me.

"What happened out there?" Latham asks. "It's like you went offline. As a goalie, that's a damn good way to get yourself killed. Not that any of us would take you out, but if we were playing a game? The enemy would figure that shit out right quick and take advantage."

"Something going on with you and your little tater tot?" Anders asks. "If it helps, I really, really like her."

Latham lifts an eyebrow. "You mean that Tinkerbell-looking chick from the barbecue? No way."

"Molly," I say. "And she's not my anything. It's over."

Anders leans one elbow on Latham's shoulder, forming a blockade so that I can't escape the inquisition. "You burnt the tot to a crisp? How'd you do that? Even you know how to turn the oven off when smoke starts billowing out of it."

"What makes you think it was my fault?" I snap.

"Uh, because you're obnoxiously in love with her?" Anders waves his free hand as if to ask, *Could this be any more obvious?* "If she'd called things off, you'd be lying in the fetal position in the shower right now. Which leads me to assume that *you* ended things, and you're now deep in the shitstorm of regret. Also, if you cut her loose, it was obviously a mistake. So, how do we fix it?"

Latham nods in agreement the whole time. It's nice to know that my friends have so much faith in me.

"There's no fixing it." I try to swallow past the lump in my throat. "Molly's uncle killed Natalie. He *killed* her, Anders. How the fuck do I get past *that*?"

Latham whistles, and Anders pulls his head back. All of his features pinch up in confusion. "Hold the phone. I was there. Viv's parents died in a car accident. You're not making any sense here, Noah."

"He killed Nat and Steve, and he almost killed Viv. Molly's uncle was the driver who crossed the center line and hit them head on."

"So, let me get this straight." Latham holds up both hands, waving the right one back and forth. "Some guy got in a car accident three years ago." He turns to his left hand, waving that one in turn. "And now you've broken up with Tinkerbell because... she shares blood with the guy? I'm sorry, am I the only one not seeing how that computes? Like was she in the car distracting him or something?"

"I, too, am puzzled by why our friend Noah has decided to punish his tater tot over something like this." Anders plants his free hand on his hip and squints at me. "Are you seriously holding that against her?"

"He's her *godfather*," I explain. Why are they looking at me like that? Like this is my fault. How are they not getting this? "She inherited the bookstore from him. I've been sleeping with the enemy."

Anders shakes his head. "This isn't the Montagues and the Capulets, and you two are not Romeo and Juliet. Seriously, Noah? Who holds people accountable for the actions of their family members? Should we round up all of Jeffrey Dahmer's family and throw them in the pen? Should we cancel Dennis Quaid because Randy Quaid is off his rocker? Listen to yourself. You're not making one bit of sense here. And you haven't been sleeping with the enemy. You've been sleeping with a nice girl who also lost someone she cared about—a pain few can understand but you two happen to have in common. Have you stopped one second to consider what she's feeling right now that she learned her beloved Uncle Arthur accidentally killed two young parents far before their time, leaving their precious angel an orphan? Christ. Is it possible you're just afraid of getting hurt and that's why you're sabotaging a perfectly good relationship? The pain you're suffering because you lost Natalie is so great that you're not willing to ever put your heart on the line again? Sounds like a shitty way to live a life. And I knew Nat. That's not what your sister would want for you."

"Well, I guess we'll never know *what* she'd want," I retort. "Because she's gone. Because Molly's uncle killed her."

Latham whispers to Anders out of the side of his mouth. "He's short-circuiting again. Must have been Marco's slapshot to the face. What do we do?"

"You could start by getting out of my business and stop trying to pressure me into revisiting a relationship that could never work," I snap. "There's too much pain. Too much derision. Too much fucking water under the bridge."

"See, man, this is what I'm saying." Anders taps his chest. "You're too reactive right now. You're going into defense mode. That's not healthy, my guy."

"None of this is healthy." I cross my arms and glare at them both. "You know what would be healthy? Sticking to the original plan and avoiding romantic entanglements altogether. Relationships are worthless. See what happens when I let my guard down even for a second?"

Latham points at me and tells Anders, "He does make a valid point."

"Like hell he does. I saw the way he looked at Molly. She wasn't some random hookup. Not even from the beginning. No matter how much he protests." He points at me. "You were crazy about her. First you told yourself that you weren't going to get attached. When your heart got all squishy around her, you tried to brush it off. When you couldn't dismiss it anymore, you finally opened up, only to realize that you had someone in your life that you were afraid to lose. Is this ringing any bells?"

"No," I grumble, although it kind of is. I glare at Anders, hating his reasoning even as I value his friendship. But he can't out-logic me away from my pain. "If that were the case, why would I break things off?"

"So that you can control when you'd lose her," Anders says, "rather than having to worry that it would happen unexpectedly. Just like what happened with Nat. You didn't have any control. She died, and you didn't have time to prepare yourself."

His words hit me like a punch to the gut. Hanging my head, I start taking off all my goalie pads and then unlace my skates. As I watch my friends, I realize they're a little *too* on the nose, and as much as I'd like to blow them off and tell Anders in particular that he's being an idiot, I can't deny that he's cut me close to the bone.

In this moment where I'm blinded by emotion like a loose cannon, he knows me better than I know myself.

"Ah, *mio amico* be unreasonable," Marco says. He's slouched on the bench near his locker, looking sour as all hell. "No hope for him. Maybe I should hit him again—knock sense into his hard head. Can we talk about real problems now? I need zee advice, because I *stesso* confusing."

"You mean 'confused?'" Anders asks. He turns to face Marco and jumps when he sees his face. A blob of brown trickles down his face, exposing a bluish mark on his eye.

"Are you wearing makeup?" Latham asks.

I couldn't see it earlier, because Marco's face was hidden by his half-shield, but sure enough, one eye is caked with concealer. The skin underneath is swollen and puffy.

A couple of the other guys come over to see what's going on, and one of them snickers. "Someone gave you a shiner, huh? Probably a good idea not to let Dante see that."

"Zees I try to tell you." Marco lifts his towel to wipe at his face, revealing a wicked-looking black eye beneath all that makeup. "I take advice from Abbot and Beck, and zees happens?"

Anders flips one thumb between himself and me. "Seriously? How is your black eye our fault?"

"You tell Marco zees passionate American taters want men to finish on zee face. So, I try it. I learn zees not true." He frowns and balls his hands into fists. "Also, I learn that American taters are very good at punching. They make *la guerra* not *amore*."

Latham lets out a snort-laugh before covering his mouth. The other guys elbow each other and snicker.

Their mirth only makes Marco's scowl deepen. "Zees not funny. What so funny? Now, I have black eye and am afraid. How do I date in this strange new country? Italian *donne*, they will yell until you go deaf, but taters do not yell at all. They go straight to zee fists, and they punch like Graziano."

Anders presses his lips together and tries to look sympathetic, but it's obvious that he's on the verge of cracking up. "Alright, new plan. We're going to teach Casanova here about a little concept known as *consent*." He walks over and claps Marco on the back. "I'll take the lead on that one. As for you, Noah? It's time to get in touch with your emotions. You've been going to group therapy for years. Put it to use. You're in love with the little tater tot and once you love someone—that means forever. Go fix this shit and make a family."

Cash glares at Marco's black eye and scowls. "Hit the showers."

Fixing anything with Molly is easier said than done, but he

does make one particularly good point. I have been in group therapy forever. Anders has no idea what I've gone through, which makes his on-the-fly assessment of my relationship troubles a little hard to take seriously. Like all he's done for his whole life is fuck loose women and collect a million-dollar paycheck playing the game he loves.

What the hell does he know about love and loss?

I do, however, know a fair number of people who've found themselves wrestling with the same grief that I've experienced. Maybe tomorrow night, I can ask for some advice from a group of people who care about me and truly understand because they've walked a mile in my shoes.

CHAPTER TWENTY-TWO

Molly

When Tuesday's story hour rolls around, I'm surprised to find Francine and Vivian in attendance. I thought Noah might have told them not to come here ever again, although now that I stop and think about it, I have a hard time imagining Fran letting anyone tell her what she can and can't do.

Vivian waves as she runs by, blowing me a kiss.

Francine stops just long enough to pat my hand. "Do you mind if we talk a little afterward?"

There's no reason to let my argument with Noah spill over into my other relationships, so I agree. I'm glad that she doesn't want to talk now, because I'm already psyching myself up to do something I've never done before.

I'm going to read my own book in my store for the first time. I've given this a lot of measured thought and keep arriving at the same conclusion. The only way out is straight through.

It's time.

Two dozen or so kids are nestled in beanbags when I step into the room, and they smile up at me in greeting. I know the regulars by name, but there are a few new people in the group too. Most of the time, I stick to happy books, ones with messages about things like embracing other people's differences, loving yourself, or caring for the environment. Today, I'm going to mix it up.

Today, I'm going to read the book I wrote after losing Uncle Arthur.

"Hello, everyone. Thank you for coming to story time." I take my usual seat at the front of the room. "How are you today?"

A chorus of '*good*'s greet me, although as always there are a few outliers, including a little boy who shouts, "Hungry!" Everyone laughs.

One girl's hand goes up, and I nod to her. "How can I help you, sweetie?"

"Why aren't you wearing your princess dress?" she asks. "I love your crown too."

"Good question." I fold my hands in front of me the way I would when discussing the theme of any story time, even though my heart's beating faster today. I can't remember the last time I got nervous before reading aloud. It's been years. This is usually one of the highlights of my week. "Today, I want to talk about something very important that involves big feelings. Do any of you know someone who's gone to heaven?"

About two-thirds of the kids' hands go up.

My heart breaks a little. "I'm going to read a book, and when I do, I want you to think about that person. We'll talk a little bit afterward, okay? And if any of you have stories you'd like to share, we can do that too."

A few of the parents look nervous, but I offer what I hope is a reassuring smile and reach for the copy of my book.

"*Where Did You Go?*" I read. "By M. A. Campbell."

"That's you!" Vivian exclaims.

I join the chorus of laughter that echoes through the room. "That's right. I wrote this book, because someone who I loved very much got very sick and went to heaven." I'm always afraid that I'm going to say the wrong thing when it comes to this subject, but I have the same concern with adults. Grief is a fickle emotion. Strong. Wild. Extreme. Just look how Noah reacted in the graveyard on Sunday.

I shake off the memory and turn to the first page that shows a little girl who looks a lot like me standing on a cliff hand-in-hand with a man whose face is hidden from view. I love how the artist was able to capture the feelings I wanted this book to convey, and how he used so many brilliant colors. It's a book about death that manages not to feel sad, and I hope like hell that it isn't as oversweet as some of the other books I've come across. It's hard to tell for sure, since I might be a *teeny* bit biased. After all, this book was wrung straight through my grief from the depths of my soul.

"After her uncle left, the little girl was full of sad feelings. 'Where did you go?' she asked. 'Why couldn't you stay here with me?'"

A few of the children sniffle, but to my surprise, Vivian isn't one of them. She watches me with interest as I turn the page.

Everyone believes different things about death, I suppose. Some people follow the teachings of their faith. Others turn to the world of the occult for answers, consulting Ouija boards and EMPs. Neither of those things helped me come to terms with my grief, and my resulting fear of not only *my* mortality, but the things that can happen in an instant to change—or end—the lives of my loved ones. Humanity has grappled with this concern for as long as we've been self-aware and able to fear it. Since every philosopher in history can't untangle the mess, there's no way I could condense those concerns into the five-to-seven hundred words that most picture books amount to. I didn't try. Instead, I chose to focus only on the concept of accepting grief as a natural part of loss, and explaining to children that those feelings are healthy, and that they should be acknowledged and processed rather than ignored.

Most of all that feelings—no matter what they are or how scary—are all okay.

When I turn the last page and close the cover, a few of the parents sniffle and wipe their eyes. One of the little girls cries into her palms. A few of the kids shift away from her, but Vivian gets up from her beanbag and goes to the girl's side, wrapping an arm around her and patting her back.

"M-my Nana died in July," the little girl says. "She was s-s-sick and she didn't get b-b-better."

"How does that make you feel?" I ask.

The girl's lip wobbles. "I miss her, b-but I didn't want her to hurt anymore. No one hurts in heaven. Is that okay?"

"Of course it is, honey." I point to the book. "You can miss someone a lot, even if you understand why they had to go. There's nothing wrong with that, and there's no *right* way to feel. Would you like to share something really *good* you remember about your Nana?"

The girl wipes her eyes on her sleeve. "Um... her name was Ivy. Like the plant. She smelled like flowers, and she always put food out for the birds in the winter. She had a dog with three legs named Cody who was really old, and she said that we should all be nice to Cody even though he was kinda ugly and had one crazy eye." By the end of this pronouncement, she's smiling again, even though her sniffles haven't quite subsided. "She made the best banana bread. The whole house would smell like it."

"Nana Ivy sounds lovely." I slide off my chair and fold my legs under me so that I can be at eye-level with all the kids. "Would anyone else like to share a memory of someone who's gone to heaven?"

A dozen hands shoot up, and I take turns pointing out the children.

"I had a goldfish named Blinky," one boy says. "We found him upside-down in the tank one morning. Dad said that he floated to the top to get closer to Fish Heaven."

I have to fight to keep my expression serious. "Is there anything else you'd like to say about Blinky?"

The boy shrugs. "He didn't have three eyes like the fish in the *Simpsons,* but he was a good fish. My brother won him at a carnival for me when I was three. Dad says he lived a long time for a fish."

Another boy talks about his old family dog who saved him from drowning in a swimming pool when he was younger. Two sisters talk about their guinea pig who escaped its cage and turned up months later in the basement. Most of the stories are about their animals, although one little boy does mention the passing of his beloved cactus that died from overwatering. Only three other kids mention family members. It always amazes me how matter-of-fact kids can be about this stuff. They aren't emotionless, but I wonder if 'forever' means the same thing to a five-year-old that it does to someone in their thirties.

I brought in a few other books, but the kids are so eager to talk about their own experiences that in the end we only have time for one more.

As we're packing up, a dad comes over to me. "Thanks for talking to my daughter about her grandmother. My wife has been having a really hard time, and I haven't been sure how to address it with Clara."

"Grief is really hard for us to acknowledge," I say. "Even for adults, it's a lot to process."

He points to the little pile of books beside my chair. "Are those ones you'd recommend?"

I nod. "Sure. Do you want to take a picture of the titles?"

"Or I could just buy them, if that's okay?"

"Of course." I pass him the stack, and when his daughter comes over, she waves to me before they head out to the front desk.

Francine and Vivian are the last two people in the room, and I make my way to Vivian's beanbag.

"It was kind of you to be there for that older girl," I say, settling down beside her. "When people are sad, it means a lot to find comfort."

Viv shrugs. "She was sad. She loved her Nana. Molly, why didn't you tell me that you wrote my favorite book! I was sad about my mommy, but whenever Unkie Noah read your book to me, I got less sad."

"Why didn't you tell *me?*" I tease. For an instant, I feel bad about the ways in which our lives intersect. I'm tempted to ask Vivian if she's angry at the man who killed her parents, but that's too much to put on her. Noah's taken his grief and anger out on me, and to ask a child for absolution for something that I know is bullshit anyway wouldn't help. Instead, I say, "The other day, you told me that you don't remember your parents. Is that why you didn't speak up during story time?"

Fran, sitting a few feet away in one of the chairs we put out for the parents, makes a soft noise in the back of her throat. I turn to make sure that I haven't put my foot in my mouth, but she doesn't look upset.

"Unkie misses them," Viv explains. "But he doesn't talk about them. I only know he's sad because of his pouty face."

I run my fingers along Vivian's curls. "Do you think you could ask him to tell you something about them? A good memory?"

The little girl nods. "Yes! I'd like that."

Out in the main part of the store, Mona is talking to the father who asked for more book recommendations. It looks like she's convinced him to add a copy of *Will My Cat Eat My Eyeballs?* to the stack. Even as I watch, she points to a shelf, and he goes to retrieve yet another title. I owe that girl a raise.

No matter what persona she likes to project, her heart is in the right place. She's a good friend at a time when I really need one.

"Molly?" Viv asks. "What happens if someone you love goes away, but not forever? Like with you and Unkie Noah? You said *we're* still friends, but what about you and him?"

This is exactly the type of entanglement Noah wanted to avoid in the first place. To be fair to him, as well as to Vivian, I have to tread lightly here.

"Sometimes people say things they don't mean," I tell her. "Noah said some angry things to me, but he was really angry at someone else."

Viv wrinkles her nose. "Why would he do that?"

I pause and inhale. "Because he couldn't tell the person he was angry at. Have you ever done something like that?"

She bites her lip and clasps her hands together, looking the picture of guilt. "One time I missed my nap and got mad at Biscuit. I yelled at her and told her that she was a bad dog, even though she isn't." Viv's eyes well up with tears. "She's the best dog, and I was mean to her."

"And when you felt better, what did you do?"

"I gave her a big hug and told her that I was sorry. And I gave her *two* treats at bedtime, so that she would know how much I love her." Viv's lip wobbles. "But that doesn't make it better. I never should have yelled at Biscuit."

"I'm sure Biscuit forgave you," I say. "If you learn from your mistakes and treat the people that you love better next time, you can move on with a clear heart." I stop, realizing that I've backed myself into a corner. "If Noah and I decide to talk about our feelings, that will be between us, okay? And like I said, no matter what, you're always welcome here. If I never saw you again, I would have a pouty face."

Fran gets up from her chair. "Are you ready to go, honey?" she asks.

Vivian nods. "Thank you for being my friend, Molly! We'll always be friends. Just like you said."

"Do you still want to talk?" I ask Fran.

"I don't think that's necessary," Fran tells me. "You're a wonderful woman, Molly. I wish that *other people* would see that more clearly and realize what they've lost by being pigheaded even when those *other people* are normally sane."

"Maybe *other people* should decide for themselves what they want, rather than feeling pressured to do anything?" I suggest.

Fran looks at me with the melancholiest expression. I almost burst into tears again on the spot. "Alright, if you say so, dear. Have a lovely day. We'll see you again soon."

I wave them off and finish cleaning up, then join Mona at the counter. That conversation with Vivian has got me thinking. A little spark has been lit at the back of my brain, a pilot light that I thought had long since burned out.

"Do you mind if I take an early lunch?" I ask Mona.

"Suit yourself." Mona shoos me off toward the back. "I'm on *fire* today."

She's not the only one. I bypass the fridge in my office and head straight for my computer, open a new document, and start typing.

What Do You Remember?
by Molly Campbell

The words pour out of me. There are too many of them all at once, and I know for a fact that I'm going to have to do a fair bit of trimming later on, but rather than worry about that, I just say what's on my mind. My last book was about grief and mourning, and I've been trying to figure out how to repeat that success.

That's not what I need, though—not as a writer, and not as a person. I need to figure out how to move on while still honoring the memory of a man I hold dear. Uncle Arthur would never have hurt another person intentionally, and I'm sure he'd be devastated to know that his final act resulted in the deaths of two strangers. Spouses. Parents. It would have broken his heart. My uncle was the kind of man who fed stray cats, who would pull off the side of the road to move tarantulas and geckos out of traffic, who made sure that everyone felt safe and welcome in this store regardless of how they were treated outside of its walls. Who made sure there were books in this store for people of every race, creed, sexual orientation, financial status, and religion.

When I'm done, I sit back and stare at what I've written. It's going to need work, for sure, but at least I've got *something*.

I fire off a quick email to my agent with the subject line, *I think I'm on to something great...*

If it took Noah's outburst to shake this loose, so be it. If he comes around, I'll hear him out, just like I told Vivian.

If he doesn't, at least I know that I have it in me to grow from our relationship and move on better for having known him. What do I remember about Noah Abbot? Only the good things.

CHAPTER TWENTY-THREE

Noah

When I get home from practice on Tuesday, Vivian is sitting on the couch, petting Biscuit and talking in a low voice. Biscuit is as happy as I've ever seen her; she's rolled to one side to let Vivian pat her belly.

"Hey." I drop my bag by the door. "What's going on here?"

"I was telling Biscuit that she's a good girl. Sometimes I forget." Vivian looks up at me, and Biscuit thumps her tail once against the cushions. "Will you come sit with us, Unkie?"

After bailing on our evening plans on Sunday, I owe Vivian an apology. I step around the side of the couch to find that a battered copy of Viv's favorite book, *Where Did You Go?*, is sitting on the empty cushion.

"Do you want me to read to you, kiddo?" I ask.

"Yes, please." Vivian pulls her knees up to her chest. "I have something very important to tell you, Unkie, so pay very close attention. Did you know that Molly wrote this book?"

"No way. Wait, *our* Molly?" The words are out before I remember that Molly's out of my life. I know this book by heart. I've read it to Viv a hundred times.

Viv nods. "Yup. *Our* Princess Molly."

I drop down beside her, examining the book. Sure enough, Molly's initials and surname are on the cover. How did I never put two and two together? My little tater tot wrote this masterpiece?

I open the book, skipping past the dedication, which I've

never paid much attention to before. I shiver when I see what she's put there.

For Uncle Arthur, a mentor, an icon, a friend, who I dearly miss.

That's crazy. The book that I used to help Vivian understand her parents' death was written about the man who killed them? How can that be possible? My insides twist into a knot of confusion even as my mind races. It's like I've stepped into some alternate universe where things that don't make sense seem like fate.

Doing my best to keep my emotions in check, I start reading. Viv nestles against my side to look at the pictures. I have to stop twice as I'm overcome with emotion. Yes, this book about a little girl's pain echoes how I feel about losing Natalie. Which means that Molly loved her uncle every bit as much as I loved my sister. Her uncle, who I said horrible things about only days ago. Who I blamed for accidental carnage all while slurring him with murderous intent.

I did that.

Me.

God save my soul, I'm a heartless asshole.

It's not lost on me that I deliberately created pain for a vibrant, breathing human being that I care about all over people who have passed away. Natalie, Steve, and Uncle Arthur no longer have the ability to feel. But I do. And Molly does too. Yet I still made the choice to put the dead before the living. How fucked up is that? Tears flood my eyes and emotion closes my throat as I struggle to read to the end. As if she knows, Viv rubs her tiny fingers along my forearm.

When I close the book, Viv looks up at me. "Unkie Noah? Will you tell me something nice about my parents? So that I can try to remember them? Molly asked me during story time today and I didn't know the right answer."

The hits just keep coming. I've told myself that I was the keeper of the flame when it came to memories of Nat and Steve, but I've been so lost in my own grief that I haven't been able to share any of those good memories with the person who needs them most.

"Yeah," I say, softening my palm against her curls. "Wait here a minute."

I hoist myself up and grab my gym bag before mounting the stairs to my room. After Natalie's and Steve's deaths, I had to go through all of the stuff that was in their house. Some things went into storage for when Viv's older, and I donated a bunch of the furniture and clothing to a local women's shelter—that seemed like what Steve and Natalie would have wanted. I only kept a few things, including a photo album Natalie put together before Viv was born. She wanted Viv to have something to look back on, but she assumed that she'd be the one revisiting these old memories with her daughter. I couldn't bring myself to box it up, but I never look at it, either. It's been sitting in a box under my bed gathering dust ever since I brought it home.

When I return, scrapbook in hand, Viv sits up straighter. "What's that?"

"Pictures of your parents," I say. "Your mom made this for you."

Viv places one hand reverently on the cover. "Did she like to make things?"

"Yeah. She was creative, like you. And your dad was handy. He was the one who fixed up your parents' old place after they bought it. There might be pictures in here."

With my heart jumping into my throat, I realize that Natalie was a genius. She set up the album as a timeline, organizing pictures by the year they were taken. Photos of us are mixed in with pictures of Steve, creating the sense that the two of them were living parallel lives that converged when they met in college.

When we reach the first picture of Steve as an adult, Viv laughs. "He doesn't look anything like you!"

"Why would your mom wanna marry someone who looked like her *brother?*" I ask. "Gross."

Vivian giggles. "I don't know. I have a daddy and I have an unkie, but I only remember you." She places one finger on a picture of Steve. "But he's skinny. I bet he smelled nice." She sticks out her tongue at me. "Not like *you,* Unkie. You smell like hockey!"

I tickle her until she squeals, and we go back to looking through photos of the wedding, and pictures of Natalie getting progressively bigger as her due date approached.

"That's me," Viv says, pointing to Nat's belly. On the next page, Natalie holds a pink, wrinkled baby, and Viv scowls. "Ooh, and that's me, too. But I look like a worm! I'm much prettier now. I'm a pretty princess."

"You were an adorable worm." I kiss the top of her head. "And you're a beautiful princess."

"Are there more?" Viv asks.

When I flip the page, however, it's blank. There are about ten pages left, and the blank white surface stares accusingly up at me.

"That's it," I say. "I guess she planned to put more pictures in there, but..." I choke on the words.

"We should finish it," Viv says.

I startle out of my funk. "What?"

"We should finish it for Mommy. You have pictures on your phone. Can we put them in here?"

I run my palm over the blank page. "Yeah, I think we could

223

manage that."

"Hooray!" Viv hops up from the couch and goes tearing through the living room. "*Nanny Frannie! We're gonna finish the book just like Mommy!*"

I sit there next to my snoozing dog, drumming my fingers against the page. When Natalie died, it felt like everything stopped. There were so many endings.

But Viv's right. There are still pages left and leaving them blank won't make anything better.

When did my kid get so smart?

And when did I start thinking of her as *my* kid and not my niece? But I do. Molly's book sits on the end table beside me, a silent reminder of the ways I've screwed up. Would she be willing to look inside her big heart to find a sliver of forgiveness? Would she even want to try?

Do I even deserve the effort?

If I were her, I probably wouldn't. What the fuck kind of partner does she think I would be to her? But we've both been through tragedy, so if anyone could understand how a normally sane man could lose his shit in the most inappropriate way, it would be her.

Everyone makes mistakes. Even me.

Even her.

Even Uncle Arthur.

After a moment's consideration and a sigh I feel from my hair to my toes, I stack it on top of the photo album and set both by the door so that I remember to take them to therapy tonight.

And tomorrow I'll ask Viv if she wants to call me Daddy all the time.

* * *

"Noah, did you get a chance to try my cookie dough billionaire bars?" Susan asks.

I lick my fingers. "I just had my second one. They're great."

"I made extra for you to take home," she tells me. "A big, strong professional athlete like you needs sustenance."

"What about the Christmas-themed macarons?" Doreen asks. "I know it's early, but I'm practicing for the school's bake sale this year, and I want them to be perfect."

I lift one to my lips and take a bite. Doreen holds her breath as she waits for my verdict.

"Ginger and apple?" I guess. "Ooh, that's zingy. Excellent flavor combo, Doreen."

"I've been having trouble getting the ginger through in the cookie," she explains. "They're so finicky."

I finish the other half. "Well, whatever you did with these is working. Let me know when the bake sale is, and I'll bring my daughter by."

All the other women gasp and immediately ask Doreen for the details.

"I'd love to meet Vivian," Jana gushes, clapping her hands together. "You talk about her so much, well, I feel like I already know her."

When the meeting finally starts, everyone is keyed up. I'm not sure what's got them all so on-edge, but when it's time to start talking, everyone turns to me.

"So." Jana steeples her fingers. "Noah. Last time we met, you were thinking about taking your relationship a step further. How did that go?"

"Well, uh…" I scratch my chin. "We broke up?"

"Oh, no!" Doreen cries. "What happened?"

I reach under my chair to retrieve the books. "So, here's the thing…" I pause, not sure how to proceed. Looking at each of these amazing women in turn, I clear my throat and just jump in. "Molly's uncle killed my sister." The more times I say the words aloud, the more absurd it sounds. "Not on purpose, but when I found out, I didn't take it so well."

Everyone stares at me, so I offer a wry grin. "Hear me out. I thought I was ready to let go but finding out the connection between my sister, Nat, and Molly's Uncle Arthur, made me feel so betrayed by the hand of fate that I couldn't be with her anymore. I couldn't even look at her. I was at the cemetery when I just happened upon her and the dates on Uncle Arthur's headstone and put two and two together." I stop and pause again. How do I tell these women what I did without breaking down again? "I freaked out. Then, today, I learned that she's the one who wrote this book. It's Viv's favorite." I hold up my copy of Molly's picture book.

"Ooh, that's a good one," says Tracy. "It helped my grandson come to terms with his brother's passing."

"Yeah," I agree. "It's a good one. But now I'm stuck. How am I supposed to get past this? The *knowing*?"

"Do you *want* to get past it?" Yolanda asks.

"Yeah." I sit back, looking at the two books I'm holding. One chronicles Molly's pain, and the other is a harsh reminder of all that I've lost. "But how am I supposed to do that? I thought I was better, and then I said some terrible shit to someone I care about. I know it's not fair, but how on earth can I fix that? How can she ever trust me again to be the man she deserves?"

We sit there in silence for a moment. Then one of the women, Amita, clears her throat. She doesn't talk much during these meetings, but I know that she lost her twenty-two-year-old daughter to throat cancer a few years back. She's been coming here almost as long as I have.

"When I lost my daughter, I was so angry," she says. Her

226

voice is soft, and her Indian accent is so thick that I have to listen carefully to catch every word. "I blamed everyone. The cancer, for making her sick. God, for letting it happen. The doctors, for letting her die. My husband, for not knowing the right thing to say. Myself, for... well, for everything." She sighs, and when she speaks again, her voice is a little louder. Then with soft eyes, she places her hand over her heart. "I was angry at the whole world, because something like that should not be allowed to happen. You all know this."

We nod, almost in unison. Doreen covers her mouth with one hand and stares at Amita with glassy, haunted eyes.

"Mira was a smart girl. A good girl. She wanted to help people who could not help themselves. In the end, I was the helpless one. Right to the end, she comforted me. *Me,* even though she was the one dying!" Amita sucks in a breath. "She was the one getting her life stolen from her right before my very eyes. Then she was gone, and I could not understand why."

"Yeah," I murmur. "The not being able to attach meaning to a travesty is the worst part."

"Noah, listen to me." Amita points a finger in my direction. "One day, I realized that my anger consumed me. I was crying, and I said to myself, *I am mad at everyone. I am even mad at Mira for leaving me!*" She opens her hands wide. "Mad at my lovely daughter, because she died before me. That is not right. I said to myself, *That's it, Amita, the anger stops here. You will find another way to mourn.* Mira would not have wanted me to be angry, and I did not want to feel anger every time I thought of her. She wanted people to be happy, so I looked for ways to make other people happy. Now, I feed cats at the shelter. My husband and I helped our neighbors fix their house after a flood. We do the things that Mira would have done if she were alive, because that way her energy lives on. The good in her heart lives on. Your sister, was she an angry person? Would *she* be angry at this woman, for loving someone who also died just as tragically as she did?"

I struggle to speak, but just end up shaking my head. I can't get the words out. No, Natalie wasn't an angry person. She'd have loved Molly. If she'd seen me crying the other night, she would have sat with me, stroking my hair and my back until I stopped. Then she'd have kicked my ass for all the angry, hateful things I said in the heat of the moment.

The things I can't take back.

"Then let go." Amita holds up two fists and slowly opens them, palms up. "Stop holding onto an emotion that no longer serves you. I strongly believe that we are here to love and be loved. Everything else is meaningless. Losing my beautiful daughter helped me to see."

Jana clears her throat. "I agree. And I probably shouldn't say this, but I went to her shop the other day.

"Me, too," Susan admits.

"Wait, did we *all* go?" Doreen asks.

Everyone, including Amita, nods.

"And you all thought that she was freaking *amazing,* right?" Jana asks.

"She seems pretty perfect," Doreen admits. "And I bet she's great with your little girl, right?"

"Yeah." I sigh. "Viv wants Molly to be her new mommy."

Susan places a hand over her heart. "Oh my God, that's so sweet. We can tell you're in love with her, too. You need to fix this, Noah. After all this time, we know you very well. You and Molly are meant to be together. Don't let anger over a tragic accident steal your joy for even one more second. Natalie and Steve wouldn't want that. They'd want you to be happy."

"And even if she doesn't forgive you, it is time to let go of your resentment," Amita adds. "It will help her let go of hers. Even if you decide to go your separate ways, please try to do so without the baggage of unresolved anger and blame."

"You *are* in love with her, aren't you?" Doreen asks.

I slide the books back under my chair. "Yup. That's why I call her my little tater tot."

The women make a collective noise of envy mixed with adoration.

"So cute." Yolanda puts one hand to her chest and pouts. "I wanna be someone's tater tot."

We move on to Tracy, whose ex-husband reached out to her when he heard about her father's death, and the group unleashes their combined life-changing wisdom on her. I chime in when I can, but I'm still processing Amita's wise words.

With the squeeze on my heart starting to ease, I realize it's time to let go.

Now I just have to figure out how to fix things with Molly.

CHAPTER TWENTY-FOUR

Molly

Our second Blind Date with a Book event takes place the Friday after Noah and I imploded from friends to lovers to mortal enemies in what seems to be more like the blink of an eye than a few weeks. I thought I'd be leaving this event for dinner and a 'sleepover,' but instead, I arrive at work knowing full well that I'll be going home alone to indulge in Netflix, Ben & Jerry's, and a truckload of regret mired down in loneliness.

It's hard not to be mad at the hand of fate. Because despite what Noah thinks, no one is to blame in this tragic situation.

At least the event is going to be fun. Not as fun as going home with a man I adore and planning our future together, but I place my focus on making my customers as happy as I can. No use ruining their night with my negative emotions. On the bright side, when we talk about the smutty chaos that is this book, I'll have a better frame of reference for how conflicted Beauty feels about her whole fucked-up relationship with the Prince.

Relatable.

At ten o'clock, the store phone trills from the counter. Only a few customers mill around, browsing the shelves. I lift the phone to my ear and try to make my voice as bright and chipper as it usually is.

"Hello, you've reached The Last Chapter, how can I—"

"*Molly!*" Angela screeches like a wild animal. With my ears ringing, I hold the receiver away from my ear. "This is great!

Just great, I tell you! I knew you had it in you."

"I take it that you got a chance to look over the manuscript?" I ask.

"I did. It's brilliant. The fact that you're tackling the same subject from a different angle is perfect. It's emotional without being too raw. I already have a new publisher in mind."

I white knuckle the receiver. "Does this mean I'm no longer in trouble?"

A pause. "Don't get ahead of yourself. I'm going to start shaking the tree in hopes of getting the next book rolling in a timelier fashion than last time." At least Angela seems more amused than annoyed now. "Do you mind if I ask what happened? Something's changed, but I can't tell what."

I look under the counter to where Noah's special-order hardback waits for pickup. I wonder how long it will sit there gathering dust before he picks it up. Maybe he'll ask Mona to courier it over to his house. "I guess I just realized that it was time I learned how to let go."

"Whatever you did, keep it up, girlfriend. The sky's the limit."

I smile bitterly to myself. Looks like Mona was right. She always told me that if I just got laid, I would get my mojo back. This isn't what she had in mind, but I suppose she gets points for accuracy and for caring enough to suggest it in the first place.

"I'm sorry, Angela, I've got to go. The store's open right now. Talk soon about the details, okay?"

"One more quick question, then. You weren't willing to go on tour for the last book, which I completely understand, all things considered. I'm sure it would help sales, though." Angela's voice lifts into a high, coaxing tone. "Is there any chance I can convince you to go on tour this time? Even a few signings would make a huge difference. Especially with a children's book. The kids love story time with the author."

I straighten up and take a deep breath. I had forgotten about that discussion. When the first book came out, I was still grieving, and I was just figuring out how to balance running the store along with everything else. Now, it's not outside the realm of possibility. Mona wouldn't be able to run the store by herself, but if I hired another staff member to help out, I would trust her to keep things going while I took some short publicity trips.

The Last Chapter would probably be fine. That's not the part I'm worried about.

I'm still holding out hope that Noah will come to his senses. The longer he waits, however, the less likely I am to hear him out. I had hoped he would be here sooner, but I suppose he's mired down in a fresh river of agony that opened up after that day in the cemetery. After all, he's had years to build up feelings of resentment and anger. He's the kind of guy who felt blindsided by pain he didn't deserve and now he doesn't trust his heart as readily as he should.

Maybe I'm a fool. Maybe there's no coming back from it. Maybe it really is over.

"I'm open to discussing it," I say at last. "It would depend on the logistics."

"Oh, honey, you know these things take time." I'm positive that Angela is waving one hand to brush these concerns aside. "Leave it all to me. I'm sure the publisher will ask, and as long as you're flexible, that will be enough for now. Take care, Molly. I'll be in touch soon."

After she hangs up, I open my texts. It's been almost a week since Noah and I communicated; his last text messages are from the morning of the barbecue. His address is followed by a smiley face and a heart and the words, *I can't wait to see you.*

I'm on my way, I texted back, followed by a kissy face and a pair of sunglasses.

And that's it. The conversation stopped. It was the last day before the hope of a loving future died. When I think of that beautiful day by the pool, I want to forgive him for what he said to me. If he loved his sister even half as much as he loves Vivian, how can I blame him for the intensity of his reaction?

Because he's a grown-ass man, I remind myself. *And he should be able to take a step back, validate my feelings, and realize that he screwed up.*

He should know that he needs to apologize and make amends, even if he can't put his emotions aside enough for us to be together.

I open his contact and change his name, from the eggplant emoji to 'Noah.' He was more to me than a hookup, and he's hurt me more than a friend-with-benefits ever could.

I don't block his number. I leave that line of connection open. If he wants to reach out, he knows where to find me, but I'm leaving the ball in his court.

* * *

Mona rolls in about half an hour before the book club convenes. She comes bearing cases of wine and charcuterie platters picked up from the caterer's.

"Hey, girl!" she says cheerfully. "How's it going? Did I miss anything?"

"I got a call from my agent," I say.

Mona grimaces as she sets an armload of sliced meats on the folding table I've just set up. "No shit? She didn't give you an ultimatum, did she?"

"No." I grin. "She called to tell me that she likes the new manuscript."

"The *what?*" Molly screeches. "New as of when?"

A rare smile tugs at the corners of my mouth. Well, rare since the anniversary of Uncle Arthur's death. "I sent it to her earlier this week."

Mona grabs me by the shoulders and shakes me. "This is huge! You've had writer's block for a million years! *I'm so proud of you!*"

"Alright, alright." I laugh as I wriggle out of her grip. "Settle down. I had to work some of my feelings out, and writing a book seemed more productive than hexing my ex." Calling Noah 'my ex' hurts, but I'm told that the truth often does.

"Yeah, well." Mona smooths her hair down. "To each her own. Don't knock it 'til you try it."

I check the clock. "Ooh, we need to get going. We need to finish setting up before—"

"Hey." Mona points through the side room window toward the front door of the shop. "Intruder alert."

I follow her piercing gaze with my own, and my heart lodges in my throat. Noah and Francine have just stepped inside, but there's no sign of Vivian. Thank goodness, since tonight is adults only. The instant I recognize Noah, my whole body goes haywire. I want to run away, but I also want to launch myself into his arms, and I *also* want to grab him by the shoulders and shake some sense into him the way Mona just shook me— although that last one sounds implausible, given the discrepancies in our height.

"Help," I squeak.

Mona pats my shoulder. "Leave this to me," she says, before marching off toward the pair of them like she's going to unsheathe her sword. I can't hear the actual words, but Noah nods amiably and gestures to the door. The two of them disappear, while Francine comes to find me.

"Whatever you've got in mind, now's not a great time," I say. "We're setting up for the Blind Date with a Book."

"I know, dear." Francine holds up her copy of *The Claiming of Sleeping Beauty*. "That's why we're here. To help Mona set up."

"O-oh." I gulp. "Fran, if you asked Noah to come in the hopes of mending fences... well, remember what I said at story time? Let's just say I don't think it's a good idea to try to manipulate him."

"I'm only here for the book club." Fran sets her purse in the corner. "If Noah's here for something else, he certainly hasn't told me. Now, how would you like the food and beverage tables set up?"

I'm not sure what's happening, but far be it from me to turn down free labor. Francine and I set to work, although inside I'm dying to know what on Earth is really going on here.

CHAPTER TWENTY-FIVE

Noah

Mona's hatchback is parked by the curb with its blinkers flashing. The second we're outside, she practically pounces on me, eyes blazing.

"You hurt my friend," she snaps. "What did I tell you about that? You're lucky I don't kick your ball sack up into your throat. If anyone doesn't deserve this men behaving badly bullshit, it's Molly."

I hold my hands up between us, thinking this bristling woman might be scarier than an opposing team's top goal scorer on a breakaway. "Listen, I'm here to make things right."

As she glares at me, it's like I'm seeing myself through her eyes—a man who's messed up big time. Damn, she's right. I hurt Molly, and realizing it feels like taking a puck to the chest without padding.

"Then why the hell are you out here and not in there groveling?" Mona demands, pointing one finger accusingly toward the bookstore. "And did I say groveling? I'm not going to be satisfied until your knees are so bruised you can't even strap on your goalie pads without an entire tube of Bengay."

I run my hand through my hair. I've been sleeping like shit all week, and between that and everything else that's been going on, I'm exhausted. Mona's well within her rights to despise me, though. I made my bed. Time to lie in it. She's shooting slapshots of truth, and I can't dodge them. I've been a goalie in life, blocking out emotions, keeping everyone at a distance. But with Molly, I want to be on the offensive, fighting for something good. For someone good.

And if bruised knees are what she wants, she'll get them. "You've spent the last week with Molly. For all I know, she told you exactly what I said. Do you really think that waltzing in the door to tell her I'm sorry is going to cut it?"

Mona crosses her arms and blows a wisp of hair out of her eyes. "Knowing Molly? Probably. She's sweet as Tupelo honey. She's a 'let's let bygones be bygones' kind of girl. I, on the other hand, am not."

My little tater tot does have a soft heart. She could easily forgive me, but do I deserve it? Have I truly learned anything if she just lets me off the hook? She doesn't have to, and I know it. But God, how I hope she'll give me a second chance to be a better man.

"I'm here to make it right," I explain. "And if I get it wrong again, you can have a lock of my hair for... I dunno, a hex bag or whatever. But I'll grovel until my knees give out if it will give us a fresh start. Even you have to admit that three dead family members adds up to a whole lot of extenuating circumstances outside of the typical male bullshit. Deal?"

Mona stares at me with narrowed eyes for a long moment. Then she extends her hand. "You've got a bargain, but I'm warning you, this is your last try at the golden ring of love. When you make a bargain with the Court of Night, you must be prepared to pay the price."

I'm not entirely sure what she's talking about, but we shake on it before we get to work unloading the rest of the car. As I make a pact with Mona, I know I'm not just making it with Molly's friend, I'm making it with myself. To be better. To do better. For Molly.

My little tater tot doesn't talk to me when I return to the

shop, and I don't approach her. Mona's right, I should lead with an apology, but words are cheap. Besides, it's not like they make Hallmark cards that say *I'm sorry that I called your loved one a murderer even though he definitely isn't.*

Ultimately, our falling out had very little to do with Natalie and Arthur, and a hell of a lot more to do with my own hang-ups and insecurities. Being so hyper-focused on Viv, I guess I never really dealt with how Nat and Steve's death upended my own life and even affected my career. I have my own grief to deal with because things definitely don't look the same as they did three years ago. And then there's the guilt about even feeling sorry for myself at all.

Molly and I orbit each other, but we go out of our way not to cross paths. Or rather, *she* does, and I resist the urge to follow her. I've missed her so damn much. I didn't realize *how* much until I saw her again, and I'm left heartsore and miserable. If she doesn't forgive me, I'll be a wreck, and I'll have no one to blame but myself.

By the time the other members of the Blind Date with a Book start trickling in, everything is in place. Fran and I take seats opposite the door, giving people plenty of space to collect their wine and cheese as they arrive.

"I assume that you *will* be talking to Molly eventually?" Fran asks. "Not just tiptoeing around her?"

I level a flat stare at her. "In the last three years, how often have I left Viv with a babysitter who wasn't you?"

"She's perfectly fine with Carly." Fran clicks her tongue. "She's our neighbor, for heaven's sake."

Meeting Fran's gaze, a sense of regret fills me. "Fran, you're almost like a second mother to me, and knowing I've disappointed you hurts almost as much as hurting Molly did. I'm here to make things right, to prove that I'm committed to her. This book," I lift it slightly, "isn't just about tonight. It's a symbol of my commitment to Molly and to the people who care about her. So trust me, I'm taking this as seriously as I've taken anything in my life."

Fran studies me for a moment, her eyes softening. "Well, actions speak louder than words, Noah. I hope for Molly's sake—and yours—that you mean every word you've just said. Because she deserves better. She deserves everything." She gives me a slight nod, as if granting me the smallest window of opportunity to redeem myself.

The group of people assembled to discuss this book are a little reminiscent of group therapy, which puts me oddly at ease. As the attendees—also mostly women—collect their cups of rosé and paper plates full of nibbles, I let my gaze wander over the store. It's a delightful mix of old and new, and every time I've walked through the door, it's felt like a safe haven. Molly did this. My Molly. She created this place through blood, sweat, and a river of tears.

This store is part of her. I wish I was too.

Maybe I can be again. Glancing up at the ceiling, I send up a quick prayer to Nat and Steve, begging them to help me. A warmth fills my heart and spreads out to my limbs. I'm not sure if they heard me, but it feels like they did.

Arthur made these shelves by hand. He probably climbed the rolling ladder hundreds of times, the same rolling ladder that Molly fell from the first time she tumbled into my arms. He arranged books on the same shelves where Viv has picked out her next bedtime story. He left Molly this amazing legacy.

"Sorry, Arthur," I murmur. "I think I misjudged you." The things that he took from me in ignorance can't be measured against what he created with intention, but if this is what he chose for himself, I have a feeling that he and Natalie would have gotten along.

What a fucking tragedy.

One without fault.

"Did you say something, dear?" Fran pats my knee.

"Just talking to myself." I scratch my facial scruff and glance toward Molly just in time to catch her staring at me. I offer her a small smile, which she returns.

So all is not necessarily lost. That slight upturn of lips and softening of expression gives me a sliver of hope I probably don't deserve.

When the crowd has mostly settled, Molly claps twice. "Good evening, everyone! We're here to discuss last month's book, *The Claiming of Sleeping Beauty.* I'm eager to know your impressions! Does anyone have thoughts they'd like to share?"

I raise my hand, and Molly blinks twice. "N-Noah? You read it? The whole thing?"

"I sure did, and I have some thoughts." I hold up my copy and look around the room. "I don't know about the rest of you, but I wouldn't call this a romance. Erotic, yes. Romantic, no."

"Even the ending?" someone asks, waving a Ritz cracker in the air.

I pause to blink a few times. It's important I get these words to come out right. "Yeah. I mean, the book literally ends up with the heroine having penetrative sex with someone on the floor of a wagon full of sex slaves." I fan through the pages. "Sure, she had some agency before the book ended, but all of her relationships center around sex. That's not romantic. That's not *love.* Sex can be part of love, but that can't be where it begins and ends. Love is bigger than that. Love is—" I catch Molly's eye again and take a deep breath. "Love means admitting when you make mistakes. Love takes root in conversations that surprise you. It transforms into sacrifices, concessions, and gestures that you know your lover will appreciate. It inhabits the biggest moments of your life, and the smallest ones, too. Love changes you. It challenges you. It expands your sense of self in ways you never expected." I tap the cover of the book. "Most of all, love is a mirror that helps you grow as a person. Become better within the circle of its warmth. I know what love feels like, and it's not this."

The women around me stare dreamily in my direction, lost in their memories and their fantasies. Molly wipes her palm across her eyes. Tears gently flow down her flushed cheeks, but she's smiling through them.

Only Mona seems immune to the notion of romantic love. She holds up her book. "You know what else isn't romantic? Getting fingered by your future mother-in-law at the medieval fantasy equivalent of Thanksgiving dinner."

Amid the swell of laughter, Molly swats her friend's arm. "Mona!"

"What?" Mona shrugs. "We all read the book. Can we please acknowledge how weird that part was?"

The conversation moves on to the salacious details of the book, with people debating the various merits and shortcomings of the novel, comparing it to the works of V. C. Andrews and Rocky Flintstone.

Fran lowers her voice so that only I will hear. "Good opening, Noah. But I hope that you still intend to offer Molly a proper apology?"

"Don't worry," I assure her. "Mona made it clear that I need to grovel as if my life depends on it. And it does. I intend to spend a long time making up for my faults and my actions that weren't born of love. And I'll atone for as long as she'll let me."

* * *

A few of the book club folks stay to help clean up while Mona and Molly start taking orders for next month's book, *Cloud Atlas,* which Fran promises me is not even remotely in the same genre. When the last customer finally leaves, Molly locks the door behind her with a happy sigh.

As I stare at the one woman who means everything to me, I realize this is my moment, my shot at redemption. And I'm as nervous as a rookie facing a penalty shot in overtime. I need to get this right. For her. For us.

"I have to hand it to you, Mona, this was one of your better ideas." She waves to her assistant. "Why don't you take out the trash and head out? Noah and I can finish up."

Fran clears her throat. "Yes, Mona, let me help. I'll go home and get Vivian settled in for the night. And if I end up making breakfast as well, think nothing of it."

While the two of them collect a trash bag each and head for the back door, Molly takes my hand and leads me back to the now-tidy side room. She retrieves two beanbags, drops them in the center of the room, and flops down into one.

"So," she says. "You finished the book. I thought you weren't going to."

"I hadn't planned on it, but it got me thinking." I join her on the other bag which, despite being uncomfortably close to the ground for a man with legs as long as mine, isn't as obnoxious as I'd assume it would be. I exhale as I snuggle in deep. "For one thing, the sex sounded really uncomfortable. The amount of consent in the book is... not great. But also, the idea that sex is the be-all, end-all of a relationship doesn't sit well with me."

"So you said." Molly brushes a golden curl back from her face. The dark smudges under her eyes tell a story of sleepless nights spent tossing and turning, probably while she thought about what an idiot I am. That makes two of us. "But you were prepared to be in a situationship with me."

"Molly, I think subconsciously, I knew I never wanted that with you. Something happened to me that night we did the tantric workshop thing. And that's why I had issues when we first started your lessons. Even though being propositioned by a hot woman for sex is every other man's fantasy, I guess I'm not cut out for that." I roll my head back and stare at the ceiling. "But what I'm really here to say is that I'm so, so sorry. Since I hurt you, I've been in agony. I said some dumb shit, and then I ran away from you. Even from myself. My buddy, Anders, thinks I'm trying to escape feelings I can't control. Some of the women at my grief group think I'm desperate for someone to blame for everything that I've been through. They're both right, but even more than that... I'm trying to work through all these big feelings—but I'm worried I'm failing. Failing you. Failing myself. That's why I didn't come by sooner. And I know that's not even close to being enough."

I force myself to raise my head and look at her. She's sitting with her knees pulled in toward her chest, arms wrapped around them, looking incredibly small. She's so breakable. So fragile. So dear to me.

She's fucking everything.

And she's strong, too. Underneath her sparkle-princess exterior, she's made of tougher stuff. She's been shaped by loss, but not broken by it.

I run my fingers through my hair, a nervous habit I can't seem to shake. "Molly, I've been an idiot. A coward. I ran from something great because I was scared. Scared of how deeply I feel for you. Scared of how much you mean to me. Scared of how you make me want to be a better man."

Molly crosses her arms over her chest, her eyes narrowing. "You think that's supposed to make me feel better? Knowing that you were scared? We're all scared, Noah, but we don't all make choices that hurt people we claim to care about. You're a *father* now. Running away is no longer an option for you."

I take a deep breath, exhaling slowly to try to calm my racing heart. "You're right. I've made mistakes, big ones. But I'm done running. Done hiding. You deserve a man who's all in, and I swear, from this moment on, that's me."

She sighs, running a hand through her hair. "You say that now, but how do I know you won't just run again when things get tough?"

Locking eyes with her, I feel my soul laid bare. "I can't give you a roadmap of the future, Molly. What I can give you is my commitment. I've never felt anything like this. It's all-consuming. And that's why I'm here groveling. I'm committed to being better, for you and for me. But it has to start with you forgiving me."

Molly bites her lip, contemplating. "Forgiving you is one thing. Trusting you again is another. How do you plan on earning that back?"

I clench my fists at my sides, fighting the urge to reach out to her. "By actions, not just words. By being there for you and Vivian. By talking to you, really talking, instead of running away. And by loving you, every damn day, even when it's hard."

Her eyes soften just a bit, giving me a glimmer of hope. "You do have a way with words, Noah Abbott. But actions speak louder. You have a lot to prove."

Feeling a sense of urgency, I lean in closer. "And I intend to prove it, Molly. Starting now. I love you. There, I said it. I'm not taking it back. And I'll spend every day proving it if you'll let me."

She hesitates, her gaze flicking to my lips and back to my eyes. "I want you to start showing me your vulnerability, Noah.

Showing up for a woman means more than just physically. I need to know you'll be a safe place for me to fall. But maybe, just maybe, we can start anew."

Hearing those words, I feel like I've just won the Stanley Cup and the lottery all at once.

"I love you, Molly," I say again. "And that scares the shit out of me. I can't change what I said to you, even though I don't really believe it now that I've had time to think. All I can say is that I'm sorry for what I said about your uncle. So very sorry. And I'm even more sorry for how I've hurt you. I was wrong about all of it. I've spent half this week with my head in the sand, and the other trying to figure out how to make up for being the world's greatest dickhead. I'm still not sure how to go about it, but I figure that apologizing is a start. So, once again, I'm sorry from the bottom of my broken heart. I'm learning how to be better, but it turns out that I'm not there yet. If you can find a way to forgive me, that might help me start to stitch myself back together."

Molly nods but doesn't speak.

"That's it," I tell her. "So, um. I'm sorry if this is weird, but I'd like to ask you a question."

"Okay," Molly says in a soft voice.

I have Vivian to thank for this next question. "What's the best memory you have of Uncle Arthur?"

Molly pushes her fingertips into the beanbag. "I wrote a book," she blurts.

"Come again?"

She clears her throat, her gaze darting toward the shelves of books. "I wrote a follow-up to my first picture book. This one's about memories."

My eyebrows pull together. "Can I read it?"

Wide green eyes stare back at me, her mouth falling open.

"What, right now?" She stares at me in disbelief.

"Now, later, whenever you want. You call the shots right now." I don't want to assume anything. "I just want to share in whatever you create. I'm so humbled by how you turned your pain into helping kids."

She flips her blond hair over her shoulder and twirls a curl around her finger. "Did you mean what you said just now?"

Hope burns through me, so intense it borders on euphoria. "Yes. All of it. Which part specifically are you questioning?"

Molly keeps twirling her hair. "The, um. The part where you said... that you... *love me? Twice?*"

I lean forward and reach across the space between us to still her hand. "Molly. I'm fucking crazy about you. Every time I try to fight it, I keep coming back to the fact that I'm absolutely mad about you. I've never felt a love like this. It's epic, and it's all consuming. I can't even imagine my life without you, and the fact that you could still change your mind and tell me to go to hell makes this even harder. But even if you do, I'll leave you alone and never darken your door again. But that won't stop me from loving you until the day I die."

Molly presses her other palm to her mouth and lets out a hiccupping sob. "I love you, too, Noah."

I hate seeing her cry, especially when I'm the reason for it. I slide over onto her beanbag and pull her to me, rubbing circles on her back as she clings to me.

"I can't promise that I won't screw up again, because I'm a man, and we do stupid shit when we can't control our emotions. But I swear that I won't run away again. I swear I'll communicate. I swear I won't let my anger get the better of me."

She sits back, removing her glasses so that she can rub at her eyes. "Noah?"

I drink her in with my eyes. "Yeah?"

Her teeth worry her lower lip. "Will you be my boyfriend again? I really liked that part."

The relief that sweeps through me is indescribable. This is more than I deserve.

How did I get so lucky? I wonder. The question itself is a shock. It's been so long since I thought of myself as lucky that I don't even know where to start.

"Gladly," I say. "Because I liked that part too." I bend down to kiss her, and the meeting of our lips feels like coming home. Her scent assaults me with memories that dance and then stop and then morph into the possibility of forever.

Of pain being sculpted into triumph.

"Can we still have a sleepover?" she asks.

Every beat of my heart seems to stretch for seconds. "Your place or mine?"

"Ooh." Her eyes widen. "I've never seen your bedroom. Or your library for that matter. And I have a first edition book underneath the counter that needs a new home."

"Er, come to think of it, maybe we should stay at your place tonight. My dog sleeps in the bed a lot. I have to change the sheets. Next time?"

"Next time," Molly agrees. "I can figure out something for dinner, and you can read my manuscript."

"I'd like that." Then I sweep Molly up in my arms for another kiss. "But right now I have something else in mind...?"

"Another lesson?" she asks. "We never successfully mastered Blowjobs for Beginners."

"Or the reverse cowgirl," I add.

"Ooh, sounds spicy." Molly links her arm through mine. "I missed you, Noah. You have no idea."

"I think I might have an inkling." I bend down for another

kiss. Every single thing about this woman lights me up. I want to kiss her all the time. Touch her. *Love* her. It's hard to imagine that I could ever get tired of it.

"By the way, I've been wondering about something. While I was waiting for you to come to your senses, I did more online research. Noah, what's a flopper?"

A grin pulls at my lips. "It's a nickname kind of like tater tot, but not nearly as delicious when you eat it."

She swats at my shoulder. "Noah! Be serious. I want to learn more about what you do and who you are."

"Well... it's a goalie that 'flops' around a bit protecting the crease and keeping the biscuit out of the basket as a dirty girl I know once said to me."

"Just any dirty girl?"

"The only one I've ever loved or ever will love. But if she wants to, she can show me just how dirty she is right now."

Love isn't always easy, but loving Molly is the most natural thing I've ever done. I plan to keep doing it for eternity.

She waggles her brows. "I'm feeling a little bit dirty. Must be all that talk of fingering at Thanksgiving. And love."

I try to think the way that she would. Each time that our lips touch, I focus on trying to map hers with my own. I try to capture every detail in my mind's eye, to think of how I would describe them on a page. I'm not sure I could ever do it as well as she does. Molly's words always sound so much sweeter than my own. When I try to talk about anything beyond hockey and books, my tongue gets clumsy and the thoughts come out all wrong.

So I stick to what I'm good at—using my hands. I skim along her lower lip until she opens them ever so slightly. I taste the creaminess of the Merlot she just drank and that magical earthiness that is so uniquely hers. It tightens something in my chest, my heart swelling so hard I worry that I might just die here and now. It wouldn't be the worst way to go. Maybe she could leave the chalk outline and move the crime novels and thrillers to the shelves right above us.

I catch her lip between my teeth, and she lets out an involuntary little moan when I tug at it. The sound diverts the blood from my heart to my groin, breaking me from my train of thought and bringing reality crashing back down around me. Molly is here, right here in front of me. Forgiving me. Loving me. The most fragile and precious thing I've ever had the good fortune to touch. One wrong move and this fantasy might dissolve, like trying to hold onto sand or starlight.

"God, Molly, I love you so damn much," I whisper, pulling back, breaking the kiss.

She whimpers at the loss of contact. My eyes find hers, and I brush my fingertips along the side of her face, tucking a loose blond strand behind her ear. Her skin feels like silk, and her pulse flutters in her throat.

"I can't believe you're giving me a second chance," I murmur, watching the way she leans into the touch of my hand and the way that her small face is cradled by my massively solid palm. "I know I probably don't deserve it, which makes it worth even more."

Molly smiles at me, warm and serene. I can see the words forming behind her eyes. She never stops thinking, like she's scribbling in some kind of mental notepad.

"I think you deserve a redemption arc, Noah," she says with an air of finality, placing a hand on my chest. "All of the best stories have them. And I think ours qualifies as one of those."

Her words are too kind, threatening to tear me right in half. I reach for her with both hands, pulling her into a kiss much harder and hungrier than the ones before, and she melts into my arms, cradled against my chest. I bring my lips to her cheek, to her jaw, to her earlobe, and down the skin of her throat. I kiss as much of her as I can reach and then some. I continue my oral assault until my lips are thwarted by the cotton of her shirt. My fingers clumsily attack the hem as I lift it higher and higher, revealing the smooth skin of her stomach, framed by a lacy pink bra.

There's a cluster of freckles on her right shoulder, the imperfection making her all the more perfect. I kiss those, too. Molly must be ticklish, because she shies away from my touch and a girlish giggle falls from her lips. I can't help but be amazed by how desirable she manages to be, even when she isn't trying.

One of my hands cups her breast, massaging at it through the delicate fabric. The other drifts down lower, ghosting along the hem of her skirt and pushing it up along her thighs. My fingertips find the skin between her legs hot to the touch.

It drives me wild, knowing that I can do this to her. That I can start a fire in her the way she does in me. With wicked intent, I slide down off the beanbag chair and onto my knees on the floor. She looks at me quizzically, head tilted to the side with a small flirtatious smile on her lips, as I push her legs apart and kiss my way up and down the inside of her thighs.

Pushing her skirt up above her hips, I reach for the waistband of her panties, dragging the thin scrap of pink lace down to the floor.

"That front door better be locked," I tease, watching a blush spread from her chest to the tips of her ears. "Because I'm about to lick you until you come all over my face."

She starts to stutter out an explanation, something about the closed sign being flipped over, but I cut her off by diving face first into her welcoming pussy.

Every moment we've been apart, I've been thinking about this. Craving it. I could do this for hours and still not feel like I've done enough. Maybe it's regret. Maybe it's guilt.

Whatever it is, I've never been so turned on in my life. Every swipe of my tongue along her folds sends shivers down my spine and makes my cock strain against my zipper. Her fingers reach for my hair, dragging her nails along my scalp in encouragement, scrambling my brain. I've taken pucks to the face that didn't make me feel half as dizzy as she can.

"What do you want me to do next, dirty girl?" I ask, dropping a kiss to her swollen clit.

I take one of her thighs and lift it onto my shoulder to give me better access, draping her leg over and down my back. I can feel the way her muscles twitch when I lick in just the right rhythm, and I know that she's close.

"Put your fingers inside me," she rasps, thrashing and bucking.

I slide one of my fingers inside of her, then another. She's so tight and wet for me that I almost lose myself right then and there. "Like this?"

"Noah," she purrs, her tiny heel digging into the spot between my shoulder blades as her hips arch upward against my hand. "Please don't stop."

Her soft plea is exactly what I need to keep going and focus on the task at hand. I tilt my fingers up, hitting that perfect angle that makes her toes curl and her eyes snap shut. Closing my lips around her clit, I suck and her body explodes at once. She pulsates around my fingers, her thighs clenching my shoulders and her hands gripping my hair and scalp. She cries out into the empty bookstore, voice echoing off of the shelves. After a minute, she goes still and limp, and I gently kiss my way along her thighs, basking in the glow that comes off of her in waves.

She laughs when I kiss the top of her knee, giggling at the sensation and pulling away from me.

"Wow, Noah. That was wonderful," she breathes, ruffling my hair affectionately as she starts to sit up and straighten out her skirt.

"You think I'm done here?" I stop her with a heavy hand on her hip and a smirk. "Not a chance, baby girl. My dick's never been so hard."

She blushes, looking away from me and casting her eyes down at the floor.

"Don't act shy now. You're crazy hot, and you know it." I crouch over her, taking her hand in mine and directing it down to the front of my pants. "Here. This should be all the proof you need. I want you, Molly. And it's so goddamn obvious."

Her fingers make quick work of my belt buckle and the fly of my jeans, and I groan in relief when she slides the clothing down over my hips, freeing my pent-up erection.

"That's really for me?" she teases, barely grazing my length with the tip of her index finger.

"Okay, now you're just pushing my buttons," I playfully snap back, bringing a light kiss to her cheek. "And we both know that you're way too smart for that."

Smart enough that she scares me, sometimes. Way too smart for my own good. I'll have to try my hardest to keep up. For now, all I can offer her is this. Something I know that I'm good at. Reaching in my pocket for a condom, I sheathe my throbbing erection. I spread her legs open with my own, and reaching between us, I guide myself into her. Since we've only done this once before, I know she's not used to my length and girth, so I take it inch by inch. Slow, painfully slow, relishing the sweet hot feeling of her around me and the sound of her breath hissing between her teeth as I come to rest fully inside of her.

I try to maintain my composure and restrict myself to this glacial pace, but my control slips with every sound that falls from her lips. Every inch of her feels incredible, from her delicate soft hands caressing my arms to her warm breath ghosting my jawline.

"Please, Noah," she whimpers. "I need you to fuck me hard and deep. Prove that you love me—body and soul."

It is all the permission I need to let go completely. I reach for each of her legs, gingerly enough that she can stop me if she wants, before slipping them over my shoulders. The new angle must be doing wonders for the both of us. Molly bites her lower lip and shuts her eyes as I bury my cock to the hilt. It's so much deeper than before, and I have to focus, or I'll blow my load too soon. Not with my Molly. I need her to come again before I do. I need to do every single thing I can to deliver that proof that she needs.

I try to grind against her as much as possible with each stroke, letting my movements stimulate her clit. I can tell that it's working, because her eyes are screwed tight, forming that cute little crease between her eyebrows that always shows up right before she comes. Neither of us care very much about how loud we are—the bean bag keeps squeaking under us, and my breath comes to me in great uneven gasps.

"I love you, Molly," I whisper, reaching between us to strum her clit. "And I want you to come for me so badly. You're mine, baby girl. Let go for me."

She inhales, then cries out sharply, her whole body tensing up underneath me. I'm not far behind, giving three unsteady thrusts before falling apart. My vision dims for a second, and I struggle to catch my breath. As we slowly drift back to earth together, we practice the tantric breathing and eye contact we learned in this very spot.

And things come full circle.

As if she can read my mind, Molly unleashes a killer grin. That brilliant smile blinds me, from the voluptuous curve of her lips to the vibrant green of her eyes, and the little dimple her grin forms on her right cheek. Returning it, I consider all that's happened in the short time we've known each other. I don't think I could bear to be the reason her smile goes away ever again. It'll be a hard road, but one worth treading for the rest of my life.

EPILOGUE

Molly

Six months later...

We celebrate our twenty-fifth official date with a zipline expedition across the Vegas skyline, to commemorate how far we've come.

For our fiftieth date, Noah lets me choose how I think we should celebrate. I suggest a Magic Mike show, which was *absolutely* the right choice. I'm all hot and bothered by the time we leave, but the joke's on everyone else, because I get to go home with the hottest guy in the room.

We celebrate our sixty-ninth date with a highly topical lesson.

After that, we stop counting.

Of course, there are other milestones to celebrate. When we decide to move in together, we say good-bye to the townhouse by defiling every surface in the place. Noah says that it's the equivalent of using sage to oust the bad energy. If he's right, the next owners are going to be mystifyingly horny at all hours of the day and night. I wish them well.

One afternoon, as Mona's relieving me at the shop, I get a text from Noah asking me to get changed and meet him at the Venetian for an impromptu date night. When I go up to our room, I find a beautiful lacy sundress laid out on the bed. It's a perfect fit. I spend half an hour getting dressed up, fixing my makeup, and putting in contacts. Before I leave, I check my phone; there's an email from Angela. She's fielding offers from multiple publishing houses, although the final numbers have yet to come in.

"Mommy!" Vivian squeals when I head back downstairs. "You look so *pretty!*" She rushes over to hug me around the waist.

"Thanks, sweetie." I bend down to kiss her head. At the rate she's growing, she's going to be taller than I am by the time she gets to middle school. "Do you still want me to go thrifting with you and Fran tomorrow?"

"Of course, Mommy." Viv steps back. "I love it when you come with us. Have fun with Daddy tonight!" She zips back to the table, where crayons are scattered across the wood. She's taken it upon herself to make an illustrated catalog of every resident of the Gnome Gloam, and since new inhabitants arrive all the time, it's an endless process.

Now if Fran could only catch one glimpse of Celine, and we could get Cash to string more than three words together at a time, we'd have an unpoppable happiness bubble.

I wave goodbye to Fran, pause by the couch to pat Biscuit's belly, and finally set out for my date. For so long, I only had Mona and the bookstore to keep me going. Now, my life is full to bursting. Everything's changed, and I'm better for it in every way.

You don't need to worry about me, Uncle Arthur, I said the last time Noah and I went to the cemetery. *I miss you like crazy, but I'm going to be just fine.*

* * *

Noah meets me in the luxurious lobby of the Venetian wearing a suit that makes him look edible. When I fling myself into his arms, he laughs.

"Do you like the dress?" he asks.

"I love it!" I twirl for him so that he can see how the skirt billows around my legs when I move. "What's the occasion?"

"You are."

I scoff as I take his proffered arm. "Flatterer."

"It's true," he insists. "I love you, Molly, and I swear I love you more every damn day. Didn't think it was possible, but here we are."

I strut down the walkway as Noah leads me toward the gondolas. I'm wearing a lovely dress on a date with the man I love. Ever since I decided to give him a second chance, he's been the best boyfriend ever. Truly, I'm living my best life, and I don't care who knows it.

At the gondolas, a familiar face waits among the gondoliers. When he spots us, he adjusts his hat and dips into a low bow. A smile breaks out because as far as Noah's teammates go, this one has a special place in my heart even though I'm not quite sure why he's here and dressed in black pants, red sash, and the traditional striped boat shirt.

"Ah, Noah and zee tater tot! Are you ready to set sail?"

I look between the two men in confusion. "Hey, Marco. What's the deal? Is this a part-time job, or...?"

"One time only." He sweeps one hand toward the water. "If you are to pretend that you are in Venice, you need a real Italian at the helm, *non*?"

"Of course." I curtsey to him, although my antennae have gone up. Something's afoot, but this can't mean what I think it does, can it?

Marco helps us onto a nearby gondola, slipping a few bills to another man in identical garb. The man nods and withdraws, which only makes me wonder more. When we're settled, Marco collects the pole and guides us out over the crystal-clear water below.

"This is lovely," I sigh, leaning against Noah. "What a great idea."

"I'm glad you like it. I wanted to do something special for you," Noah says, his eyes never leaving mine.

Just when I think he's about to ask *the* question, he reaches into a bag placed discreetly at his feet. "Before we get to the real reason we're here, I have something else for you."

He hands me a beautifully wrapped package, the paper so exquisite it could be a work of art on its own. My hands tremble as I open it to reveal a rare, signed first edition of "Charlotte's Web."

"Noah, this is—"

"Let me explain," he interrupts, taking a deep breath. "I chose 'Charlotte's Web' because it's a story about love and sacrifice. It's about stepping up when someone needs you, even when it's hard, even when you're scared. Charlotte the spider didn't have to help Wilbur, but she did, out of love and friendship. She used her talents to save him, much like you've saved me with your love and your kindness. This book is a rare, signed first edition—kind of like what we have. A rare love that I'll forever cherish. Every time I see it on our bookshelf, I'll be reminded of how you make me want to be a better man every single day."

My heart feels like it's expanding, filling up the space that's been hollow for so long. This gift isn't just a book; it's a bridge to my past, to Uncle Arthur, and to all the lessons he taught me. In this moment, it feels like Noah has not just heard me, but understood the very fabric of who I am. He's mending torn pages in the story of us, giving us a fresh chapter. And God, does it feel like forever.

I can't hold back the tears any longer. "You don't even know how perfect this is. 'Charlotte's Web' was my favorite book as a young girl. Uncle Arthur used to read it to me. He said it taught him how to be a good friend."

Noah's eyes brighten, the emotional weight of the moment clearly hitting him too. "Then it's settled. This book will be a tribute to the two most influential people in my life—my future wife and the man who made her who she is today."

I'm at a loss for words, the emotional impact of the gift not lost on me. Noah takes the moment of silence to shift gears.

Did he just say *wife*? My already squeezing heart shoots up into my throat.

Noah swallows and shifts away from me, taking both of my hands in his and staring into my eyes. "You're special, Molly. You're perfect for me. When I'm with you, I'm the kind of man I want to be. I've come to think of you as part of my family, which is why I'm hoping to make it official."

I let out a high-pitched squeak and grip his hands like he might disappear, and I need to hold him to keep him inside the gondola.

"Molly Campbell, will you marry me?" He wriggles his fingers in mine, then breaks into a huge grin. "You've got to let go of me for a second here, though, so that I can get out the ring."

"*Of course, I'll marry you!*" I cry the words so loud that people in other gondolas turn to look. With my emotions already raw, I start bawling again even before he manages to retrieve the ring from the pocket of his jacket.

"Ah, what I tell you, *mio amico*?" Marco exclaims, clapping Noah on the shoulder. "All you need is gondola, a proper Italian, and boom! Zees *legit*." He gives Noah a thumbs-up and a hearty wink.

Noah finally manages to get the ring on my trembling finger, and we kiss as we drift underneath the bridge, just like I've always wanted since I was a girl watching *The Little Mermaid* for the first time. Sadly, there's no singing hermit crab to serenade us, but the rest is pretty spot-on.

Kiss. The. Girl.

As people on the other boats whistle and clap, I place one hand on each of Noah's cheeks.

"I'm going to find the frilliest, fluffiest, most princess-y wedding dress," I warn him. "Don't forget the diamond tiara. I don't think you're prepared for how girly I'm about to go. You've unleashed a monster."

"I'm well aware." Noah grins. "Between you and Viv, I expect that it's going to be an intensely girly wedding. In fifty shades of pink. I figure it's probably better if I just step aside and wait for marching orders, right?"

"Right." I kiss him again and settle my head against his shoulder.

Above us, Marco clears his throat before breaking into a lilting libretto. He's tall, dark, and handsome in the truest sense of that description, but I don't really notice him. He's not my Noah. I don't understand Marco's words, but his voice is incredible, echoing off the structures around us and filling the space with the haunting melody of what I'm sure is a love song.

"Wow," I breathe. "He's even better than Sebastian."

Noah's brow wrinkles. "Pardon?"

"You've got to bat your eyes like this." I sigh and flutter my long eyelashes, looking forward to the days and years ahead, imagining everything that the future holds in store. "You've got to pucker up your lips like this."

Without knowing what I'm even talking about, Noah takes my protruding lips as in invitation to kiss me senseless right underneath another bridge of selfie-taking tourists. Marco smiles and waves to their applause, blowing a kiss and tipping his straw hat.

One teenage girl even squeals, "That's Marco Rossi! He's my favorite Venom player!"

When I snuggle back into Noah's solid chest, my heart overflows. I know from bitter experience that life can change in unexpected ways without a moment's notice.

So, I take a deep breath, and as I exhale, I feel like I'm releasing years of pent-up sorrow and regret. Because life's too short for what-ifs and could-have-beens. It's time to seize joy, embrace love and build something lasting out of the wreckage. With Noah's hand in mine and Vivian's laughter as our soundtrack, we're becoming a family. Together, we're turning the page, writing a new chapter filled with passion, love, and endless possibilities. And just like that, I know we're not a tragedy waiting to happen. Not even close.

We're a love story for the ages.

And we're just getting started.

ABOUT THE AUTHOR

"People are like stained-glass windows. They sparkle and shine when the sun is out, but when the darkness sets in, their true beauty is revealed only if there is a light from within."
— Elisabeth Kübler-Ross

Are you willing to discover the beauty within the flaws?

Then this is your tribe.

These are your books.

Colleen Charles is the USA Today Bestselling author of Perfectly Imperfect Romance for perfectly imperfect readers.

Take a chance and join her... you won't be sorry you did.

Colleen loves to hear from her readers and she answers all communications personally. You can find her at:

ColleenCharles.Com

Subscribe to my Newsletter online and receive email notices about new book releases, sales, and special promotions.

New subscribers receive an EXCLUSIVE FREE NOVEL as a special gift.

www.colleencharles.com/free

Printed in Great Britain
by Amazon

32181510R00155